# AUCTIONED FOR HER BLOOD

THE VAMPIRES' ILLUMINANT BOOK 1

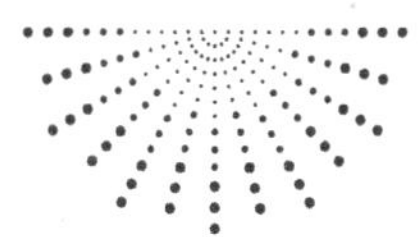

MARA LEIGH

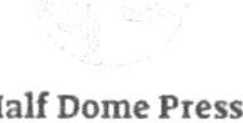

Half Dome Press

Cover design by Covers by Juan
ISBN: 978-1-989318-18-8

# CHAPTER ONE

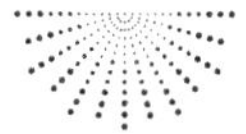

## *Ember*

"Ember! Hide!" Mom yells. "In the cellar! Now!"

I open my mouth to object—Mom can be so *extra* sometimes—but her eyes are wide, full of terror. Serious terror.

She tosses the vial of blood she just drew from my arm into the fireplace and smashes the glass with the poker.

"What are you waiting for?" she yells as she runs to the door to make sure it's locked. "Cellar!"

This isn't a drill. It's the real thing, even though I have no idea what that *thing* is, only that she's been preparing me for it since…forever.

Heart galloping, I scramble past her and into her bedroom, and as I enter the room, her massive cherry wood armoire shifts to the side like a feather blown in the breeze. A brass handle appears on one of the thick pine floorboards, just like it has every time she's run these drills.

The handle is unnaturally cold in the hot humid air,

and when I touch it the edges of the cellar door appear in the floor like magic.

Not *like* magic. It *is* magic. Magic I don't understand, and my mother refuses to even name. I've had little contact with other people outside my mom, but I've read enough books and seen enough TV to know that the things my mother can do aren't normal.

"Faster!" Mom yells, her arms stretched wide above her. "I can't hold them off for long!"

I want to ask who "they" are, but don't. Tugging on the handle, I pull up the door and quickly descend into the cold, dark space of the cellar, and then take a few steps back from the ladder as I wait for my mom to join me.

Above me, the door slams shut and steals the light.

"Mom!" I reach for the ladder to climb back up to her, but it's gone.

Did I descend the *illusion* of a ladder, or can she make physical things disappear just like she can move that heavy armoire?

"Mom!" My scream scrapes my throat, but gets no response.

In the blink of an eye, the cracks of light around the cut floorboards vanish, and the armoire lands above me with a thud, moving back into position and landing as if accidentally dropped. Not my mother's style.

The space around me glows, an ethereal deep blue, like I'm submerged in illuminated smoke, but the glow is thicker than smoke, more like a heavy liquid, and then it dissipates, plunging me back into darkness.

"Where is she?" asks a loud voice above. An unnatural voice, distorted, deep and menacing.

"Who?" my mother answers.

A slam echoes. Dust and dirt falls around me as our house shakes.

"You will pay for your disobedience!"

My mother screams. At least I think it's my mother, but the piercing sound hurts my ears and stabs my heart. Then the bloodcurdling sound fades, as if all the air behind it was consumed.

I pry my hands off my ears, not sure how they got there.

"Where is she?" another voice shouts and it echoes in my bones.

*Who are they looking for?*

*Me?*

Still in total darkness, I want to scream out for my mother, but I'm choked by fear that makes me feel weak and childish. I'm fourteen—fifteen in seven months—and I shouldn't be cowering in a cellar while my mother is in danger above, especially if she's doing it for me. I need to save her from whatever monstrous beings attacked our house, attacked her.

Hands in front of me, I search the space. I've been down here so many times that I know it by heart, and I reach for the stone foundation to get my bearings, my nostrils filling with musty, humid air as I step forward, moving farther and farther, expecting my hands to strike damp stones at any moment, but the wall isn't as close as I expect.

In fact, no matter how far I step, I can't seem to reach the edge of the room. I turn back, moving toward the middle where the ladder and trap door were.

The voices have grown quiet upstairs but I hear the scraping of furniture legs on our pine planked floors, the smashing of glass and the thud of footsteps—but I can't tell how many feet are making those noises.

The sounds from above go quiet and the footsteps vanish. And still I haven't found one wall of the cellar room.

"Mom!" I shout. "Mom!" I stumble around the space again, trying to find any marker or indication to orient myself in the utter darkness.

Finally, I sit, the ground cold under my butt as I hug my bent legs into my chest and shiver.

It's not cold down here, at least I don't think that it is, and yet my arms and legs are covered in goose bumps and the hair at the back of my neck is prickling up to salute my terror.

I rock, counting to keep track of time, and then when the numbers get so high that the plan seems futile, I start to sing to myself. Kid songs, pop songs, ads from the TV—whatever comes into my mind.

Fatigue is threatening, so I pinch my arms and then slap my face. I've never done well in the dark, never even stepped outside our house after sunset, and it's so quiet down here that I'm not certain my ears even work.

I can hear my own voice but that doesn't prove much, so I clap a few times to verify that I can hear.

"Mom!" I yell again, crying now.

My nightmares visit me, even though I'm awake—recurring dreams of being trapped in a much smaller space filled with terror, smoke and screams. At least I know my nightmares aren't real. Unlike what's going on now.

She's dead. My mother is dead. Even if I escape from this tomb, I am alone, an orphan. Suddenly fourteen feels like a baby, not the near adult I believed it to be. But I can't give up. I need to be strong. And if there's any chance that Mom is still alive, I need to get up there to save her.

Standing, my legs are stiff from the cold and inaction; pins and needles scamper through them as I move. Hands ahead, I search for the walls, for the ladder, for anything that might help me orient myself and let me escape.

But what feels like hours later, I'm still pacing the room, turning each time I'm certain I've gone too far, and I've yet to find the edges of a room that I *know* has four sides, and I *know* is only about twenty feet in both width and length. I'm going insane.

It doesn't make sense, and I know it's not meant to.

This illusion of distance must be part of Mom's magic. A glimmer of hope flickers through me. If her magic is holding, does that mean she's alive? I have no idea.

I wish she'd answered my questions about how magic works, about why we stay isolated, but she refused so many times I stopped asking.

Closing my eyes, I draw deep breaths, longing to calm myself, to decrease my heart rate, to convince myself that all is well.

Light glows through my closed eyelids. I open them and gasp.

My mother is standing in front of me. I reach to hug her, but my arms go straight through.

"Mom!"

She smiles and nods. "Ember, the immediate danger has passed."

"What danger? Who was that up there?"

Not reacting to my questions, she keeps talking. It's some kind of recording.

"But, my daughter, the danger you face will never pass. Not fully. I have done what I can to protect you, but at some point you will have to face the darkness."

How could anything be worse than the total darkness I've suffered through these past hours?

My mother's arm rises, and a light glows, illuminating the corner of the room that's not more than five feet away from me. Her magic, or someone's, kept me from finding that corner before.

"In this corner you will find a box," says the apparition of my mother. "In this box you will find documents, access to money, the deed to the farm that will be yours at eighteen. Until then, stay hidden. Tell no one you are alone, and—I cannot emphasize this enough—never go outside after dark. Not ever."

Her image disappears.

"Mom!" I step forward and turn but the image of her has gone.

The room fills with light, starting as a blue shimmer that brightens to a white light, revealing all four walls of the room, the box in the corner, and the ladder leading up to the trap door above.

I grab the box, climb the stairs and push against the trap door that opens easily as if it's being pulled from above.

Hope again grabs my heart. "Mom?"

I climb out.

But she's not there. And her bedroom is in shambles.

The armoire, standing to my left, is the only thing in the room that's where it was when I hid in the cellar. Her mattress is slashed, its guts strewn everywhere. The photographs and paintings are all on the floor, their frames twisted and the glass smashed. I shake the glass off a photo of mom and me making chocolate chip cookies when I was six.

Holes are punched into the plastered walls where the artwork and memorabilia once hung. There are holes too in the ceiling and the floor, and although I know the cellar is directly below her room, the holes in the floor open only to a small crawl space, less than three feet deep.

Somehow her magic hides the cellar, or is the cellar itself an illusion?

I decide to look under the trap door, but the armoire is back over the opening. Distracted by the destruction, I didn't hear it move back. But its movement gives me hope that my mother is still here, still working to protect me.

I search the rest of our small farmhouse, but it's more of the same. Furniture slashed and broken, holes everywhere, books and clothes and dishes tossed to the floor. Even the kitchen cupboards and appliances have been yanked from the walls, their wires spilling out like veins onto the damaged floors.

Clutching the box against my chest, I search and search, but there's no evidence of her. I should feel glad that I can't spot any blood, but while I know little about magic, I know that the absence of blood doesn't mean she survived, or didn't suffer.

A wind arises, blowing torn curtains into the house and the front door slams shut.

I rush into the front room. It could be my mother and not the wind that made the door close.

A message is scratched into the back of the wooden door. My breath freezes in my lungs as I step closer to read it, every instinct inside me telling me this is *not* another message from my mom.

"Gullveig the Illuminant," it reads, "wherever you are, we will find you. Evanora will pay for her crimes."

I stagger back from the message. The words Gullveig the Illuminant mean nothing, and I'm a tiny bit relieved that whoever was here wasn't looking for me. Evanora could refer to my mom, Nora Cross, but I've never heard her called that.

As I try to make sense of the message, it fades, disappearing before my eyes. I run my hands over the wood, but it's smooth again, no hint of the words that were carved deeply into the surface.

Was the message just my imagination?

I turn around. The entire farmhouse is back to normal. No gutted furniture, no broken glass, no holes in the walls or ceiling or floorboards.

I rush from room to room and it's all the same. Everything is back where it was.

Breaths coming too quickly, I grab a paper bag from the drawer where Mom keeps them, and then sit and breathe into it until my light-headedness fades.

Was this, all of this, just my imagination? Will my mother step into the farmhouse at any minute, coming back from Henderson's General Store? Was this all a dream?

Is it still? I pinch my arm and feel it.

And the box from the basement is sitting on the counter, above the drawer where I got the paper bag. The box is real. I'm not insane—or at least there's evidence to argue both sides.

And if I'm *not* insane, then whoever was here was looking for someone or something called Gullveig the Illuminant, and more importantly they have taken my mom.

I drop the box on the table, take my head in my hands, and weep.

# CHAPTER TWO

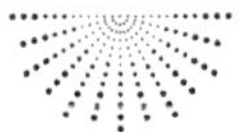

## *Ember*

### *Eleven years later*

"CAN'T our new benefactor come here?" I ask my boss, Shana. "That way he'd be able to see the operations first hand."

Shana puts her hands on her ample hips. "With the amount he's offered to donate, I'd agree to meet him on the moon." She forces her notebook and planner into the vegan-leather backpack she's already stuffed full of pamphlets, financial statements, and other documents about Sanctuary House. Then as if that weren't enough, she adds her obsolete iPhone and, for some strange reason, a full-sized stapler.

I open my mouth to ask her why she needs a stapler, then snap it back shut. Shana's eccentric, but she's still my boss.

"Have you got the financial records?" she asks me.

"Yup." I pat my leather tote bag.

The deep brown skin on her forehead wrinkles into a frown as she looks at my tote. "Are you sure? I'll bring my financial file."

She reaches into a filing cabinet and pulls out an overstuffed manila folder that gives way and spills papers onto the floor. "Crap."

"I'll get them." I crouch to gather her papers, coffee stained and covered in doodles, and then set them back on her desk. That's all normal, but today is the first time I've seen Shana nervous.

"No need to bring your file." I smile as we stand. Hoping to reassure her, I pat the side of my tote again. "I've got hard copies of the last two years' annual reports, ten years of our financial records on my laptop, and I can e-mail him anything else he needs. Plus, I've got a spare thumb drive if he wants to take digital copies right away." I don't even mention the many other options better than her massive, disorganized folder.

Shana eyes me with trepidation, then closes her office door to give us some privacy. "Ember, I know you understand the severity of our financial situation."

I nod. Without new funding, the not-for-profit we both work for might have to fold.

"How much is he donating?" I ask.

"*If* he makes the donation…a lot. It all hinges on this meeting." Closing her eyes, Shana draws a long breath, her equivalent of a prayer.

"Wow." My gut tightens as the stakes sink in.

"Let's just say," Shana continues, "if he donates even half the amount he dangled, we'll have enough to cover our operating budget for at least two decades, plus expand our service offering to serve more at risk youth."

I mentally calculate the ballpark number, based on twenty times our operating budget. The number of zeros turns me light headed. "All that from a single donor?" This man could definitely save us.

She nods.

"Is he a billionaire?"

"Yup. And one with a reputation."

"What kind?" My teeth scrape my lower lip.

"Tough. Difficult. Abrupt. Plus, he's *very* picky about choosing charities. We've got to handle this just right." She glances at her watch. "Ack! We've got to run. The car he's sending might already be waiting."

My already racing nerves go into hyper drive. It's only 4:00 pm, but it's fall, the days are getting shorter, and I don't like to be anyplace in the afternoon where I can't be sure I'll be home before dark. "How far are we going?"

"He didn't say." She bustles out of her office, and I race to keep up as she crosses the small cluttered area that houses the desks of the Sanctuary House staff—all the staff except me, that is. I work from home most days—another way to make sure I never have to be out at night. I follow her down the four flights of stairs to the street.

I glance at my watch. "How long will the meeting take?"

She stops on the last flight of stairs, halting so suddenly I nearly smash into her, and then she turns, her impatience as clear as glass. "Ember, I let you work from home and you've done a great job—way better than our last accountant." Her large eyes roll as she shakes her head.

"I don't think it's too much to ask you to go to one offsite meeting with a donor. Especially one so important."

"No, it's not, but I…" I close my eyes, wishing I could get past my irrational fear of the dark.

She squeezes my arm, and I open my eyes to find hers full of empathetic kindness. "Don't you worry, lamby, we'll get you home before nightfall."

Her words are kind—both in meaning and delivery—but I can't help but feel foolish. I'm twenty-five years old and I'm still afraid of the dark.

---

### *Ember*

SHANA TAKES A LONG DEEP BREATH AND SHOOTS ME A smile. We're standing in front of a metal door just inside a narrow alley behind a center city office building. Above us, camera lenses dip to take obvious note of our presence.

"Are you sure this is the place?" I ask her. The alley is clean, pristine really, but this is definitely the back of this building—the opposite of inviting. Super sketchy.

She pulls out a crumpled sticky note from her pocket and reads, "When the car drops you off, enter through the metal door on the left of the alley." She glances around. "This has to be the right door."

"This doesn't seem *strange* to you?" *Or dangerous?* I moved to Philadelphia not long after I turned eighteen, but after growing up in the country, I'm still cautious.

She shrugs. "Rich people are eccentric."

Shana should know. My earthy, scattered boss, who

buys most of her wardrobe at used clothing stores as a protest against fast fashion and waste, is actually the youngest daughter of the man who's family owns the largest real estate company in the state.

Shana holds open the door for me, and the space we step into is narrow, but belies the simple steel door. The entrance way is sleek and tasteful, modern and yet somehow classic with long, teal curtain panels hanging at intervals over crisp white walls that rise at least twenty feet up to a ceiling covered with gleaming metallic ceiling tiles. The lighting is recessed, it's source unclear, creating the illusion that the white and black floor tiles are floating over a bed of light.

A shiny black door opens at the back of the room, and a tall, elegant man appears, dressed in a tuxedo complete with white gloves. "Welcome." He bows slightly. "Shana Johnson and Ember Cross, I presume?"

"Mr. Zuben?" Shana walks forward, extending her hand, but the man shakes his head.

"He will meet you inside the club."

*Club?* I've never been outside after dark, never mind inside anything that could be described as a club, and a frisson of excitement races through me. Or maybe it's fear. I'm not sure my body knows the difference. "What kind of club is this?" I ask.

Shana hip checks me and shoots me a look that says, 'shut up'.

"It's a social club," the man answers as we pass him. "Exclusive to the most senior executives of DEFTA."

DEFTA. That's where we are? I know little of the

mysterious company whose name graces the top of this major high-rise in center city Philadelphia.

The man shuts the door from the lobby, leaving the three of us in a wide hallway painted deep black. At least I think it's painted. The texture of the walls seems cushioned, and it's hard to resist touching them to test how far my fingers would sink in if I pushed. But before I can act on my impulse, a door at the other end opens and light floods the dark hallway.

We enter the most beautiful room I've ever seen.

"Wow," Shana says, clearly impressed too, even though I'm sure she's seen way more beautiful spaces than I have. "This is really something."

I nod as my attention is pulled from one place to another—red velvet and satin, gold detailing, wood paneling, rich leather chairs in a deep blood red, antiques galore—and, although it's super-fancy, the space also feels comfortable, as if the room is literally asking us to make ourselves at home.

"...and this is our accountant, Ember Cross," Shana says.

My attention snaps from the surroundings to her voice, and I realize that, while I've been lost in the decor, she's been in the middle of introductions.

Focusing on my hand, I reach forward to shake the man's, and his engulfs mine. His touch is warm and soft, his fingers long, his skin light brown, and his face... Raising my gaze, I can't draw a full breath as I take in the most handsome man I have ever seen in the flesh.

His warm, brown eyes are rimmed with the kind of

thick, dark lashes women yearn for, giving the illusion that he's wearing black eyeliner, his eye whites shimmer in contrast, and his deeply tan skin luxuriates over sharply chiseled features so perfectly symmetrical it's hard to believe the man's real. He's more like an artist's interpretation of male beauty, and his thick, well-groomed brows rise as he stares.

Stares at me.

His gaze on me is so intense it makes me feel naked, and heat rises to bake me from the inside. I suck on my cheeks, desperate for enough moisture to allow me to speak.

"Ms. Cross?" His intense attention turns to a look of concern, pooling in the depths of eyes the color of chestnuts that I can't stop staring into. "Are you quite well?"

"Yes." My heart racing, I drop his hand and step back. "Yes, fine. I'm very well. This…this is a beautiful room. I've never seen anything like it." *Or anything like you…* And I've certainly never felt anything like the reaction his handshake and attention set off in my belly.

"Mr. Zuben," Shana interjects, reminding me she's there. "We're very excited to answer your questions and to show you how much your generous donation will help homeless youth in our city."

His eyes flash with what looks like a message directed at me, one I don't understand, then he turns toward Shana. "Ms. Johnson, I requested a meeting with your accountant."

"This is her." Shana smiles, trying to hide her confusion.

"Alone." The man's intense glare turns back to me again and my belly tightens.

Shana grabs my forearm and tugs, urging me closer toward her—and away from the handsome man. I smile at her mothering instincts, saving me from the big bad wolf. As if a wolf would dress so well, or smell so good, or be so amazingly handsome.

Shana clears her throat. "Mr. Zuben, I assure you that I can answer any questions about our finances. I am the executive director of Sanctuary House and have been for nearly twenty years—"

"Precisely why I would like to speak to your accountant on her own." His tone is abrupt, his voice low and deep.

Looking stunned, Shana shifts her huge pack up to her shoulder, but it slides down her arm again.

"My request was for an in person meeting with your accountant," the billionaire says sharply. "Check your correspondence."

"But—" Shana shoots me a look of alarm.

I force a quivering smile onto my face as I nod and mouth, "I've got this." I certainly hope I've got this, because if I don't, that will be the end of Sanctuary House.

The man who brought us in, gestures for Shana to follow him out of the club.

Another tuxedoed waiter appears out of thin air and pulls out the table of a semi-circular booth to make it easier for me to slide onto the shiny leather seats, such a dark red they could have been dyed with blood.

"Ms. Cross, shall we sit?"

Nodding toward our potential benefactor, I perch on the edge of the seat, and he slides in next to me.

The waiter pushes the table in, trapping me. "What can I get you?" he asks.

I shake my head. "I'm fine." I reach for my tote bag.

"There is no doubt that you are fine," Mr. Zuben says. "But you must accept my hospitality. I insist." He smiles at me with what seems like genuine kindness, but his eyes dance to an entirely different piece of music—one part amused and the other…this man seems *fascinated* by me, like I'm a strange creature he's never before encountered.

A dance starts low in my belly, but at the same time my chest widens with confidence. "If you *insist*, then you might as well choose my drink for me too."

His eyebrows rise, his face flashing amusement, but then his eyes narrow as he studies me in what feels like an academic way, like he thinks my drink preferences can be found in the pores of my skin.

"Ms. Cross will have a sidecar," he says without turning to the waiter. "And I will have one too."

"What's in a sidecar?" I ask.

"Cognac, Cointreau and a dash of lemon," he answers.

My limited drinking experience is another side effect of avoiding the dark. Beyond the occasional glass of wine, I don't drink and have no idea what those ingredients taste like, aside from lemon, but I don't want to appear unsophisticated or ungrateful.

"Sounds delicious." *And strong.*

"It is." He smiles again and everything inside me flutters.

I nod slightly, then remembering why we're here, I pull my laptop out of my tote and set it onto the table. Thumb in the indentation, I start to open it, but Mr. Zuben puts his hand on the lid.

I turn toward him, shocked.

"I have studied the organization's financial statements in great detail." His hand brushes over mine as he moves it from my laptop and my breath catches. "I will contact you if I require additional details."

My shock vanishes as I'm fully absorbed in this man's eyes. I don't think I've ever seen so many dimensions to the color brown. At first they seemed like chestnut, but now I see that deep brown and amber flecks dance through his irises, combining into the sparking light brown color I saw from a distance.

But up close… Up close…

I turn abruptly away, alarmed by the intensity of his gaze and the resultant stirring in my belly—and down lower. "Mr. Zuben," I say softly.

"Just Zuben."

"Okay, Zuben." I draw a long breath to settle all the crazy things going on inside of me. The survival of Sanctuary House depends on this meeting—on me. "If you don't want to see our financial statements, what exactly can I do for you?"

"A lot I suspect."

My back stiffens.

His long elegant fingers shift on the table and he leans back against the padded leather bench. "My main objective today is to meet you. I never make donations of this size without getting to know the people responsible for keeping track of the money."

The waiter arrives and sets down two cone-shaped

glasses on stems, one in front of me and one for Mr. Zuben. No—just Zuben.

"It's imperative that I inherently trust an organization's accountant," he says.

I nod and shift my focus to my drink.

Our glasses are rimmed with something crystalized, maybe sugar or salt, and the contents are amber, shining under the warm lighting. The drink's almost clear, but with a slight murkiness that I suspect comes from the lemon.

"Shall we drink to Sanctuary House?" Zuben raises his glass.

"And to you." I lift mine. "Your generous donation will transform our organization."

He takes a sip of his drink and I tip mine to my lips.

It's definitely not salt on the rim. I'd guess sugar, held there with lemon and something else I can't quite make out. Passing my lips, the liquor burns my tongue and then my throat as I swallow. I try to stifle a cough.

"Do you like it?" Zuben asks, eyeing me with concern.

I nod, taking another small sip when the burn subsides.

"What flavors do you detect?" he asks.

Closing my eyes for a moment, I run my tongue around my mouth, not wanting to say something obvious like sugar or lemon. I want to impress him. There are flavors I recognize, but I'm not sure—"Orange?"

Zuben nods. "Orange peel is used in the distillation of Cointreau."

Taking another sip, I hold the bittersweet liquid in my mouth as I inhale, and the flavor floods my senses.

"I've never had Cointreau before." I smile at him. "What was the other thing in the drink?"

"Cognac," he replies. "It's a type of brandy, made in specific regions of France." His voice is rich and soft, like velvet at this low volume, and I even though I've never had a big interest in alcohol, I want to hear more.

He tells me more about the origins of brandy and what makes cognac special amongst brandies and why this particular cognac is extra special, or something, and then he starts using French and Dutch words for equipment and places. But I don't even try to keep up with the details. I just like hearing his voice and the heat of his attention as it floods over me. I nod and smile as I take small sips of the drink.

I'm mesmerized by this man—by his voice, his eyes, and the way he looks at me, and by his long fingers and how they are such a inconsistency of strength and grace as he gesticulates to emphasize points. My gaze follows as his index finger drops to the white tablecloth and draws an invisible outline of what I believe is a map of France, and then circles little areas of it to show me where the best cognac is made.

His hand moves to his glass, and my gaze follows it to his perfectly formed lips as he takes a sip of his drink—only his second sip, I realize—even though mine's halfway gone. After he drinks, his eyes close and his cheeks and lips move slightly as he takes obvious pleasure in the flavors.

"Are you a liquor expert?" I ask. "Is that your profession? I don't know much about DEFTA."

His eyes snap open. "Why do you ask?"

"You sure know a lot about brandy."

"Cognac," he corrects, then shakes his head. "I went into too much detail. Sharing an excess of knowledge is my worst vice." He smiles. "Please. Tell me more about yourself."

"Me?" I shift slightly. "Sanctuary House provides support for homeless and at risk youth through a variety of programs which—"

"I know all that." His words, cutting me off, are abrupt, but the way he looks at me is the opposite. "I asked about you."

I want to slide closer to him, to feel the touch of his fingers again on my skin… But that's the effect of the alcohol. And there's nothing interesting about me to tell—nothing I share anyway. I need to focus, to sell him on making this donation.

"May I tell you about our upcoming fundraising event?" I ask.

He shrugs.

"It's a black tie gala and based on ticket sales it should raise thirty percent of our annual operating budget—and more if the silent and live auctions go well."

Zuben nods.

Grateful that he hasn't cut me off again, I continue on the topic. "This year, Shana decided to add a live auction with a very exciting element."

"And what is that?" Zuben takes a sip of his sidecar.

"Patrons will have the opportunity to bid on an evening out with—well some are dates with local celebrities, and others with some of our staff."

Zuben frowns. "Shana is prostituting the staff?"

"No!" I exclaim. "It's all in good fun, I assure you. All of the volunteers for the auction are of legal age and have willingly agreed to participate, and none of our patrons would expect…" My cheeks are burning.

Shaking my head, I close my eyes for a beat.

When I open them, Zuben's leaning forward slightly, his attention directly on me. "Will the pleasure of *your* company be on the auction block, Ms. Cross?"

"Me?" I shudder. "No, I…"

Setting down my cocktail glass, my fingers slip and the glass tumbles forward. I reach for it, and the top of the thin vessel ends up sandwiched between my palms.

I crush it.

"Oh!" Embarrassment floods me and I catch the stream of blood with my other hand to make sure none lands on the white tablecloth.

"You are bleeding." Zuben's elegant fingers take my injured hand, and he studies it with a brazen intensity that makes me feel unbelievably vulnerable. Inhaling deeply, he studies my cut palm.

His hold is at once gentle and firm, his skin transferring an electric heat into mine that makes me ignore the pain from the cut. My heart races as he bends forward and pulls a tiny shard of glass from the wound.

Blood oozes from the cut, and he bends to press his mouth against my palm.

An intense shiver of pleasure races through me that I don't understand, and my face heats as if I'm too close to a raging fire. His lips on my skin feel foreign, his action's shocking, but my pain eases, and time seems to stop as I relish the thrill of his lips moving against my skin and his tongue unmistakably flicking over my wound.

Still with his mouth on my palm, his gaze lifts to meet mine, and I realize my mouth is open, my breath thready, and even more shocking, desire is pooling between my legs. Desire like I've never felt before, not even reading the hottest romance novel or making out with the few boys I briefly dated in college.

"Mr. Zuben," Shana says.

I pull my hand back and turn to see that she's returned, standing just in front of our table, her eyes wide.

"That was—" her back stiffens, "—I'm sorry, but that was *highly* inappropriate. Not to mention unsafe, your mouth against an open wound..."

Zuben nods to acknowledge her, but continues to stare at me, and something in his expression has changed. Something in his entire body, his entire presence. There's now something animalistic, something wild lurking under the staid and elegant businessman's formal exterior. It scares me.

"Ms. Johnson is right," he says looking at me, "but the alcohol will kill any bacteria from my lips. Do you have any blood borne illnesses Ms. Cross?"

I shake my head.

"And did I make you uncomfortable?"

I shake no again, because uncomfortable isn't the word I'd choose to describe how he made me feel, although I do admit that the damp heat between my legs is making me feel some kind of way, especially as he leans closer again and inhales, like he can smell my unexpected arousal.

"Interesting." He leans back.

"Excuse me?" My voice comes out hoarse. Can he *tell* I'm aroused!

"Please forgive me, Ms. Cross." He's all business again. "Seeing you injured, I acted on instinct."

"Of course." My heart is racing a million beats a minute, and I have so much energy flowing through me I'm finding it hard to stay still. My body, so normally cautious—especially around men—wants to get closer to him, to touch him, to have him touch me again.

The waiter appears and pulls out the table.

"Ms. Cross." Zuben stands and bows his head quickly. "I do hope that we can move past my faux pas. I very much look forward to seeing you at the gala."

He turns to Shana. "I will give you my decision at the event." He steps out from behind the table and once again directs all his attention on me. "Perhaps I will make a bid on your lot in the live auction, Ms. Cross."

"Call me Ember, please." I try to regain control of my trembling voice. "But I'm not going to the gala."

His head cocks to the side. "Why ever not?"

My chest tightens. "I'm not a party sort of person."

"But the organization's accountant should be present at such an important event." He turns to Shana.

I take a step back, my throat tightening. Shana and I have already hashed this out, and she agreed to let me off the hook, just as she has for our past galas and nighttime board meetings, but shame is stretching its monstrous hands inside me. My irrational fear of the night is impacting my job.

"I've worked with our fundraising manager to develop airtight procedures and controls for the event," I tell

Zuben. "I assure you that the auction bids and other donations will be properly handled."

"Since you are so well prepared—" Zuben smiles "—you will be free to enjoy the evening."

"Ember can't go to the gala," Shana interjects.

"Why ever not?" he asks, his persistence leaving me both flattered and full of shame.

Shana's lips twist, a clear sign she's trying to figure out how to explain, without being rude or betraying my confidence—both things she's loath to do. "Are you making her attendance a condition of your donation? Because that's not—"

"I'm afraid of the dark," I blurt to rescue my boss. It's my issue and I certainly don't want to do anything to jeopardize the donation.

Zuben's attention snaps toward me. "I don't understand. Surely the event will have adequate lighting?"

"Yes. Of course." I shake my head. "It's just that…" I've never felt more like a toddler, and his gaze is filled with intense interest, like a scientist with a newfound discovery.

"I apologize," he says, "if I have again overstepped."

"No apology required," I say offering an embarrassed smile. My fear is foolish, not to mention childish. I draw a long breath. "I'll see you there."

A smile spreads across his unnaturally handsome face, and my body heats as his gaze penetrates my skin.

# CHAPTER THREE

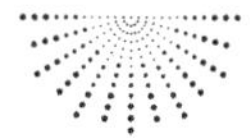

## *Ryker*

My eyes open slowly. It's dark, wherever the hell I am, and my tongue, thick from hunger, drags off the roof of my mouth like Velcro, leaving the taste of my own blood.

Holy shit, my body aches. Did I fall asleep on a rock?

Shifting, I discover bindings around my wrists, and wince as they burn. Fucking silver!

Panic grips my chest, but I take long breaths to hold that particular monster at bay, one that hasn't plagued me for nearly a century. *Keep calm,* I tell myself. *I might have been captured, but I'm not at sea. That nightmare is long over.*

And yet I *am* captive. Somewhere. This isn't a nightmare.

My night vision improves to offer a few clues. What the bloody hell did I get up to last night?

The last thing I remember…

Oh! That human wench! I took her vein right after I

fucked her… Was her blood dosed? She *did* seem too good to be true.

"Fuck!" I yell into the dark void that's clearly an interrogation room. Shit. It's got to be DEFTA, the biggest and most powerful vampire syndicate in the North East—hell, the entire country. How the hell did they snag me this time? I can think of several reasons as to *why*…

Using my night vision I confirm my suspicions, spotting DEFTA's ensign on a plaque at the end of the room—a lovely little number featuring a seventeen century carving of a man, ridiculously wearing a tall, wide brimmed hat and fancy long coat while wrestling a bear.

The Dutch and English Fur Trading Alliance publicly rebranded themselves as DEFTA during the anti-fur movements of the last century. Not that DEFTA was much involved in the fur trade for the better part of two hundred years before that.

Instead, the syndicate has been in the business of controlling the vampires of the Philadelphia area and beyond, under the guise of protecting us from humans and their wooden stakes. But humans are easily tamed—evidence the thirsty wench I fucked last night. These DEFTA assholes are just out for power and they hate vamps like me who refuse to join their little club and play along with their rules.

But it is true that humans have become a more lethal annoyance the past couple of decades. The unveiling of vampires as real has made it more challenging for an honest vamp to get a tasty meal without hassle. Dishonest ones like me, too.

Past several years, humans have gotten better at spotting us, more proficient with stakes, and have started using unfair tricks like silver netting, and I sure as shit hope humans don't know about whatever got into my bloodstream last night.

Lights come on, and I blink against the sudden change.

Behind me, a door opens and the distinct scent of two vampires enters the room—presumably along with their actual bodies. I grin at my unspoken joke.

One of the vamps positions himself in front of me and, dressed in an overstuffed business suit, he spreads his muscled legs beyond hip width, like some kind of power stance. What a joke.

Slowly, as if I could care less, I let my gaze drift up his body, finding his arms crossed over his chest—typical—and I glare with hatred when my eyes reach his gloating face, framed by unnaturally blond hair, even though it's been that color for the couple of hundred years that I've known the asshole.

Diederik Van de Berg, DEFTA's chief gorilla.

"Hello *Ricky*," I say to the security head. "Nice place you have here. Thanks for having me over."

The side of his mouth quirks up in a half grin that develops into a full on sneer. The vampire's eyes are a dull hazel made even more dull by his personality.

I tug up on the bindings. "Is this really necessary?" I fight my reaction to the pain and the smell of my burning skin.

"Can I trust you to behave?" Diederik asks.

I want to smack the arrogance right off his face. "Don't I *always* behave?"

"If you did, I wouldn't have had to resort to such measures."

"Touché." I glare at him, but he makes no move to release my cuffs. "Who's your buddy?" I ask. Whoever else is in the room, it's another vampire, male, and standing just out of my sight, even when I look over my shoulder.

Diederik shifts his gaze to his companion and a tall vampire with smooth, light brown skin steps into view. He's also dressed in a business suit, but his is way fancier and so pristine it's like it's hanging on a mannequin. I wonder if he's ever sat down in the thing.

"This is Zuben," Diederik says, "Senior Vice President of Research and Compliance."

The expressionless man is carrying a tablet in his left hand, and standing so stiffly he might have a literal pole up his ass. His skin is so smooth, his features so perfect and striking, it's hard to believe that he's real. I much prefer my fuck partners to be female, but even I can't deny this guy is hot.

Given the name Zuben, he's probably Egyptian, or was at some time in the past. But he doesn't seem old, definitely not one of the Ancients. The guy can't have been a vampire more than a few hundred years. I'd guess we're contemporaries in terms of time spent sucking blood.

I lean toward Diederik. "Cute robot."

"Very funny, Ryker," Diederik replies.

"I'm a veritable barrel of laughs." I stretch a leg forward, or rather I try to, but discover they're bound as well. At least my leather slacks partially shield my ankle from the pain. "Take these fucking things off."

"My security team is watching the room," Diederik says. "If you try *anything*—"

"What would I try?" Lifting my fingers, I shake my head. "Seems this time you've outsmarted me, *Ricky*."

His lips twitch, and I try not to grin. Yes, he *did* capture me, and I may currently be trapped inside his little room—and I hate being trapped—but we both know who has the upper hand, who *always* has the upper hand. That would be me. Even if I don't play my trump card.

Reaching back to the desk behind him, Diederik touches a button, and the silver cuffs snap open around my wrists and ankles.

Gripping the arms of the cast iron chair, I bite down on the hiss that escapes my mouth when the burning metal leaves my skin.

"How did you snag me?" I ask. "Was it that tasty human I had for my midnight snack?"

"Yeah." Diederik laughs. "You should be more careful what you eat. DEFTA has plenty of safe blood sources, if you'd join—"

"Why am I here?" No way am I joining DEFTA.

"I just want to talk."

"If you're *that* desperate for a fuck—" I leer at Diederik "—you could have just asked."

"Asshole." Diederik leans back against the table.

"What did you give me?" I ask. The woman didn't taste like garlic.

"Colloidal silver," Diederik answers, like the predictable Bond villain he is. "We gave her a transfusion, and as soon as you showed signs of drifting, one of my team injected more silver straight into your jugular."

He looks so fucking proud of himself, and I suppose he has a right to, but there's no chance I'll ever let something like that happen again, no matter how gorgeous and tasty the morsel that's dangled in front of me. No shortage of fish in the sea.

But…silver in my veins? No wonder I'm so groggy and thirsty. How long have I been here?

I slouch back in the chair, folding one leg up over the side and slinging my arm over its back, as if the uncomfortable interrogation furniture is a plush easy chair. "Come on Ricky. Spill. Why am I really here? Surely you're not *that* desperate to fuck me." I adjust my package, delighted to get a reaction from Diederik. The homophobe is so predictable.

The robot, on the other hand, hasn't moved a muscle since he arrived in my eyesight.

I turn my attention to him. "Reuben was it?" I say knowing full well I've got the name wrong.

His back goes even stiffer. "Zuben."

"And what is it *you* do for this lovely crime syndicate, Reuben?"

He blinks. First sign of emotion. "DEFTA is not a crime syndicate, and as Diederik already informed you, I head up the Research and Compliance departments." His eyes are alert, full of interest.

And…I hate to admit it, this Zuben dude is beyond handsome.

I prefer to be the prettiest in the room, and I can't shake his cool. I may have underestimated the robot. Time will tell.

"Compliance." I nod, leering at him. "That's secret

code for BDSM, right? Kinky." I wink. Maybe the same buttons will work with him as with Diederik.

"No." He backs up a step and shifts his tablet to the other hand. "If you must know, I oversee and conduct research and other investigations related to DEFTA's interests."

"What kind of investigations?" I ask casually, small talk.

"This particular matter relates to finance."

"Numbers guy." I yawn. "Figures."

I get a reaction—finally—a small adjustment of his shoulders, and his chin tips up a fraction of an inch. He did not like that characterization. And when I find someone's buttons, I'm like a toddler with a remote.

I smirk. "Bean counter. Pencil pusher. Figures." I raise my fist to my mouth and fake cough. "Nerd."

Not getting the reaction I hoped for, I push that button again. "Women must find you *fascinating*. I bet you know *all* the prime numbers."

The right edge of his mouth lifts just a little. "Are you asking me for romantic advice?" he asks. "If so, I would recommend staying away from listing prime numbers on a first date, and your joke was blatantly sexist. Many women are interested in finance and science."

"Good to know." It's interesting that he brought up science when that wasn't even on the table. I file that away too.

"Ryker." Diederik draws my attention. "If you're done trying to provoke Zuben—good luck with that, by the way—it's time to get on with the interrogation. I don't have all day."

"Neither do I. Places to go, people to drink." I turn toward Zuben and scan his body with the most salacious look I can muster. "Ruben and I can continue our flirtations later." I lean forward. "He already seems plenty…stiff."

Zuben steps back. Clearly I've found another button to press. His cheeks darken and his fingers pick at the stitching of the leather cover on his tablet. He's rattled. And I don't feel as good about that as I usually do.

I turn to Diederik. "Okay. Let's get this over with. What can I do for you, Ricky? Why go to such lengths for a visit? Or *are* you looking for a little action?" Grabbing my package, I thrust.

Diederik rolls his eyes. "Once an asshole, always an asshole."

"Sorry, Ricky. But I'm going to have to say no to that. I'm a top. *Hard limit.*" I grin. Laughter always greases the wheels.

But Diederik frowns, clearly reaching *his* hard limit with this conversation. "Ryker Stone, you've been detained on suspicion of piracy."

"Piracy?" I hold up my hand toward him. "Okay, okay. Let me stop you right there. That's all in my past. I haven't been a pirate for at least two hundred and fifty years."

"But you do admit to acts of piracy at one time." Zuben steps forward, his striking, brown eyes focused hard on me.

Leaning back in the chair, I shrug. "Sure." I wink. "Do pirates turn you on, Reuben?"

"Enough!" Diederik interrupts. "This isn't a joke Ryker."

I cock my head to the side. "Really? Because you two are cracking me up. Have we time travelled to the eighteenth century? Shit. I haven't even been on a ship—pirate or otherwise—for at least fifty years."

"No." I raise my index finger to my lips in mock dismay. "You crack detectives have caught me in a lie. I took a booze cruise the last time I visited New Orleans. Best I recall, I got shit-faced on the blood of my fellow partiers. Think that was in the mid-eighties… The *nineteen* eighties if you want to get technical."

"Piracy takes many forms." The tall Egyptian lifts his tablet, opens the cover and starts swiping the screen. "What do you know about a thousand gold bars that vanished from a container at the Port of Philadelphia in 2008?"

"That was a bad year for a lot of people in finance," I say. "I'm sorry to hear you lost some of your gold trinkets during the recession." I pout at him and keep my tone light, but my neck muscles tighten.

I don't remember the exact number, but I did manage to…um…*shift the ownership* of a whole lot of gold bars in 2008. I had no idea any were DEFTA's. Not that it would have made any difference. Once a pirate, always a pirate.

"And in 1993," Zuben continues, "five million US dollars worth of bearer bonds disappeared in the Caymans while they were being transferred by armored truck from our vault—at night."

"Fascinating." I nod in interest. "Sounds like you need to be more careful about where you leave your toys." I grin. I am particularly proud of how I pulled off that heist in the Caymans. I had to get past four vampires and at least a dozen human guards to pull it off.

"Thing is," Diederik's eyes narrow, Zuben's team discovered that *you* cashed that same dollar value of bearer bonds in Panama two days after ours vanished."

"Did I?" I shrug. "I don't think I've been in Panama since the canal was built."

"Yes you have." Zuben swipes and pokes his tablet several times, and then turns it toward me. "This account in the National Bank of Panama is in your name." His expression is smug, and I hate smug—unless of course it's coming from me.

"It's *possible* that I have a bank account or two in Panama." I flip my hand. "I have financial interests worldwide. Can't keep track. Hey!" I exclaim as if I've just had a brilliant idea. "I should hire someone like you to help me keep track." I lean toward Zuben. "Are you looking for a change? You interested in a position—*under* me?"

Zuben's eyes narrow.

Diederik steps forward. "Did you, or did you not cash bearer bonds in the amount of five million dollars in Panama on December 16, 1993."

"Doubt it. I hate the tropics." I cross one leg over the other. "Too much sunlight, even in winter. Then again..." I draw a long breath and sigh. "Some days, don't you just yearn for daylight?"

"All the time," Zuben says under his breath and I grin to myself, finding another button to press.

"Speaking of sunlight." I stand and stretch. "If that's all, chaps, I'd like to get home before that bugger of a burning star shows its face."

"It is currently 6:30 pm," Zuben says.

"No shit?" I've lost a whole day, but at least I know that once I talk my way out of this room, I can leave the building. "How long have I been down here?"

"Seventeen hours, more or less," Diederik says. "Seems we overdid it on the silver."

"No shit." I frown. Unconscious and full of silver so long, no wonder I'm famished, not to mention groggy, and now that I'm standing, the room is swaying as if I've got sea legs. "Great talk guys, but no need to go to so much trouble next time you want to chat."

"I do not believe that you would have come in if we'd simply asked," Zuben snaps.

"I guess we'll never know." I turn toward the door. " I'm off."

Diederik steps in front of me. "Who said you could go?"

"Are you saying I can't?" Time for my trump card. "Because if you are, I think we should talk to your boss."

"I am his boss," Zuben says behind me, and I try to hide my surprise. This guy has more power at DEFTA than I thought.

"I meant *your* boss, then," I say to Zuben. "The CEO?" I smile at Diederik who's fully aware of my relationship with the head honcho here.

"You have no right to—" Zuben says, but Diederik shakes his head, and steps away from the door.

"Zuben." The fear in the big vampire's voice is obvious. "I don't think we want to bother the CEO about this."

Zuben nods sharply. "I concur. It is premature to

involve her, but this is not over. Not by a long shot. My investigation has only just begun and I have a long list of thefts with which I suspect you are involved."

I turn slowly toward him. "With which you suspect I am involved?" I mock his tone, and then chuckle under my breath. "Well, la-di-da. When you put it so eloquently, so *formally*...I almost take you seriously." I tip my head to the side. "Still. If you fellows plan to hold me, we really should check in with the boss. Not sure if Reuben knows that Octavia and I go *way* back."

Sure, not all of our history is good, but it's well known in the city that the head of this vampire syndicate was my lover for a time, and our past relationship has gotten me out of a multitude of scrapes. Typically vampire syndicates only protect their members, but Octavia's makes an exception for me. I'm safe in this city.

"Shall we call Octavia?" I ask again. She scares the shit out of me, but I'm sure she'd set me free. Pretty sure.

Zuben's repressed anger and frustration are reaching a boiling point—I see it simmering under his skin, hear it in his pulse. Perhaps I've pushed his buttons one too many times.

"Call the CEO if you must." Zuben's tone is clipped and sharp. Is he not afraid of Octavia? "I have twelve other thefts about which I would like to question this pirate."

"About which..." I chuckle under my breath.

"Look," Diederik turns toward Zuben. "With all due respect, we need solid proof before getting the CEO involved."

"I *do* have proof!" Zuben's cheeks darken again. "Or

will soon. I am certain that Octavia will agree that this suspect needs to turn over his financial records…"

"Financial records?" I chuckle. "All I know about my money is that I've got a shit ton of it. That's another argument for you to work under me." I raise my eyebrows and Zuben looks away.

Diederik shrugs. "Even with proof, we can't hold him longer than eighteen hours without going to the judiciary committee…"

Zuben blinks at the burly security head, nods sharply, and then drops his tablet to his side and turns toward me. The Egyptian's lashes are so thick and black they look fake.

"This isn't the end." Zuben steps toward me, frustration still clearly bubbling inside him. "Not the end by a long shot. You are a *pirate,* and I will prove it, and then you will be brought to justice for your crimes."

His clear determination makes my nerves spark, but I raise my hands in mock fear. "Oooo, so *scary*!"

Diederik's been a thorn in my side for decades, but today the asshole's last argument is my ticket out of here. With the King's return, the local syndicates have less freedom to interpret vampiric laws without oversight. Long live the fucking King.

The door audibly clicks.

I open it and stride down the hall, push open the glass doors at its end and then wait for the elevator. This fellow Zuben is going to be a problem for me. While the King's return means DEFTA can't act above the law, it also means that if Zuben goes above her head to the Crown, Octavia may no longer have the power to protect me.

To get leverage, I need to find out what this Egyptian

vampire knows, what he cares about, who he *loves*—assuming robots are capable of love. Everyone has secrets, pressure points; I'll discover his and exploit them.

Until he lets this go, I plan to stick to the robot like glue—make his life miserable.

There is no chance in hell I will ever let myself be locked up again. I'd rather die.

No...If I'm ever locked up again, I *will* die.

# CHAPTER FOUR

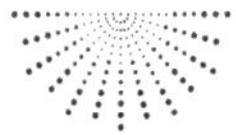

## *Ember*

"THE ROOM LOOKS FANTASTIC!" Shana smiles as we survey the results of all our hard work. "Way better than I expected."

"Thanks. I guess?" I turn to her, not sure if she meant that as a backhanded compliment.

"Seriously, Ember," her genuine smile puts me at ease. "I've been to a *lot* of posh parties. You've got a real talent for this."

"Thanks." Pride warms my body. I did do a good job and working hard distracted me from thinking about tonight. I don't know which scares me more, seeing Zuben again or staying out after dark.

Shana pats my arm. "Plus, you saved Sanctuary House several thousand dollars by designing the decor and setting it up yourself."

I hope that helps Shana from urging me to go on the auction block tonight. I can't imagine I'd fetch much, anyway. Our volunteers for the auction include prominent socialites and politicians, plus some models and local TV personalities. Even if I participated, no one would bid on me.

*Or would Zuben?* My body heats, considering the possibility. But I'm sure I read too much into his attention last week.

I turn back to Shana. "Thanks for appreciating my work, but all I did was google a bunch of pictures and combine my favorites." My words are modest, but I am proud of the results. Despite the hotel's fancy address and reputation, the room wasn't much when we started and it took tons of planning and a full day of work to set up. "Maybe I should go into the party planning business."

"No way," Shana says quickly, and the stab of reality bursts my pride bubble.

I shake my head. "You're right. I plan one party and—"

"No, No." She pats my arm. "You'd be *great* at it. It's just that I'd hate to lose you."

Pride reheats my cheeks, but then I notice that one of the centerpieces isn't placed correctly, and I head to adjust it.

Shana follows. "Who knew my accountant had such hidden talents." She looks at her watch. "We'd best get changed. The patrons will start arriving soon."

"Really?" All the air sucks out of my chest as the nerves start to set in. "What time is it?" I glance around the room for a clock. My phone is with my party clothes in a closet, and absorbed in the decorating, I lost track of time.

Shana puts her hands on my shoulders. "Lamby, the sun went down over an hour ago. And look… You haven't turned into a pumpkin." Her warm smile offers comfort as my anxiety rises. "Relax. You're perfectly safe."

Easy for her to say. I chew the inside of my lower lip, trying to pump up my courage. I agreed to attend this event and I've got to live with the consequences. While it might be the first time in my life that I've been outside my own house after sundown, I am not a baby. I am no longer afraid of the dark. *I'm not.*

Drawing a deep breath, I survey the room one final time. This fancy, Rittenhouse Square hotel ballroom doesn't have windows, and so if I don't let myself think about what's going on outside, I can ignore the fact that I'm out after dark.

Shana drags me to the ladies room and we put on our party dresses and heels. Exiting my stall first, I turn back and forth, admiring my outfit in the full-length mirror at the end of the room. It's my first fancy dress and I'm still getting used to how I look.

Never going out after dark eliminates the need for outfits like this, and the red dress the saleswoman convinced me to buy, has miraculously transformed me into an entirely different person, a different *species* perhaps.

But I feel naked without a bra, and the thong underwear is strange and intrusive, but the saleslady was right to talk me into those choices too. The barely there underwear does improve the line of the soft, clingy fabric that's hugging my hips and butt and skimming over my breasts.

The longer I look into the mirror, the less the reflection looks like me. Maybe that's the key to surviving this evening—disassociation. I'm not here, my alter ego is. An alter ego who happens to be adventurous and up for fun. An alter ego who might even flirt with the stunningly hot Zuben if given a chance.

After tucking strands of dark hair behind my ears, I press my hands into my belly to calm the butterflies—more like bats—flapping their wings in there.

The door to the handicapped stall opens, and Shana steps out in a floor length gown in a bright African print that's gorgeous on her. She digs into a big cloth shopping sack, pulls out a huge flowered cosmetic bag and plops it onto the counter. She glances toward me. "Oh, Ember!"

"What?" I ask, looking over my shoulder into the mirror, hoping I don't have a stain on the back of the dress.

"You look *amazing*," she says. "A-ma-zing. Who knew you had a body like that hidden under all the loose clothes you wear."

I cross my arms over my chest, suddenly self-conscious. Digging into her cosmetics bag, she steps up to the mirror and applies deep purple lipstick.

"Want some?" she asks, holding the tube toward me.

I shake my head.

"You're right." She nods. "With your pale complexion, you need red." She digs into the bag, extracts a dark black tube shaped like a bullet, and squints at its bottom. "Can't read for shit these days." She shakes her head. "But I think this is the one."

She hands me the lipstick, and I lift the cap and slowly roll out the lip stain. It's a very deep red—the color of blood—and goes well with my dress.

"I don't know..." I've never worn make up.

"Trust me," she says. "With your pale skin, dark hair and violet eyes, this will be per-fection."

Leaning in close to the mirror, I paint my lips, careful to stay inside the lines, and then step back to survey my work.

"Oh!" I stare at the woman in the mirror, amazed at how the tiny bit of make up has transformed me even more than the dress did. Now, I really don't recognize myself.

"Perfect. Told you." Shana has a smug, but proud look on her face when I turn, and I reach out to give her the lipstick.

"You keep it, lamby. For touch ups."

I nod and slip it into the tiny silver purse that matches the strappy high heels that I've practiced walking in every night since I bought them.

"Ready?" she asks.

"Ready as I'll ever be."

"Great. Let's stash our day clothes in the closet and get ready to raise some serious dough."

I call on my alter ego to take over for the night. My alter ego is brave. She can do this.

# CHAPTER FIVE

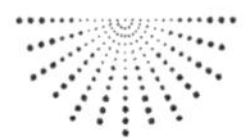

### *Ember*

"Did you eat?" Shana asks after dinner, and I shake my head.

She frowns. "They're holding plates for staff in the kitchen. Grab a break before the auction starts."

I nod, but I couldn't possibly eat. The set up was hard work, but it was nothing compared to the actual event so far. I've been running non-stop for three hours and adrenaline's pumping through my bloodstream at a hurricane's wind speed.

"Have you seen him yet?" Shana asks.

"Who?" But I know exactly who she means.

She cocks her head to the side. "Zuben, our mysterious potential benefactor."

I shake my head. "Not yet." The cloud of bats goes berserk in my belly.

Shana frowns. "If he's a no show…" The worry on her face is clear, but she draws a deep breath and smiles. "If his answer is no, then our short term survival hinges on the live auction's success. It's due to start soon. Let's focus on that. After you eat."

"I'll check the silent auction tables," I tell Shana. "I'll grab a bite after that."

She shakes her head, feigning disapproval, but I see the opposite in her eyes. I head to the silent auction area, where dozens of patrons are chatting as they peruse the various items up for grabs.

I move the velvet rope set up to block off the backs of the tables, and then walk down the line, making sure that none of the sheets are completely filled, and checking to see whether there are any items without bids.

Mia, the fundraising manager spots me, heads over and puts her hands on her hips. "What are you doing back here?"

"Just making sure that everything's running smoothly."

Mia frowns. "My team and I have this."

"Yes. Of course you do." I let myself out from behind the tables, leaving Mia to her area of expertise.

She's right. Technically I don't need to be involved in the silent auction while it's running—not even once it's closed. My being here wasn't in the original plans, and the staff are well set up to collect the winning bids smoothly without me, but the busier I am, the less time there is left to think about everything else.

Keeping to the shadows at the side of the room, I look for anything out of place.

"I'm sorry, sir, but this is a ticketed event." A voice rises at the front of the room and I quickly make my way to the entrance area. Most of the patrons arrived hours ago, but a few are still trickling in, even though dinner is over.

Henry, one of our former clients who now volunteers as a mentor, is blocking the entrance. Seeing why, I'm grateful that we picked a large person like Henry to guard the door. The man he's blocking looks dangerous.

Fear gathers inside me as I step toward the pair of men.

The gate crasher isn't doing anything physical or overtly intimidating, he's smiling as he talks to Henry, and yet…everything about him reads danger: his long hair, partially tied up in a messy man bun, the well worn leather jacket that looks like it's from another time—another place. He's probably from New York or Montréal, somewhere way more fashionable than Philly.

I step up behind the table that Henry's guarding and see more of the man.

His pants are leather too, a dark grey that perhaps was once black, and his boots are heavy, out of place but oddly stylish. Whether or not he has a ticket, he's certainly not dressed for the occasion, not even close. Is there a motorcycle club gathering in another part of the hotel? Or a pirate themed costume party? I grin to myself to tamp down the fear racing through me as I drink in this intimidating man.

"Can I help you?" I ask.

His head swivels toward me, his eyes flashing interest, and then a smile breaks onto his face. "I can think of *many* ways *you* could help me."

My ankles wobble.

Light glints off his bright blue eyes, gleaming like a

beacon and drawing me forward, my body reacting before my brain catches up. The beacon is more likely a warning than a welcome.

The man shifts until he's across from me, his body projecting confidence and strength as he leans onto the table that separates our bodies. Even his hands broadcast danger. Laden with heavy rings, some gold, some silver—one has a skull—his thick, powerful fingers also sport tattoos, a series of stars and dots in a seemingly random pattern, all black against his skin.

My focus drifts behind his hands, where his thick leather pants stretch over powerful hips and thighs, molding around a very obvious bulge.

My mouth goes dry.

It's not like I haven't seen male genitalia—well, in photos—but this is my first time exposed to such an obvious display. I can't look away.

"My eyes are up here," he says.

Cheeks heating, I snap my gaze up to find his eyes laughing, and his grin even wider than before.

"I'm so sorry," I say, then I shake my head, realizing I've probably made the situation worse, all but admitting my illicit ogling.

"No worries, luv. Looking's free." He winks, but then his expression softens. "But my joke embarrassed you. I apologize." He puts one of those scary looking hands over his heart.

"That's okay." I laugh, shocked at how quickly he's set me at ease. "I embarrass easily."

"I can see that." His eyes study me intently, and I can't

figure out whether the glint I see there is kindness or mischief. Maybe both?

Stepping back from the table, he bows. "Ryker Stewart Stone, at your service." He reaches forward toward me. "And you are?"

"I'm Ember. Ember Cross." I reach out to shake his hand, but turning mine in his, he kisses my knuckles.

An electric shock races from his lips to settle deep between my legs. I suck in a ragged breath.

Holding my hand, he presses his lips against my skin longer than seems necessary—or proper—all the while looking up and into my eyes—even while straightening as he finally lets go.

I'm left breathless and more than a little unsettled. "What can I do for you, Mr. Stone?" I stammer.

"Ryker. Please." He smiles. "You must call me Ryker."

I nod.

"I live in the hotel," he says, "and thought I spotted a friend of mine coming in here." He looks past me into the ballroom.

"Oh?" I say. "Who is that? We can look him up—or her?—on the guest list."

"I might have been mistaken," he says. "But now that I'm here, your party seems festive, your cause worthy. Might as well attend."

"He doesn't have a ticket," Henry interjects, and my eyes snap to the burly young man I'd forgotten was there.

"With your permission," Ryker says bowing slightly, "I'd very much like to *purchase* a ticket. And of course I'll also make a handsome donation on top of the ticket price to apologize for my tardy arrival."

"We don't actually sell tickets at the door." I drag my teeth over my lower lip, wondering why I didn't make a plan for same day admissions. "We don't typically get walk-in traffic. Plus—" I gesture behind me "—dinner is over. You've missed everything except the live auction."

"I'm not hungry." He leans onto the table. "Not for dinner, anyway." His words come off predatory, but his grin doesn't, and both stir up whatever's fluttering inside my body.

"To be honest," he continues, "it was your saucy little auction that drew my attention." He tips his head to the side. "Humans for sale? How very eighteenth century."

"It's not like that!" I blurt, but then I smile, as his eyes reveal he was teasing again, joking.

"Perchance," he asks, "are *you* on the auction block?"

I shake my head.

"Aw, what a shame." His chest expands under his white shirt and leather coat, as he heaves an exaggerated sigh. "Nevertheless, I'd love to attend your little soiree and, as I said, I will make a sizable donation."

"Is there a problem?" Shana arrives beside me.

"This gentleman would like to attend the gala," I tell her.

"*And* make a sizable donation," he adds.

"He doesn't have a ticket," Henry interjects.

Shana clears her throat. "The tickets are $500." She crosses her arms over her chest, clearly assuming this will close the matter and send him away. "We accept all major credit cards—and no discount because you missed dinner." Shana is clearly hoping to get rid of this guy, and I'm shocked to find myself disappointed.

Ryker reaches into his jacket, pulls out a gleaming gold bar and sets it onto the table. "I assume this will cover it?"

"Is that real gold?" I ask, breathless.

"Sure is, luv." Raising his eyebrows at me, Ryker runs a thick finger down its gleaming metal side, and the gesture is so sensual I can feel its effect on me.

"Sir." Shana leans onto the table. "I'm afraid we can't accept your stage prop or whatever it is. But as I said, we *do* accept all major credit cards."

"Too generous?" His finger traces the markings on the bar. *AU 999.9, 400 oz.*

I'm not sure what an ounce of gold is worth, but suspect it's a hundred dollars at least, so if I'm right and this is four hundred ounces of gold, it's worth…forty thousand? Is that right?

"Is that really four hundred ounces of gold?"

He looks into my eyes. "Sure is, my very, *very* bonnie lass." He taps the bar. "This puppy's currently worth about seven-fifty, more or less."

"Seven hundred and fifty dollars?" I inhale. It's less than I thought, but still… "That's very generous." I turn to Shana. "At least fifty percent more than the ticket is worth."

Frowning, she shakes her head. "He means, seven hundred and fifty *thousand* dollars."

I gasp, turning back toward Ryker. "Three quarters of a million?" My heart races; my head buzzes. I've never seen so much money.

"But it's clearly fake," Shana adds flatly.

"Madam." Placing his hand over his heart, Ryker leans toward Shana. "I assure you, it is not."

Shana's eyes narrow. "You're saying you carry gold bars around in your motorcycle jacket?" Her voice drips in disbelief.

"This, madam is most definitely not a *motorcycle* jacket." He runs his hand over his leather coat, like he's a tailor proud of his finest fares.

"Listen." Shana's voice rises. "If you and your fake gold bar don't get out of here, I'm calling security."

"Heavens," he says in a mocking tone. "Not hotel security! What a terrifying threat."

"There's no need for sarcasm." Shana folds her arms over her chest. "If you prefer, we can skip past the hotel and go straight to the police."

"Might I be of assistance?" says a deep warm voice from behind us.

I turn to find Zuben standing a few feet away, even more shockingly handsome in a tuxedo, one that fits him so well it looks tailored to the millimeter. The light from the hall sparkles in his dancing brown eyes and their attention is directly on me.

I back up, running into the table behind me, my body trembling at the close proximity to not one but two men I find immensely attractive. Two men who couldn't be more different.

"Mr. Zuben!" Shana's voice draws my attention and a grin spreads over her face. "No one informed me you'd arrived." She glares at Henry, who's now leaning against the wall and scrolling on his phone, so engrossed he doesn't notice the reprimand.

"Just Zuben," he says. "No need for the mister, and I

arrived only moments ago." He glares at Ryker. "Perhaps I was followed."

*Followed?* Is Zuben the friend that Ryker claimed to be looking for? The vibe between them doesn't seem friendly.

Zuben turns toward Shana. "Did I hear you were calling the police? Is something amiss?" Looking down at the table, his eyes open wider. "Is that LGD?" The two men make eye contact, distrust written all over both of their faces. Whoever they are to each other, they are not friends.

"Zuben," I say, hoping to smooth the situation. "This gentleman offered to pay for his ticket with a gold bar, but we're not sure that it's authentic."

"May I?" Zuben asks.

Shana steps to the side, a smug look on her face, like she's glad to have an ally, and the two men stare at each other. It's clear that *something* is going on, but I can't make out what.

"Do you know each other?" I ask Zuben.

"Haven't had the pleasure," Ryker says quickly, extending his hand. "Ryker Stone, and you are?"

"An expert in gold bullion," Zuben replies without looking up from the bar.

"Well now, that is helpful." Ryker says, and then raises his eyebrows as he looks at me. "I'm very happy to have someone settle this." He leans across the table, moving his lips close to my ear. "So that you and I can get better acquainted."

A shiver races through me—the tremor a mixture of fear and something else—and I shift closer to Zuben, inappropriately closer I realize too late, but instead of moving away, Zuben presses his hip against mine.

Warmth, and what can only be called electricity, sparks from the connection, but Zuben acts as if he hasn't even noticed as he picks up the gold bar and examines it, flipping it over, running his fingers over the indentations, holding it up to the light, testing the weight of it in his hands and examining some faint indentations on the back.

"Where did you get this?" he asks Ryker.

"None of your fucking business," Ryker replies, and then he nods toward Shana and me. "Ladies, please pardon my French."

Ryker captures my gaze and something stirs deep inside me. Something that leaves me uncomfortable, yet craving more. *What is going on with me?* Here I am pressing my hip against one man and flirting with another.

Perhaps *this* is why Mom warned me not to go out after dark. Maybe she cast some kind of nymphomania spell on me that only activates after dark.

I shake my head at that foolish thought. More than a decade after mom disappeared, I'm not even sure I believe in magic anymore. My childhood is like a bad nightmare, mostly forgotten.

"This bar is authentic," Zuben says to Shana. "And based on today's spot rate, I would estimate its value at… seven hundred and eighty-six thousand, four hundred and fifty eight US dollars, give or take."

"You're shitting me!" Shana exclaims, then raises her hand to her mouth. "It's real? I mean—really?"

Ryker shrugs. His body reads, *I told you so,* but casually, like it's no big deal, like his pockets are full of those bars. Maybe they are.

"And you want to donate this gold bar to Sanctuary House?" Shana's voice is a mixture of wonder and skepticism.

"Sure," Ryker says, "why the hell not." His eyes flash wider, like he's had an idea, and he leans toward Shana. "And that isn't the limit of my finances. In fact, I'm very much looking forward to your live auction."

Shana tips her head to the side, considering the suggestion, then she turns to Zuben. "Are you absolutely certain this is real?"

"Yes. I am afraid so." He glares at Ryker. "Very sure. And as your new benefactor, I would be happy to advise you whether you want to sell it, or store it safely as an investment." He hands her the bar and she grips it in both hands as if it might run away.

"So..." Shana's breathless.

"Yes. I have decided to pledge my funding in the amount we discussed." Zuben nods sharply and his hip slides against mine, eliciting a sharp intake of breath combined with a tight contraction between my legs.

"For now," he continues, "might I suggest the hotel safe for this gold bar? I will be happy to escort you there, if you desire."

"Yes. Please." Shana nods. Her hands are shaking, and she looks at me, wide-eyed. "Can you find the emcee?" she asks. "Tell her to get ready to start the live auction. We'll begin as soon as Mr. Zuben and I get back."

"Sure." I say, my voice quivering with excitement. In the last few minutes, Sanctuary House's financial problems have been erased by these two wealthy and handsome men.

Zuben gestures for Shana to walk ahead of him. Waiting for her to pass, he turns back and makes eye contact with me, and his gaze is so intense, so focused, that heat explodes inside me. Heat I can't explain, but don't want to end. I watch, agog, as he holds the elevator door open for Shana and then follows her inside. Even the way Zuben walks is a study in masculine elegance—the perfect fusion of grace and strength.

"Guess that means I'm in like Flynn," Ryker says, snapping me out of my daze. Passing a bored Henry, he holds his elbow toward me. "Shall we?"

It takes me a moment to realize that he's offering me his arm, like in an old fashioned movie, and I take it. The leather of his jacket is softer than I expect—but the arm under it firmer. This man just donated over three quarters of a million dollars to Sanctuary House, and then there's the multi-year endowment from Zuben. This is going to be our best year for donations, ever. By a million miles.

"Ember," Ryker says as we stroll through the ballroom. "That is a beautiful name."

"Thank you. My mother claimed it was a family name, but I never got the chance to ask her more about it."

"I'm sorry." Stopping, he turns toward me. "Did your mother pass?"

"Yes. Well…" I draw a breath to push back rising tears that totally catch me by surprise. "I'm not totally sure, to be honest. My mom disappeared. She's been missing for over a decade."

"Oh, my." He puts his hand over mine that's still

resting on his arm. "You must have been a child when she vanished. How terrifying."

I nod, shocked that I've shared more with him than I've shared with anyone, ever. Shana doesn't even know anything about my family. Ryker and I just met, but even though he stirs up a mixture of fear and desire inside me, the compassion in his voice and expression make me feel like I can tell him anything, like I want to.

"That explains your interest in Sanctuary House." His fingers, over my hand, gently stroke. "Did you partake in their services as a teen?"

"No, but you're right. I understand the plight of homeless teens." Although I can't begin to compare my experience to that of our clients.

I had money. A place to live. And living out on the farm, I was able to evade child services until I turned eighteen.

"And your father?" he asks, his voice soothing like hot chocolate.

"I never knew him."

"Brothers and sisters?"

*Only in my dreams.* "I'm an only child."

His expression is painted with what looks like sincere empathy. "We orphans make our own families, right? A beautiful young woman, such as yourself, must have many good friends."

I look down, both embarrassed and sad as I'm hit by how totally alone I am in the world. I do know my fair share of people, but have never made any real friends—not before mother disappeared and definitely not after.

We were so isolated at the farm and now I avoid everyone. Mostly because it's hard to explain why I don't go out after dark. And I certainly don't like to go into how my mother disappeared, or how crazy I probably am to believe the things that happened that day. By avoiding friendships, I can keep those things to myself.

"My beautiful Ember." Ryker's voice draws my gaze from his chin to his eyes.

"If you permit me," he says. "I'd like to apply for the job."

"What job?" My brain is scrambled, my attention distracted by memories, and now by the flecks of teal and ice dancing inside the sky blue of his eyes. His eyes are like twin glacier-filled lakes.

"I make a *very* good friend," he says. "I'm loyal to a fault, understanding, and many find me amusing." He leans forward. "I've even been called *charming* by some." His expression has changed.

I step back, pulling my hand from under his and off his arm. I don't want to offend this major donor, but with the way he's looking at me…

I suspect he has something far beyond friendship in mind. I'm inexperienced with men, but no fool, and my gaze drifts back down to his bulge. Catching myself, I jerk my eyesight to the side. Clearly I have something beyond friendship in mind too.

"What are you drinking?" he asks, as if no awkwardness just happened.

"Drinking?"

He nods toward the bar. "Yes. What can I get you?"

"Oh, just water."

He lifts his elbow for me to take again, and when I

don't, he shifts his arm forward as if he was simply gesturing for me to follow, and we head toward the bar.

"Good evening barkeep," he says when we arrive. "We'll take two glasses of your best champagne."

"I've got a sparkling wine," the bartender says, looking bored. "It's got a twist off cap."

"That will do," Ryker answers.

"I'm not drinking—" My heart is already beating too quickly.

He holds up a finger to stop me. "Ember, as your oldest friend—"

"Oldest friend?" I laugh.

He grins. "Well, if I'm your *only* friend, then by definition I am also your oldest—not to mention dearest."

I smile at his logic and boldness. And I admit that the danger vibe I felt earlier has morphed into charm. But charm can be dangerous in its own right.

He leans toward me. "A little birdie told me that your organization received a *huge* donation tonight. I say that's cause for celebration, and you *cannot* celebrate with water. It's against the law."

I laugh. "What law is that?"

"The law of celebrations," he says. "The law of parties."

"And I suppose you're an expert on this particular area of the law?"

He lifts the two flutes of sparkling wine, and hands one to me. "I'm an authority."

"I see." I take the glass and our fingers brush on the stem. "And where did you study law?"

"Study?" He tips his flute toward me. "I am the *author* of the party laws."

Our glasses clink together, and he moves his toward his lips, pausing before he reaches the target. "Please, Ember," he says over the rim of his glass. "I would very much like to be friends, and friends do not let friends drink alone. Especially when celebrating."

He winks, and the effects of his charm spread through my body, making me feel drunk, even though I have yet to taste the beverage.

"To new friends," I say raising my glass.

"To our friendship," he responds. "One I hope will last forever."

I take a small sip of the wine, hiding my smile in my flute.

His words are sweet, but nothing lasts forever. If anyone knows that it's me.

# CHAPTER SIX

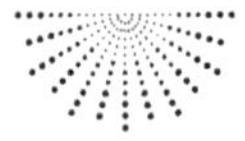

## *Ember*

"DISTINGUISHED PATRONS AND GUESTS," Shana says over the sound system. "It's time for our live auction!"

Completely engrossed in my conversation with Ryker, I snap out of my euphoric haze and turn toward the stage. My nerves are over-stimulated, my thoughts so fully immersed in his attention that I've completely forgotten I'm here for work.

"What is it?" Ryker asks.

My heart swells. We've only just met and he can tell when I'm worried.

"I should go up there," I tell him. "I'm the accountant for Sanctuary House, so I need to make sure all the bids are properly recorded."

"Stay," he says in a way that stirs in my lower belly and makes me want to obey his quasi command.

But at the same time, his demand encourages me to run. This attention from him, and from Zuben, it's all too much. I'm not used to it, especially not from two very different men, their apparent and inexplicable interest in me the only thing they have in common.

"Please excuse me." I step away, but he touches my hand before I can escape and leans forward, moving his lips close to my ear.

Electricity wakes parts of my body I barely knew existed as he traps my hand, preventing me from running up to the stage.

"Come back to me." His voice growls against my ear. "Soon."

His voice vibrates into my body and his heat radiates, increasing the strength of the strange electricity already coursing.

My fingers still engulfed in his, I look up into his eyes but can't fully read what I see there. This man is interested in me, of that I have no question, but I'm confused about the nature of his interest.

While we talked, his attention seemed romantic, and when he growled in my ear—unmistakably sexual—but right now, his interest seems more like curiosity, like I'm some kind of puzzle he's not finished solving.

Dropping my hand, Ryker grins and winks in a charming, joking way that's already starting to seem familiar. Perhaps I projected my own desire onto his earlier expressions and words. I overreacted to his friendly flirting. It doesn't mean anything.

"Are *you* going on the auction block?" he asks.

I shake my head.

"You should. I've heard it's for a good cause." His eyebrows rise. "I dare you."

"Sorry." I back a few steps away. "I've got to go."

Turning quickly toward the stage, I bump into a rotund patron, his belly hanging over his cummerbund. "I'm so sorry." I stammer to the man, and then dash through the crowd to take a seat at a table at the edge of the stage, next to Mia and her intern Rico.

Mia and her assistant Rico can handle this auction without me, but I need something to do, something to distract me from the way I feel around Ryker—dangerous, mysterious Ryker.

On stage, Zuben is reading a short script that Shana prepared, and I remember the touch of the tall elegant man's lips on my injured hand, the way he looked into my eyes when he tenderly kissed my cut palm.

So much for distractions.

Another round of heat shudders through me and dampens my barely-there panties. I can barely breathe now, barely think. Clearly it's not just the nighttime I can't handle, because I met Zuben in the daytime.

As overwhelmed as I feel, I have no doubt about one thing—something inside me has awakened tonight. Something scary and exciting. Something I dread, yet want to explore. It's all confusing and crazy, but every instinct inside me is screaming that nothing in my life will ever be the same again.

Up on stage, Zuben shakes his head, lowers Shana's notes, and then goes off script.

"Sanctuary House helps hundreds of young people each year," he says, his voice strong and clear. "This is a good cause, run by competent, caring people, so please, open your wallets and bid generously. Some of Philadelphia's finest restaurants and venues have donated dinners and tickets for the dates on the auction block, so I encourage you to bid on the chance to share an evening with one of the individuals who have volunteered their time."

"Now." He gestures to the side. "I will hand the microphone to our auctioneer, radio host Gloria Sanchez."

He walks off the stage as our emcee calls up the first person to be auctioned—a former player from one of the local sports teams. The date with this sports guy includes dinner at a fancy restaurant and floor seats at a sporting event—basketball, I think. I should know who the tall man is, but the electric charges buzzing through my body are scrambling my thoughts.

I need a task. Something to keep me occupied and distracted from my wild sexy mood and this raging desire inside me.

Standing, I turn to Mia. "I'll help Shana escort the winners to the front, okay?"

Mia shrugs, and I join Shana at the edge of the stage.

"Hey," I say to her. "Need some help finding the bid winners? Two sets of eyes are always better than one."

"Sure," she nods. "Teamwork makes the dream work." Shana's glowing. I've never seen her so elated, and with the huge donations from Ryker and Zuben, I guess she has a good reason. Unless…do these men affect her in the same way they affect me?

Nah. I've got nothing to worry about there. Shana is hopelessly devoted to her wife of sixteen years, even if only the last few years of that marriage have been official.

The final bid for the basketball date comes from a

middle-aged woman, and a spotlight is trained to where she's standing. She looks like she's had way too much plastic surgery, her skin unnaturally smooth and her eyes too open above her clinging and sparkling gown. Shana goes into the crowd to escort her up to Mia as I watch the crowd bid on the next "lot", a dinner and symphony date with our communications director, Shelly.

The bidding for Shelly is slow at first, only a single hundred dollar bid from a man I suspect is Shelly's husband, but then Ryker jumps the bid up to three hundred dollars, and another older man joins in. That sparks a four-way war that ends with the older man bidding six-hundred-and-fifty dollars.

I head out to escort the man up to pay, but before I reach him, Ryker steps into my path.

My breath catches in my chest. "Thanks for bidding," I stammer as the buzz revs up inside me again.

"I'll bid on everyone if it makes you happy." His eyes widen and fill with desire.

"You will?" I know it's hyperbole, but my heart thumps hard in my chest as my entire body heats and tingles. I feel paralyzed under his gaze, trapped.

Shana touches my shoulder, startling me. "I'll make sure the winning bidder gets up to Mia."

"Sorry." I shake my head, trying to clear my mind.

Grinning, she leans in close and whispers, "No worries, lamby. You entertain our donor."

Embarrassed, I keep my gaze trained on the carpeted floor and on Ryker's leather boots, which are oddly both rugged and elegant, like the costume from a period film.

In fact, his entire ensemble could be the costume from a movie now that I think of it.

"Penny for your thoughts?" His voice draws my gaze up to his face that's full of handsome amusement.

"I've never met anyone like you," I blurt before thinking.

"That's because there *is* no one like me." He grins.

I laugh. "Plus, you're so humble."

Chuckling, he brings his hands to his heart. "I'm no braggart. Just stating the facts." He shifts a few inches closer—or maybe it was me who moved?—and the heat of his body penetrates mine.

"And I've never met anyone like you," he says, his voice so deep and delicious I swear I can taste it.

"Excuse me." Another voice breaks into my consciousness, and I step back abruptly.

My lower back runs into Zuben's hand. Or did his hand purposefully catch me?

Drawing a deep breath to regain control of my senses and thoughts, I shift away from the fire of Zuben's touch on my back.

"Mr. Zuben—" I say.

"No mister," he corrects me. "Just Zuben."

I nod. "Yes, sorry—*Just* Zuben." I grin. "Thank you for kicking off the auction."

"It was my pleasure to participate," he says. "But now, I wonder if I might have a moment of your time, Ms. Cross."

"Just Ember," I say my cheeks heating.

"Just Ember." He nods, a smile dancing over his lush lips.

I glance toward Ryker who's glaring at Zuben, but his expression quickly changes back to something more neutral when he notices me looking.

"I hope I am not interrupting." Zuben looks at Ryker.

"As a matter of fact," Ryker says, "you *are* interrupting."

"Apologies," Zuben says. "But I assure you, my business with Ms. Cross is most urgent."

Squaring their shoulders, the two men face off in silence, as if each of their stares holds the power to slay the other. My body pulses, inexplicably drawn to both of these men. They aren't the only attractive men in the room, so whatever's going on with my body, not *every* good looking man is a trigger.

A shameful thought enters my mind. Am I attracted to wealth?

"What's wrong, Ember?" Zuben asks me. "You look ill. Did this cad offend you? Touch you inappropriately? Say something crude?" He shifts, like he's about to attack Ryker.

At first glance, the tall, elegant Zuben shouldn't be a fair match against the rugged, wide-shouldered Ryker, but as Zuben's chest expands and his chin rises I sense the immense power inside both of these men. If they fought, they'd tear each other apart, and I'm ashamed to be a little excited by the idea of watching that hypothetical battle.

Hoping to calm them, I lightly touch both of their arms, dropping both my hands before I give my fingers their fair chance to sense the solid muscles under their jackets.

"Everything's fine," I assure Zuben. "Great, in fact."

Zuben looks at me with concern. "I'm glad to hear that, but I really do need to speak to you. Alone."

I nod, but Ryker's clearly annoyed. At this moment, I can't choose which man to please and which to disappoint. I want to please them both, for reasons that have nothing to do with the money they've donated to our charity. I'm intrigued by both of these very different men.

"Thanks again for bidding on the first date," I tell Ryker. "You helped drive up the final donation. But if you'll excuse me for a moment—"

"It was nothing." Ryker leans down to my ear and whispers, "I'd part with a dozen gold bars for an evening with you."

A flush washes through me at his obvious exaggeration, yet I can't help but glance back at Ryker as Zuben leads me away.

A couple crosses my field of view, breaking my eye contact with Ryker, and I turn forward and continue alongside Zuben, without speaking, barely thinking. This night has been the strangest, most exhilarating of my life to date, and I feel like I'm floating, a balloon pulled on a string held by Zuben as we cross the ballroom floor.

We stop in a shadow at the edge of the ballroom, and he hands me a glass of champagne.

"When?" I shake my head, embarrassed that I didn't even notice him picking the flutes off a waiter's tray as we walked, because that's the only explanation for how he got them.

"When what?" He looks into my eyes and I'm mesmerized again by their color, by their interest in me.

I take a quick sip of the sparkling wine to avoid answering. "What did you want to talk to me about?"

"Everything." His eyes darken and he leans toward me. "You evaded my questions at our first meeting, and I want to know everything about you. No detail is too small."

"Oh." My cheeks heat and I take another sip of champagne. "There's not much to tell." My teeth scrape my lower lip as I scramble to think of something to keep this sophisticated man's interest, because as scary as it feels, more than anything, I want to hold his attention.

"Have you always resided in Philadelphia?" he asks.

"No." I shake my head. "I grew up in a rural area of Pennsylvania. In the mountains. Pretty isolated, really. How about you?"

"Are your parents still there?" he asks. "Your brothers and sisters?"

I shake my head.

"They came with you to Philadelphia," he says. "What year was this?"

My eyes threaten tears, and I look down. It's been ten years, and I thought I was over the loss of my mother, but I'm not.

Zuben's finger gently urges up my chin, and my mouth opens to draw a ragged breath. I can't believe how his light but intimate touch radiates inside me, spreading down my throat, into my chest, and lower.

"You are all alone," he says softly, his eyes full of concern and empathy.

I nod.

"I too am alone." A wistful look bathes his eyes.

"I'm sorry."

His sad expression vanishes as quickly as it arrived. "I lost my family a long time ago."

I nod, feeling a connection to this man; we have something in common. "It feels like a long time ago for me too."

"And what happened to your parents?" he asks.

"It was just me and my mom." I take another sip of the wine while I consider how to respond. I've never told anyone what happened to my mother, and I'm no longer sure I even trust my memories of what happened. Over the years, my memories have become intertwined with nightmares and false memories—of fires, of other attacks, of losing people I don't even know.

"Mom was…she disappeared." The verb *taken* would open too many questions.

"Disappeared? How?" He gestures to a passing waiter and then reaches for my flute, and I'm shocked to find it's nearly empty. He exchanges our glasses for two full ones.

"She disappeared into thin air." I shrug, covering my feelings and wishing I'd just claimed she was dead. "Just up and left me."

He frowns, clearly not satisfied with this answer. "Thin air? She did not leave any clues?"

"None that were useful." I sip my champagne, hoping to disguise how much that day haunts me. How my memories, although vivid, no longer seem real.

Once I left the farm and discovered the world, the internet, I did look for my mom. And I asked questions at the bank where the money she left me was held, talked to the lawyers who set up the trusts, but no one could, or would, tell me a thing.

But I don't want to come off as the poor little orphan girl.

Discomfort rising inside me, I change the subject. "That guy with the gold bar, Ryker, do you know him?"

Zuben's demeanor changes. His muscles tighten, his spine and jaw stiffen, and a dark cloud settles around him. A chill traces down my spine, as if he changed the room's climate.

"Stay away from that man." Zuben's voice is harsh, losing its silky smooth texture.

"Why?"

"Ryker is dangerous. The worst kind of scoundrel."

"He seems nice to me." I raise my chin. "He's very charming, and he made such a generous donation." I don't know why I'm arguing. Dangerous is exactly how Ryker first seemed to me. Still does.

"Ryker Stone is a criminal," Zuben says crisply.

I gasp. "That gold bar? Was it stolen?"

Zuben nods.

"From whom?"

"My employer."

"DEFTA?"

He nods.

"Should we call the police?" My eyes widen and I scan the room, looking for Ryker, spotting him thirty feet away, leaning against a high-top table, staring at me and Zuben. Okay...staring at me.

I turn my attention back to Zuben and lean in close to whisper, "Did you already call the police when you and Shana went to the front desk?" The police crashing in here would *definitely* change the room's climate. I should warn

Shana, but she might already know. Part of me wants to warn Ryker.

"No police." Closing his eyes for a moment, he sighs. "I do not have sufficient evidence to prove his thievery. Not yet."

"So, it's just a suspicion?" I glance back toward Ryker who nods and winks.

"Ember." Zuben reaches forward and our fingers brush. Alarmed by the warmth that floods through me. I sway slightly, momentarily knocked off balance. Or maybe it's these high heels.

"I cannot stress this enough," Zuben says, his voice serious. "Stay away from Ryker. He is a dangerous criminal—a pirate."

"Wait a minute." Smiling, I tip my head to the side, assuming he's joking. Are the two of them playing a prank on me? "A pirate?" I chuckle—although now that the word's been mentioned, he does dress like one. Maybe that's what put the idea in Zuben's head.

But Zuben remains stony faced—and gorgeously handsome. If he's joking, he's got an amazing poker face.

"So… You're claiming he's a pirate. Like a swashbuckler on the high seas?" Is this jealousy talking? If it is, I'm not sure I like this side of Zuben.

"You may simply call him a thief," Zuben says, "if that makes it easier to understand in a modern context. Whether he seizes his bounty at sea or in port, from a plane or an armored truck, Ryker's modus operandi has been and always will be that of a pirate."

"Okay…Listen." His accusations seem way over the top, and donating three quarters of a million dollars to a not-for-profit does not seem like something a thief would do. And if this is Zuben's way of competing for my attention with Ryker… I don't like to be told who to like or who to spend time with.

Wanting out of the conversation, I glance to the front of the room. "I'm supposed to be helping with the auction. But it was nice talking to you." I turn to go.

"Ember." He grabs my hand, and I'm nearly pulled off my feet at the abrupt stop.

"Please," he says, looking apologetic, but not letting go of my hand, his very tight around mine. "You do not understand the severity of this situation, the danger a man such as Ryker poses—especially to you."

I tug, but my fingers are trapped by his larger and much stronger ones. Fear invades my chest and my belly, freezing out all the warmth. "I understand enough," I say coldly. "Let me go. Please."

He releases my hand and my fingers ache from the pressure. He bows his head slightly then looks back into my eyes. "Please accept my apologies. My actions in physically detaining you were abhorrent, but your safety is my only concern."

I draw a long breath, reminding myself that this man is a major donor, a man who, until the last minute, I felt an unbelievable attraction to and connection with. And as he gazes into my eyes, I feel that connection again and believe him when he says he wants to protect me. In fact, given the intensity in his eyes, I get the distinct feeling that he'd kill anyone who tried to harm me.

But that's silly.

"Ember, I suspect you are very special."

"Suspect?"

He raises his hand to his forehead. "Forgive me again. I am not well practiced in speaking with women."

"I don't believe that for a moment."

"Nevertheless, it is true."

I shrug. No point in arguing on that one.

"You are *clearly* special," he says somewhat awkwardly, "and a man…a man like Ryker…He poses a great threat to you. I do not want to see you get hurt."

I smile softly. "Thank you, but I can take care of myself." Two wealthy men fighting for my attention seems like something out of a fantasy—not real life. And Zuben's warning is clearly driven by jealousy.

My fingers graze Zuben's arm, and he inhales at my touch.

"I do appreciate your concern," I say firmly. "But I really do need to go help Shana."

Walking away on shaky legs, I can feel the heat of Zuben's gaze on my back.

## CHAPTER SEVEN

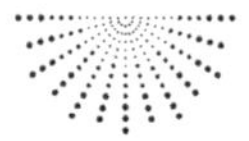

### *Ember*

"Hey, Ember," Shana says as I approach. "We're on the final lot."

"I'm sorry I haven't been here to help."

"Not a bit." She squeezes my arm. "Everything's gone swimmingly. Plus, I spotted you having a drink, not only with Mr. Stone, but also with our mysterious Zuben." Her eyebrows rise a few times. "Both men seem to have taken quite a shine to you."

My cheeks rage again with heat, a searing combo of embarrassment, shame and anger. I can't begin to sort out my conflicting emotions, especially given all the champagne I've consumed, another possible source of the flames now I think of it. At some point I lost count of the number of glasses and realize I never went to the kitchen to get the dinner that the hotel staff were kindly holding for me.

"Let yourself enjoy their attention," Shana says.

"Zuben raised a few red flags for me at our first meeting, but now that I've gotten to know him, I approve." She winks. "He's very smart and a serious man, not unlike you. Perfect for you."

I nod, unable to express to Shana how I feel about Zuben. His negative words about Ryker annoyed me, but now that it's been a minute, I'm starting to wonder if his warning was based on something more than jealousy. Ryker does seem dangerous…

"Plus. He's not hard to look at." Shana winks. "I haven't been with a man since the nineties, but if I were a few years younger…hell, even at my age, I wouldn't kick him out of bed."

"Why, thank you." Ryker arrives out of nowhere. Hand on his heart, he winks at Shana, then turns to me. "You ladies *were* talking about me, right?"

Shana laughs uncomfortably. "Of course not."

"Ah well," he says. "A fellow can dream." He turns to me. "Are you ready?"

"Ready for what?" My body buzzes under his attention.

"For me to win you on the auction block." He grins, cocking his head slightly.

"What?" I take a step back. "No." I shake my head so vigorously it makes me dizzy, and I stagger on my heels.

Ryker gently touches my back to support me.

"The emcee's about to call you," he says. "I'd be thrilled to have the opportunity to make another donation to the charity. Even more if it's for an evening with you." Closing his eyes, he leans a little closer and inhales, as if in some kind of ecstasy, and it thrills me way more than it should.

"The bidding, you know it's just for a *date*—just dinner," I blurt.

"But of course." He raises a hand to his chest. "A gentleman would never expect anything more than your delightful company."

"Thank you." I like Ryker and won't take the warnings from a jealous man as gospel.

"Glad it's settled." Hand lightly on my back, Ryker steers me toward the stairs leading up to the stage, and his lips move close to my ear. "Of course, a man can always hope for more."

"More what?" I smile at him, chuckling in spite of the nerves going off inside me. Even without Zuben's warning, I know exactly what Ryker means by *more*, but while it could be the champagne talking, my body is throbbing at the idea of a dinner date with Ryker turning into *more*.

Zuben's warning suddenly feels like a dare. A dare that makes me want to test the waters with a man like Ryker. Although I had plenty of daytime flirtations and dates during college, I've never gone for *more*. I'm twenty-five. It's time.

It's time to come out of the shell I've been hiding inside—a mental shell my mother molded around me with her irrational fears. Plus, if Sanctuary House can benefit from my going on my first date, all the better.

The emcee calls me on stage, and as I draw a long breath, bracing myself to go up the stairs. Ryker's hand brushes softly up and down my spine, a gesture that I expect is supposed to be comforting, but instead excites every nerve in my body.

"I will win you," he says close to my ear. "And I cannot *wait* to have you for dinner."

Stirred by his innuendo, I quiver as I walk up the stairs, but when I reach the stage Zuben's danger warning flashes again, and I glance back at Ryker. His smile is charming, encouraging, supportive—not a hint of menace or predation.

Well, maybe a little predation. In spite of my undeniable connection to both men, I'm puzzled by Zuben, but Ryker I get. I know exactly what he wants.

Stepping to the center of the stage, I'm struck by the heat and glare, feeling exposed, almost naked under the spotlight's scrutiny.

"Ember Cross is the accountant for Sanctuary House," the emcee says to the crowd. She flips the card she's holding. "Other than that, I don't have much information about this lovely young woman, or the date that's planned, but ladies and gentlemen, I'm sure she'll be wonderful company for an evening out."

If I felt naked before, now the full heat of the lights and the gaze of the crowd are penetrating the thin fabric of my dress and licking my skin. I press my hand to my belly to verify the dress is still there and then force a smile as I hear the first bid—one hundred dollars.

I can't see the bidder, the lights shining on me are too bright, but whoever it was, they're quickly outbid, and then again, as the price for a date with me rises quickly to a thousand.

"Do I hear, eleven hundred?" the emcee calls out.

"Come on ladies and gentlemen. This is the last lot of the evening, let's make it the highest."

"Five thousand," calls a voice.

Shading my eyes, I step to the side. Zuben is standing near the front of the crowd, looking at me intently. He holds the highest bid.

# CHAPTER EIGHT

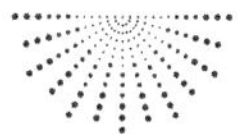

## *Zuben*

THE CROWD MURMURS, reacting to my dramatic jump in the bid, but the thump of Ember's heart underscores the crowd's sounds—a strong, rapidly increasing drumbeat that calls to me with the enticing promise of her blood.

I will win her. I must. That despicable pirate may have been the one to coax her onto the stage, but in the end, she will be mine.

*Mine?*

I catch myself. Ember is very attractive and extremely appealing, as humans go, but no chance will I claim her as mine. I don't believe in the notion of love—it is nothing but temporary hormonal reactions—and she is too important to sully with physical urges.

I have the winning bid. Our dinner will give me time to discuss my research with her, help her to understand how important I suspect she may be—and will keep her away from the pirate.

Ryker steps into view near the side of the stage. Most vampires have the sense to change their clothing to fit with the times, but Ryker's outfit is beyond outlandish, drawing unnecessary attention. I shake my head at his long leather jacket and tight breaches, his heavy belt and a silk shirt I expect is voluminous under that jacket—not to mention those farcical boots. For a man who denies he is a pirate, he most certainly dresses like one. All that is missing is a parrot for his shoulder.

"Ten thousand," Ryker calls out, and then smirks at me.

I frown. For a brief moment, I believed he had no additional resources on hand to bid against me tonight. Certainly such a freebooter would have nothing resembling a credit card or local bank account.

I clear my throat. "Twenty."

"Twenty *thousand*?" The emcee looks at me in dismay.

I nod to her, and then turn my full attention back to Ember.

Her slender body is trembling, her chest rising and falling as she breathes rapidly under the hot lights and attention.

"Fifty thousand," Ryker shouts, and the crowd goes wild, making me lose the sound of Ember's heart for a moment, but I can still detect the scent of her blood over that of the other hundreds of humans in the room. She is beyond special.

"Fifty thousand going once!" the emcee calls out.

I snap out of my thoughts. "One hundred thousand."

Ember sways on her feet, and every instinct in my body wants to leap onto the stage to steady her. But moving that quickly will expose me to this crowd, and while I can defend myself from the hotel security staff's stakes, I cannot risk exposing myself—or DEFTA—in such a reckless manner.

Based on myths and works of fiction, humans fear vampires, but we are grossly misunderstood. And out of such ignorance, under the human laws of most countries, shoving a stake into a vampire's heart is perfectly legal. No questions asked. Barbaric.

"Two hundred thousand." Ryker jumps onto the stage, arms raised, and the crowd cheers. His leap was beyond the athletic ability of most humans, but distracted by his absurdly high bid, no one seems to have taken notice—at least not enough to pull out a stake.

"Three hundred!" I shout, and then head for the stage, taking the stairs in a civilized manner, and striding across to a spot near the center, where I take the opportunity to glare at my opponent.

This auction is akin to a ridiculous duel of the past, the pair of us facing each other with Ember and the emcee between us. Ryker looks determined, but there are no bounds to how much I will bid.

"Four hundred." Ryker widens his stance and crosses his arms over his chest.

"Five hundred thousand," I declare.

Ryker turns toward the opposite side of the stage and beckons someone forward. Shana walks up to him, looking dazed but euphoric as Ryker whispers into her ear. From this distance, I should be able to hear easily, but I'm too focused on Ember's heartbeat, on the rush of blood in her veins, on the whoosh of air in her lungs—all overpowering other sounds.

Shana steps up to the microphone. "Didn't I promise that a live auction would be exciting!"

The crowd cheers.

Ryker moves toward Ember and I move closer too.

Gasping, Ember raises her palms, stopping us both a few feet away from her.

"It seems we may be at an impasse," Shana says. "An impasse that I'm pleased to say will prove very beneficial to Sanctuary House, and more importantly, to our clients."

She clears her throat. "I am calling and end to the bidding, so that these two gentlemen can discuss their final bids in a less public forum. Who knows?" She shrugs. "Perhaps our Ember will agree to have dinner with them both."

The crowd roars, and I glare at Ryker. But then I coax my competitive side to stand down, calling instead on my intelligence, and on reason.

This auction means nothing. Even if I allow him to win, I can prevent him from actually going on the date and discovering what I suspect are the miraculous features of her blood. I will protect her no matter what.

"Let's let these gentlemen talk," Shana continues. "I'll come back to let you all know the final bid, but for now, please enjoy the rest of your evening. Dance! Drink! And if you're not staying overnight at the hotel, please have a safe trip home."

The roar of applause fills my ears, but it still cannot drown the sound of Ember's sweet, pounding heart.

Ryker pulls back the side of his leather jacket, and my

body tenses. For a split second, I expect a stake, but instead, he flashes several gold bars stashed in the coat's lining, letting me know that he is willing to pay millions to win her.

Fine. He might be attracted to the lovely Ember, he might even sense that she is special, but there is no chance that he knows what I know. I have been researching the possibility of her existence for centuries, and this lazy, likely illiterate pirate might be drawn to the scent of her blood; he might want to feed from her, to bed her, but he does not want her in the same way that I do.

In fact, bidding at all was foolish on my part. Ryker's attention on Ember is only to raise my anger—payback for having him brought in for questioning.

Well, I have a payback plan of my own. Glaring at the pirate, it is hard not to smile. I will let him win this auction. But first I will make sure that Ryker empties that foolish jacket of all its gold bars, providing me with even *more* proof of his crimes. And with that proof, I will have him imprisoned, clearing my path to complete my research with the beautiful and delicious Ember.

# CHAPTER NINE

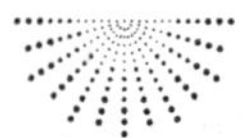

### *Ember*

Nerves scramble like a million ants loose inside me, but through that discomfort I can't deny that my nerves are at least in part fueled by excitement.

After Shana stopped the live auction—was that just last night?—Ryker and Zuben held a private discussion that ended with Ryker donating another three gold bars to Sanctuary House for the privilege of taking me out to dinner. In total, Ryker donated four bold bars to our charity, counting the one he gave to cover his ticket, and that's well over three million dollars. Nuts.

Nuts doesn't begin to describe it.

And even stranger, in spite of his warnings to me about Ryker, Zuben didn't seem all that disappointed once it was settled and, once again, offered to help Shana handle the gold bars.

I immediately wondered if Zuben had some scheme to steal the gold, but today's events proved me wrong. With

Zuben's help, Shana sold two of the four gold bars, and the transactions were verifiably real—I've seen the records of the deposits into our bank account. And the other two bars are in a safety deposit box at our branch as a long-term investment for the charity. The board has scheduled an emergency meeting for Monday to discuss plans for our organization's windfall.

Ryker's massive donation is verifiably real.

I have irrefutable proof of his incredible generosity, and I can't believe that a man like Ryker is interested in dinner with someone like me. Interested enough to pay millions.

Counting the minutes until he's due to arrive, I lean against the large window of my ninth floor condo apartment, as the late afternoon sun glints off the center city office buildings in the distance. Tonight will be my second time out after dark, and it can't possibly be as eventful as the first. I push away from the window. It's time to get ready.

At Shana's urging, I went shopping after work, buying the second fancy dress of my life. I was planning to wear something more casual, or the red dress from last night, but Shana's right: there is no chance that a man who dropped nearly three million dollars is going to take me someplace casual. And I shouldn't wear the same dress two nights in a row.

A quick shower and blow dry later, I slip into my new dress and stare at my image. The pale pink satin skims my body and shines when it catches the light. I can't do a bra or proper panties with this dress either—do people not wear undergarments anymore?—and the dress leaves most of my back exposed, with only a thin strip of vertical fabric, just wide enough to accommodate the zipper, stretching from very low on my back and up to my neck. The dress has a sheer jacket, so I won't be quite this naked.

I reach back to pull up the zipper. But no matter how much I struggle and twist, there's a point that I can't pull the zipper past. In the store, the saleslady did the zipper, and it didn't occur to me that I wouldn't be able to do it myself at home.

Frustrated, I give up momentarily, and finish getting ready, putting on my strappy silver shoes, some of the red lipstick that Shana gave me last night, and then I fasten my hair back with two rhinestone covered clips.

Determined, I try for the zipper again, hoping my shoulders were just tense on the first attempt. I fold one arm back and push up while bending the other behind my head, trying to catch onto the zipper's tag. My hands refuse to meet.

*Just a little bit further. I've just about got it.*

My doorbell rings.

I drop my arms, and my shoulder's throb. But that sensations quickly forgotten as my heart pounds and my mouth goes dry. I glance at my phone. It's 6:05. Ryker said he would pick me up around 7:00. I remember, because I knew it would be well after dark. Did I misunderstand? Is he early?

I make one final attempt at the zipper, but there's a second knock at the door, this one louder and more urgent, so I grab the sheer jacket and small handbag and make a dash for the entrance.

Ryker knocks a third time—so eager to see me!—and I open the door.

But it's not Ryker. It's Zuben.

Mouth gaping I step back. "What are you doing here?"

A thrill races through me as I take in his imposing presence, tall and dark and devastating, with his heavily lashed eyes, his long, sculpted nose, and his lips that… I've never seen such richly, red lips that weren't sporting lipstick, and while he's dressed more casually today, a fitted crew neck cashmere sweater under a blazer, he's still so put together and gorgeous he could be straight off the page of a fashion magazine.

"Good evening, Ember." His voice is rich and flavored with an accent I still can't place, but is one of the sexiest things I've ever heard. "I am here to apologize," he says. "I am exceedingly sorry that I made you uncomfortable last night. I would very much like the chance to explain."

Is he here to try to stop me from going out with Ryker? Does he even know my date is tonight? "How did you get my address?"

"From Shana."

I frown, shocked that my boss would give this man my address, no matter how much money he's donated to Sanctuary House. But I'm glad that he plans to apologize.

"I mean you no harm." Zuben clasps his hands behind his back and bows his head slightly, his eyes cast down. "I can promise you that."

His posture works. He really does seem harmless. Especially compared to Ryker who I'm expecting in less than an hour.

"Okay." I back a few feet from the door. "But I don't have much time."

He nods, lingering in my doorway.

"Come in." I turn and walk toward the seating area of my condo, in an old building that contained rentals for almost a century before the units were offered for sale. Financed with the sale of the farm, my condo is beyond the means of most people my age, but I'm sure it seems like a dump to someone like Zuben.

"Your home is very comfortable," Zuben says as he enters, then closes the door behind him.

"Comfortable?" I turn slowly, trying to read between the lines and determine his meaning. Comfortable could be taken as an insult.

"It is lovely." He steps toward the window. "And what a beautiful view. How long have you lived here?"

"Why did you come?" My heart is racing as I watch him take in my home, the furniture I picked out piece by piece at various used furniture stores around the city.

"Ember." He runs his hand across the back of my mid-century Danish sofa. "You have impeccable taste."

"Thank you." My shoulders start to unfurl, and I remember my manners. "Please. Make yourself comfortable. Can I get you a glass of wine?"

"Only if you are having one." He nods, with a hint of smile sparkling in his chestnut eyes.

I head for the kitchen where I have a bottle chilling in the fridge. I picked it up thinking I should have something on hand if Ryker comes in when he picks me up—or when he drops me off…

Heat bubbles inside me, thinking about how my night

might unfold with the uber masculine Ryker, how it might feel to embrace, to kiss, to do even more with such a dangerously sexy man.

"May I be of assistance?" Zuben asks.

I jump back from the counter holding the cork screw and bottle to my chest as if they can protect me.

"I am once again finding myself with the need to apologize." Zuben bows his head. "I startled you."

"No need." Smiling, I set the bottle and cork screw down on the counter. "I'm just feeling jumpy tonight." I'm feeling *something* anyway… "To be honest, I don't often have company." I never do.

And certainly not such handsome company. In spite of how things ended last night, every time I look at Zuben, every time he speaks, my body stirs and my mind is swept off to far away places that I can almost see in his eyes, hear in his voice. But…I shake my head…tonight I am going out with Ryker.

"Please, let me assist." Zuben takes the bottle and easily removes the cork, and I turn to grab two glasses from the cupboard.

"I don't have proper wine glasses." I set two juice glasses on the counter. *Why didn't I buy wine glasses?*

"Those will do very nicely." He pours some wine into each of the glasses, and then he hands one to me and raises his. "To what shall we drink?"

I shake my head, so foggy with adrenaline and confusion I can't begin to form an answer.

"How about: to new friends?"

I raise my glass to meet his. "New friends." I swallow some wine, more than I probably should, hoping it will take the edge off my overly active nerves. "Would you like to sit?" I turn to lead him toward the living room.

"Ember," he says, stopping me short. "May I first help with something else?"

I look back over my shoulder. "With what?" Should I have offered him food?

"With your dress," he says softly.

My hand rises to my chest. "My dress?"

He smiles. "The zipper?"

"Oh!" Heat rages beneath the skin on my cheeks and I press my back against the broom closet door. "I forgot. I'm so embarrassed."

"No need to feel embarrassment." His expression is understanding, gentle, and he sets his wine down on the edge of the counter. "May I?" He holds his elegant hands toward me.

Nodding, I slowly turn toward the closet door, and my entire body hums as I feel his approaching. Then the hum's volume turns up as he slowly sweeps my hair to the side, his fingers barely brushing my neck.

I reach to hold up my hair for him. "I tried to get the zipper myself, but my arms don't twist that way." I laugh awkwardly.

His hand glides down from the base of my neck, barely grazing my skin as it moves. I'm not even positive he is touching my skin, but it's as if I can sense the small space between his fingers and my back, as if there's something connecting us, something warm and unseen and electric.

One of his hands stays lightly on my lower back, where the zipper starts, while the other takes the tab and raises it slowly, so, so slowly, and as his hand rises, his knuckle brushes along my skin. It's all I can do to keep still, my body wanting to make involuntary motions under his gentle, barely-there touch.

The pressure on my lower back grows heavier, his hand there hot and firm as the zipper draws near the top, and then his breath washes over me, hot on the nape of my neck, and then brushing over my ear. He stands still, so close behind me, one hand resting barely above my butt and one at my neck, and the heat of his entire body penetrates mine. I've never had sex, but can't imagine anything better than what I'm feeling right now.

"Ember." His voice, barely audible, brushes through me, and my spine arches, pushing my head and butt back. The latter grazes his mid section—I don't want to guess where.

"Oh!" I pull my hips forward. "Sorry."

He backs away from me, and I take a long breath, my cheeks and body aflame, then slowly turn toward him.

Cool as a cucumber, he takes a sip of his wine. "Shall we sit?"

I nod. "Yes." My voice is hoarse. "Thanks. For the zipper."

"My pleasure." He smiles, and the way he says *pleasure* bathes me in renewed warmth, like he means so much more, and I feel entirely naked, utterly vulnerable, as if he lowered the zipper instead of raising it.

But I tell myself that my attraction and adrenaline have joined forces with my overactive imagination to add double meanings to all of his words.

In the living room, I gesture toward the sofa and then grab the sheer jacket, slipping my arms into it quickly.

"Are you feeling quite well?" He sits on the sofa. "I hope my actions were not too forward, offering to assist with your dress."

"Not at all." Shaking my head, probably too vehemently, I sit in the chair opposite him. "I appreciated your help." I drain the rest of my wine, starting to feel its loosening effects. I'm being ridiculous. This man might be rich and unbearably sexy, but he's just a man—a normal, ordinary person—and there's no need for me to act like a foolish child around him.

"More wine?" he asks.

"No thank you." I set my glass down on the table next to me. "But...would *you* like more?" I am the hostess, after all.

He shakes his head. "When I am around you, Ember, I need no further intoxicants."

I draw a shaky breath. Maybe this crazy chemistry between us *isn't* just in my head.

"Have I once again made you uncomfortable?" He looks annoyed with himself. "It seems that I have been too direct." He grimaces. "But I must risk doing so one more time, because you must let me explain my interest in you."

"Explain?" My stomach keeps flipping. I don't need intoxicants around him either, especially not now that I can feel the wine's effects.

"Yes, I must explain why Ryker poses a grave danger to you."

My back stiffens. "Look, you're not going to talk me out of this dinner. Ryker won the bidding fair and square."

"Ember, Ryker will use you. He poses a particular danger to you because you are most unique. Very special."

"That's flattering, but—" My insides are squirming and not in a good way. Is Zuben trying to give me a parental sex talk?

"It is not just flattery," he says quickly. "While you are comely and charming, that is not the kind of special I mean."

*Comely?* "Then what *do* you mean?" My exasperation and discomfort are growing.

"Your blood—"

"What?" I lean back into the sofa. The way he says *blood* makes me feel exposed again, unsafe, and the mood shifts, my attraction morphing into fear.

"I am a scientist," Zuben says. "And one of my areas of research is rare blood types."

I gasp. "My mother—" I clamp my lips together and my heart rate accelerates. All the air vacates my lungs as memories flood in of events I'd forgotten or blocked.

My mother claimed there was something rare about my blood... In fact, after I turned twelve, she drew vials of it weekly. But her claims were a lie.

After I moved to Philadelphia, I discovered my mother's deceit.

"My blood is totally normal," I tell him what the Red Cross told me when I went to donate. "It's O positive. Plus..." I narrow my eyes "...you said you were in *finance* not science."

Zuben draws a long breath as I call out his lies. "I have many interests," he says calmly, like we haven't just been discussing my blood. "At this moment, finance is my official area of work for DEFTA, but for years I have been searching for…

"The exact details do not matter." He shakes his head. "I have detected something very rare in your blood, Ember. Something that could hold the key to solving a mystery which I have been studying for cent—for most of my life."

"*Detected*? You mean when you *tasted* it?" My stomach rises in my throat, remembering how he licked my cut palm.

He nods.

Freaked out, I try to sink into the sofa to escape his close scrutiny and my recollection of my reaction that day. I should have been repulsed when he kissed my cut palm, but instead I was…I was turned on.

*What is wrong with me?*

I'm ashamed by my reaction that day, not to mention my intense attraction to him not minutes ago.

"I sense your discomfort and fear," he says carefully, "but I assure you that I mean you no harm. My interest in you is not of a sexual nature. It is entirely related to your blood."

His blunt words are not only gross, they wipe away the last of my temporary hormonal insanity that made me feel attracted to him. It's time to get Zuben out of my apartment. "I think you should leave."

"I suspect you're upset," he says, and he leans forward. "Did you already *know* that your blood was unique? You mentioned your mother before. Did *she* know? Do you already know what you are?"

"What I *am*?" I stand on shaking legs. "What the hell do you mean?"

"I most certainly did not mean to offend you." He stands, shaking his head, clearly regretting his choice of words. "I am referring to my strong suspicions about your rare blood type."

"Like I already said, there is *nothing* rare about my blood."

Although he's made me question my certainty—my sanity. Is there something about my blood the Red Cross didn't detect? And if so, did my mother *know*?

"Ember." Zuben clears his throat. "How much do you know about vampires?"

"Vampires?" Blinking, I drop back down to the sofa. This night just keeps getting weirder. "Are you accusing me of being a *vampire*?"

"Of course not." He stands there across from me, calmly waiting for me to say more. His expression's intense, his eyes trained on mine as if he's urging me to trust him. And in spite of all this creepy talk, there is something about Zuben I do trust. *Why?*

"I don't know much about vampires," I answer his question. "I know they're monsters, vicious killers. But to be honest, I'm not sure I even believe they exist." Then again, I never go out after dark, and vampires are never out in the light.

"I can assure you," he says. "Vampires are real. Very real."

My mouth dry, I lick my lips, wishing I'd said yes to more wine but unable to muster the will to get more. "What do vampires have to do with me?"

"Assuming my hypothesis is correct," Zuben says, still so calm through this weird conversation. "Your blood, it is very…*extremely* attractive to vampires."

"What, like fairy blood?" I smirk, remembering a plot line from an old TV series I watched.

He leans forward, his expression serious. "No, not fairy blood, Ember. Something else. Something far more ancient and powerful."

"Ancient? I'm in my mid twenties."

He leans toward me. "There are myths, legends about a goddess and a coven of witches who hide her."

*Goddess*? "Okay." I stand again, trying to look confident while my body trembles inside. "This has been fascinating." *Vampires, goddesses, witches, oh my!* "But I don't believe any of it. No offense."

He stands. "No offense taken. But your belief in something does not impact its existence."

"Look." I gesture toward the door. "Thanks for stopping by, but I am expecting someone."

"Ryker Stone." His eyes narrow.

"Yes." I raise my chin, trying to look confident. "So, if you don't mind."

I walk toward the door. But he beats me there, shifting positions so quickly and gracefully I didn't detect any movement until he was ahead of me.

He looks down into my eyes. "Do not go out with Ryker tonight." His tone is pleading and serious.

"He won the auction." I blink, surprised that I'm even arguing about this. "Plus, you can't tell me what to do."

Zuben's hand slides onto the back of my neck.

I gasp. He's completely invaded my personal space, but

for some reason nothing about it feels threatening. Instead, his touch is warm and gentle—I could easily pull away from his hold—and it's so intimate. It's the first time I've had a man hold me this way, and I'm shocked at my body's reaction, more turned on than frightened, as I struggle to normalize my breathing and heart rate, both soaring.

"There is something else you should know." He looks into my eyes. "Ryker, he is a vampire."

His words snap the spell, and I pull away, stepping to the side and crossing my arms over my chest. "You really are something."

"What do you mean?"

"You're nothing but a sore loser." I raise my chin. "You lost the auction. Deal with it."

"But that is what I am doing." He tips his head to the side. "I *am* dealing with it. Today, I helped your boss with the gold bars, and now I am helping you—attempting to help you, that is."

"I don't *need* your help."

"Yes you do.'

Anger and determination rise inside me. This guy is certifiable. And I can't believe my instincts ever claimed otherwise. I can't believe I was attracted to him, trusted him.

"First you claim Ryker's a pirate," I snap, "even though he made a generous donation to Sanctuary House, and now you say he's a *vampire*? You certainly can come up with original accusations against your rival. I'll give you that. A-plus for effort."

"I have not made *accusations*," he says. "I have stated

facts." He swallows, hard, as if he's trying to tamp something down. "And Ryker will use you, enslave you. He only wants you for—"

"For sex?" I raise my chin.

"For your blood."

I scowl at him. I can't begin to understand why these two men have decided to compete over me. I'm no one special, and I refuse to be a pawn in Zuben's little game, whatever it is. "I think you should leave. Now!"

"Ember. I am warning you. If Ryker discovers what you are—"

"What I *am*?" I shake my head and thump my first against my chest. "I am a *woman*. A *human* woman who wants you to get out of her apartment."

Taking another step back, I run into a chair, and then grip it to steady myself. "Leave. Now. Please."

"But."

"Now!"

Zuben's head bows. "I will leave, but I implore you: Do not keep your date tonight. Ryker is dangerous."

I grab my little silver bag and dig into it for my phone. "You're the one who's dangerous, and I'm calling the police. I'll tell them that *you're* a vampire and they'll stake you!" Who cares if it isn't true.

He holds up his hands in a gesture of surrender, then turns to open the door.

But before closing it, he looks into my eyes. "You might not yet believe that you are special, Ember, but you are, *very* special, and I vow to protect you—always."

I slam shut the door. "Stalker!"

# CHAPTER TEN

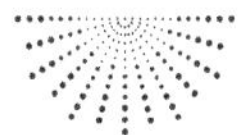

## *Ember*

"CHAMPAGNE?" Ryker uncorks the bottle without waiting for my response, and the cork strikes the roof of the limousine, landing on the shiny black leather of the seat facing ours.

"Oh!" I giggle at my outburst that revealed my still jagged nerves. This car is like something out of the movies, and while it probably sits eight, the two of us are side by side on the long seat facing the barrier separating us from the driver. Above us, the moonroof is open and streetlights whoosh by, creating a light show inside.

Ryker showed up about fifteen minutes after Zuben left, and the second glass of wine I downed while waiting did little to soothe the effects of that unsettling discussion, and Ryker brought with him another catalyst for nerves —himself.

He's wearing leather again, dark black slacks and what looks like the same long jacket over an off-white shirt without buttons. It's open at the neck and looks so soft it's got to be silk. My finger itches to touch it, not to mention his broad chest underneath.

His shoulder length hair is down tonight, looking wavy and soft and Ryker raises his eyebrows and smiles as he pours me a glass of wine. Then looking at him through the tiny bubbles rising through the liquid to burst at its surface, I feel like I'm about to burst too.

"To us," he says.

"Us?" I peer over my flute.

"Too early?" He laughs. "Let me try again." He settles his shoulders as if thinking, then leans forward, reaching his glass toward mine. "To new beginnings."

"To new beginnings." I smile, then tip my head to the side. "Aren't all beginnings new?"

Chuckling, he winks. "You've got me there."

We clink glasses, and then I take a small sip of champagne. The taste bursts on my tongue, a million times nicer than the sparkling wine at the gala.

Already feeling floaty, I need to make sure I drink this glass slowly. Zuben's warnings were absurd but I need to keep my wits about me. My first impression of Ryker was, after all, danger, and now that I'm on to second and third impressions I can't deny that he's dangerously…hot…and the feelings he's rousing in side me feel dangerous too. Dangerously exciting.

The gala may have been my first time out after dark, but this is my first real date, first time in a limo and first time to what I assume will be a fancy restaurant and… while I don't know what will happen later, I've decided, if it feels right I'll say yes if he wants to have sex.

Taking another small taste of champagne, I coach my courage to rise, just like the bubbles pricking my nose. I am a grown ass woman! It's perfectly normal for me to be out on a date with an attractive and charming man—even at night. It's time that I stop acting like that paranoid teenager, deserted by her mom.

"I'm glad to see you smiling," Ryker says, shifting to turn slightly toward me. "But you seem pensive. Penny for your thoughts?"

"They're only worth a penny?" He used that expression last night too.

"It's an old expression." His arm stretches across the top of the seat behind me, and I resist the urge to lean my head against his strong arm as I look into his eyes.

"I'd love to know what you're thinking," he says. "What put that beautiful, soft smile on your lips?"

I take another sip of champagne, hoping to buy time to find an answer that's not—'You're super hot,' or 'I think it's time for me to start having a sex life,'—which is the truth of what's going on in my mind.

"I'm just happy to be here with you," I finally answer. "It's my first limo ride." I look out the window, noticing that we're on the highway now, going south on the I95. "Where are we going?" I thought that most of the good Philly restaurants were downtown or by the museum.

"To a little restaurant I think you'll enjoy." He smiles, looking down into my eyes.

"Keeping our destination a secret?" I didn't expect to be headed for the suburbs.

Shrugging one shoulder, he winks.

"You're certainly a man of mystery."

He leans toward me, so close I can feel the air heat between our foreheads. "I suppose I am."

"Here's to solving mysteries." I raise my glass, forcing him back a tiny bit and he clinks mine before we both drink.

"I'm ready." He pours more champagne into my glass and his own.

"Ready for what?" Nerves and desire make my belly contract. Although I've decided that I'm game to have sex with Ryker tonight—if the opportunity comes up—I assumed we wouldn't be anywhere near that stage until after dinner.

"For my interrogation," he replies. "Do your worst, madam detective."

Relief floods through me, and I take a sip of champagne to hide any facial evidence of my misunderstanding.

"Where are you from?" I ask, wanting to know everything about him. Not sure where to start, I remember the questions Zuben asked me. "Have you always lived in Philadelphia?"

"No, not always." His fingers stroke the leather seat above my shoulder, the soft sound somehow erotic. "But I've lived here, on and off, for a very long time."

"How long?" In spite of his confidence and wealth, Ryker's young. He can't be more than thirty based on his appearance, and his reference to a very long time seems out of place.

"You want my life story?" He clinks his glass against mine.

"Very much."

He reaches for the bottle and pours more champagne

into my glass, and then his. "I was born in the north of England."

"You don't have an accent."

"That, my dear, is a matter of perspective." He sets the bottle back into a hole in the shelf where it fits tightly. "Everyone has an accent."

"Okay, okay." I shake my head. "What I mean is, you don't have a *British* accent." I don't even hear a trace.

He grins. "Like I said, I've been here a while."

I nod, understanding his need to fit in after moving across the ocean as a kid, starting out in a new place. Even though it was the same state, my move from rural Pennsylvania to Philadelphia felt like relocating to another planet.

"My turn." He shifts on the car seat, moving just a fraction of an inch closer, and a thrill races inside me. "How long have you been with Sanctuary House?"

"Two and a half years."

"Joined right after you graduated?"

I shake my head. "It took me a while to land a full time job because…" I look down, feeling foolish.

His finger gently glides to lift my chin and he looks into my eyes. "There's nothing you can't tell me."

Surprised at how easily he perceived my hesitancy, I gaze into his eyes, so brightly blue in contrast to his dark hair and eyebrows. Heat flutters inside me in the anticipation of what might happen later this evening, even though we haven't even arrived at the restaurant.

"I have this strange phobia of being out after dark," I confess. "It puts a limit on the hours I can work—especially in the winter."

He leans forward slightly. "It's after dark now."

"Yes." I shake my head, feeling foolish. "But… This is so embarrassing."

"Don't be embarrassed." He shifts and whispers close to my ear. "I want to know *all* your secrets."

Desire shivers through me—cool and then raging hot—and I close my eyes against the intense thrill. "Tonight—right now—it's only the second time I've been out after dark." I turn to look at him. "In my entire life."

His eyes widen. "Really? How come?"

I look away. "It's ridiculous."

"Ember." His finger grazes my cheek, gently nudging my gaze from the window and back toward him. "Nothing about you could ever be ridiculous. Not to me." His hand drops from my cheek to my shoulder, and its heat reaches far below the surface of my skin to penetrate my bones.

Adjusting my body as it absorbs his warmth and support, I draw a breath and let it out slowly. "My mother…"

"Who disappeared."

"Yes." He remembered. "My mother forbade me to go out after dark." I laugh. "It's funny, now that I have some perspective, but… I'm not really sure what her issue was. I guess it was because we lived in the wilderness with wildcats and bears and no neighbors for miles. I guess that's why her rules were so strict.

"But even after she disappeared, her warning stuck with me, and it turned into a…a kind of commandment I couldn't break. I developed a phobia." How else can I explain my bizarre behavior?

"If it is a phobia, you're facing it now. Be proud of that." His hand slides back up to cup my face, his thumb gently stroking my cheekbone as he looks into my eyes. "You lost your mother, the most important person to you in the world. It makes sense that you'd adhere to her rules, even long after she was gone."

I nod, relishing the sensation of his hand on my face, his callused thumb strumming my skin.

Heat and wetness gather between my legs—a sudden flood that makes me fear I'll discolor my dress—and then his thumb grazes my lower lip, and the heat and wetness throb.

I've never felt anything like this. The ache. The need. I can barely breathe.

*Kiss me*, I think, hoping I'm sending the right signals.

I've never been kissed, not properly, not seriously or with passion, and my lips are quivering, all the blood that's not pooled between my legs moving up to my mouth, burning and twitching my lips, and they part as my breaths continue to shallow, coming too fast now to pass through my nose.

Ryker bends toward me, his lips hovering there, waiting, teasing, sparking messages across the millimeters that divide his mouth from mine and intensifying all the desire roiling inside me. Closing my eyes, I wait for him to make his move, my anticipation building so high that my head, my whole body feels like it's about to explode.

He pulls back. "We're here."

Gasping I realize the car stopped. "What?" I can barely breathe, barely speak. I can't remember where we're going or why.

I shake the fog from my head. "Oh, yes. The restaurant. Right." I squeeze my eyes shut for a moment, hoping to regain my center—my sanity.

"We're not at the restaurant quite yet, luv." The limo door opens, and Ryker reaches back for my hand as he slides out.

Hand in his, I step out of the limousine, confused. We seem to be in some kind of industrial location near the river, the area lined with warehouses, and Zuben's warnings about Ryker flash through my mind again. Is he going to torture and kill me in one of these warehouses?

Far in the distance, the lights over the Ben Franklin bridge shine, and much closer, I see and hear a helicopter.

Eyes widening, I turn toward him. "Is that…is that for us?"

He nods. "The restaurant's in New York." He leans down, his lips next to my ear. "And as for that kiss… I'm saving you for dessert."

# CHAPTER ELEVEN

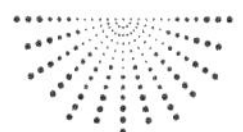

### *Ember*

I FEEL like I'm flying. Well, technically we *are* flying, but it's way more than just the helicopter causing this exhilaration, more than the cocktails and wine I had with dinner too. The restaurant he took me to was intimate, the food delicious, and the staff treated us like celebrities or royalty.

As the lights of Philadelphia come into view, I've never felt happier, and Ryker intertwines our fingers and raises them to his lips. The soft press of his kiss on the back of my hand makes my insides contract.

I look into his eyes. "Thank you," I say. "Thank you for the most amazing night of my life."

"You might have already thanked me—once or twice." Ryker winks, but other than that small gesture he doesn't break eye contact, and I can no longer remember seeing anything beyond what I see in his strikingly bright blue eyes.

They're so brightly blue they don't seem real, and I feel

different under his gaze, the same person and yet utterly changed, more mature, more desirable, more fully myself, and yet also someone who *needs* Ryker, needs his touch, his kiss, his body in a way I'd only imagined before tonight. Sexual desire—now that I've experienced it—my imagination did not do this feeling justice.

"Your car has arrived at the Heliport, Mr. Stone." The pilot's voice breaks into my fantasy world, and Ryker pushes a button and speaks into a small microphone. "Thank you."

I'm panting now, like I've been running, even though I've been sitting for the forty-five minute flight, and I look out the windows to see we're about to land back at the port on the Delaware River. Soon after that, we'll get into the limousine and the driver will take me home.

But I'm not ready for this night to end. Assuming I can find the courage, I plan to invite Ryker up to my apartment, and then I'll invite him to do other things, invite him to do anything he wants. My chest is heaving now, my breaths short and shallow.

"Nothing to fear," Ryker whispers, and I wonder if he realizes what's causing my anxiety.

The helicopter lands and Ryker gets out first. I shift to the door, and Ryker puts his hands on my waist, lifting me and gently setting me down on the ground. He releases me, but the expanse of skin he touched pulses with the sense memory.

He takes my hand, and we bend slightly against the wind of the helicopter's blades as we walk to the car, where the driver is holding the door open. I slide inside.

He still hasn't made any kind of a move on me—didn't

even kiss me for dessert like he promised, or threatened—but I'm certain of his attraction, certain his desire is building alongside my own. I might lack experience, but I'm acutely aware of the intimacy growing between us. I sense it with every fiber of my being, with every shallow breath I inhale.

Is Ryker the one? *My one*? I know it's foolish to be thinking in those terms on our first date, but some claim love at first sight is real, and on our travels and at the small Italian restaurant in Manhattan, we talked nonstop about everything and nothing, and the conversation flowed so naturally. Even the moments of silence between us seem filled with the dichotomies of comfort and discomfort, relaxation and excitement, safety and danger. He makes me laugh, he makes me feel special and he makes my body sing with want.

I've never wanted *anything* the way I want Ryker.

"Cognac?" he asks as he pours amber liquid into two ornately carved crystal glasses. The drink reminds me of Zuben, and of his warnings, but all of that seems so ridiculous now. A vampire. Seriously?

Our fingers brush as Ryker hands me my glass, and desire ripples through me, parting my lips and arching my back—both things happening outside my conscious control. His expression darkens as his tongue grazes his lips, and he maintains eye contact as he takes a sip of his drink.

I taste mine too, even though I don't need or want more alcohol. I've had more than enough to loosen me up, and don't want to cross over to a place where I might fall asleep or be too far gone for a gentleman like Ryker to accept my consent—because as dangerous as he looks, he is a gentleman, and I plan to consent the hell out of whatever he wants.

Zuben's warnings flash again and I smile as I swallow their absurdity. A vampire. A thief. A pirate. Ha!

"Something's amusing you." Ryker says, his body turned toward mine, one arm across the back of the car seat and the other holding his glass, resting on his knee. "What's so funny?"

He reads me so well. "Nothing really. Something Zuben said."

Ryker blinks, masking what looked like an instant of anger that flashed in his eyes. "And what did my good pal Zuben have to say?"

I shake my head. "I'm embarrassed to repeat it."

"Come on, luv… As I've already said, you can tell me *anything*."

The way he says *anything* whips up everything he's already ignited inside me—the attraction, the affection, the lust—and I feel like I *can* tell him anything, in the same way I'm sure that I'll let him *do* anything he wants with me tonight.

"First—" I shake my head "—Zuben claimed you were a pirate. Arr, Billy!" I grin.

Ryker just nods, swirling the cognac in his glass.

"And then he said you were a *vampire*. As if."

Ryker's fingers slide from the car seat to the back of my neck and then slowly stroke my sensitive skin there. I fight my body's desire to writhe on the seat, to slide into his lap, to press the burning hot core of me into his hard thigh—or into the obvious bulge against it.

"But…" He licks his lips. "You don't believe him."

I take another small sip of cognac. "Of course not. Vampires, if they even exist, they're monsters, killing machines. I know you're not that."

"You're right. I am not that." He nods, and something new flashes in his eyes. Uncertainty? "But what if I *were* a vampire, or even a pirate?" he asks, his voice deep and soft and dangerous, like the purr of a tiger. "If that were true, would you still be here with me? Would you still *want* me?"

The way he says want, stirs my desire, but then a nervous laugh rattles through me. I love his sense of humor almost as much as I love how he makes my body feel—and my heart—but I'm not sure I get this particular joke. Is he trying to scare me?

"Would I still…like you, if you were a vampire pirate?" I grin, but his expression doesn't change. "You're not serious."

"There's a lot of misinformation in the press about vampires, you know."

"And about pirates too, I'll bet." Taking a sip of my drink, I realize my hand is trembling. I don't love the direction this conversation has taken. Why is he giving any bandwidth to Zuben's crazy accusations?

"I'm not even sure I believe in vampires," I say. The press is so sensationalized.

"You don't believe in the supernatural?" he asks.

*The supernatural…* I swallow, and the cognac burns on the way down. "I grew up believing in magic." Another thing I've never told anyone. "But…" I look down.

"But what?"

I raise my gaze and his eyes show intense interest, and more than a little surprise, but then they soften, filling with so much warmth and not a hint of judgment about my strange confession.

I shake my head. "I believed in magic when I was a kid, but I realize now that my mother had some kind of delusional mental illness." And somehow she drew me into her delusions. It's the only explanation for my childhood, for how she disappeared.

Ryker lightly strokes the back of my neck, the base of my head, threading his fingers into my hair. "Did your mother ever *tell* you why you weren't allowed out after dark?" he asks softly.

I shake my head.

He nods, but the limo stops and he turns his head to the side. We're in front of my condo building.

"May I walk you up?" he asks, turning back to me.

"Yes. Of course." I set down my barely touched glass of cognac. "I'd like that." My jets were cooled by this strange conversation, but they're still running, and I still want to invite him inside. Invite him inside my house, my bedroom. Maybe even inside my body.

I tremble.

The driver opens the door, and Ryker holds out his hand to guide me from the car. After I enter my code, he holds open the door to my building, letting me go inside first where I use my keycard to unlock the door from the vestibule. Even if Ryker still has an air of danger about him, he's a total gentleman. Suggestions of his being a pirate or a vampire are laughable. Even if I don't quite get the joke.

# CHAPTER TWELVE

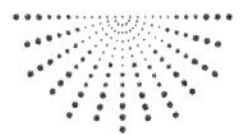

### *Ryker*

THE ALLURING EMBER pushes the elevator button for the ninth floor of her building, and I lightly trace my fingers down her back. Under my touch, her body reacts in the most delicious way, so responsive, almost like I just sucked on her love nub or plunged my fangs into her neck.

My cock throbs at those thoughts, but I tell it to calm the fuck down. I do want to fuck her, not to mention feed from her sweet vein, but although I've had countless opportunities—in the limos, the helicopter, the private dining room—for some bloody reason I've thus far refrained.

There's something about this woman, her effect on me, I don't understand. At the gala I admit my attention was largely driven by pissing off Zuben, whose carnal interest in her is clear, but it quickly became much more than that. How else to explain why I lay down bars of gold for a night with her? Something I could have claimed without such a bold and expensive gesture. But what it is about her, I can't comprehend.

There are so many wenches in the sea that I've never found myself craving any particular one.

Ember's attractive, no doubt about that—her pale skin, her long silky hair and eyes the color of violets in spring—but attractive women are a dime a dozen, so it can't be just that. As the elevator rises, her body trembles slightly, almost humming, and I stroke her back.

She turns her delicate facial features toward me and smiles, her violet eyes flashing in the light and all of it forming a transparent expression, full of nerves and desire, but also innocence and hint of darkness and pain.

The pain in her eyes is something I've seen often in vampires—lifetimes of pain in the eyes of someone appearing young—but I've never seen it in a human, at least not in this excessively comfortable century.

I follow her down the hallway, and her body… Fuck, the girl is smoking hot. Unsuccessfully trying to put the key into her apartment door, her hands tremble, and my eyes feast on the curve of her back, the round mound of her ass as it presses against that silk dress.

Finally penetrating the lock with her key, she looks back over her shoulder, and my cock throbs with near painful desire.

But my interest goes far beyond Ember's obvious physical charms—otherwise I'd already have taken her. Or perhaps I'm learning the benefits of delayed gratification? I almost chuckle at that idea. I'm going to gratify the hell out of myself with this wench.

"Would you…" her voice is quiet, and she sucks on

her cheeks for moisture and courage "...would you like to...to come in?"

I lean against the wall next to her door. "Yes. Very much. If you'll *have* me—inside."

She fumbles to remove the key now, her cheeks turning bright pink as they have many times this evening. Everything about her body is responsive, she can't hide a thing, and she's been close to an orgasm several times this evening, even though I've barely touched her.

Her physical attributes explain her effect on my cock, her youth and vitality explain her affect on my fangs, but what remains a mystery is my compelling desire to protect her from...from everything—from me.

But I remind myself who I am. Who she is. Ember is tempting and easy prey, and I am a fucking pirate. A fucking pirate who loves to fuck, so it's time to step up, to snap out of whatever spell I've been under and act like one.

"Can I get you anything?" Inside the apartment, she turns to walk backwards, leading me into her humble home, her nipples taut under the silky fabric of her pale pink dress, barely shielded by a see through jacket. "I have some white wine open in the fridge."

"Well, I *am* very *thirsty*." Wrapping my hand around her slight waist, I pull her forward.

Her body makes contact with mine, and she exhales—hard. My fangs pulse, determined to spring into action and plunge into her vein, but I catch myself.

I want to fuck her first, fuck her before she's under the effects of my venom. Even though the bodies of sleeping humans respond to pleasure under the influence of vampire venom, vampires who fuck unconscious humans are depraved. There are few lines I won't cross but that's one.

Besides…for some reason I want her to remember the feeling of my dick ramming inside her. I want to imprint myself in this woman—both in her cunt and her mind.

"I, ah…" Her heart gallops, sending her sweet, sweet nectar racing through her body, and the scent of her blood is intoxicating, heightened by the hormones that reveal her emotions and desire.

Poor thing can't decide whether to be excited or afraid at the moment, and I can't help savoring the knowledge that I am inciting both.

Her fear—fear and anticipation of what she thinks I might do to her—hardens my cock to a point that's unbearable, and I hold her tighter to make sure she feels it pulsing against her hip and belly.

Her breathing grows even more thready and her lips part. She is beyond ready to be fucked. Leaning toward me, every part of her body is inviting me to do whatever I want.

I step back.

"Wine would be lovely. Thank you."

Her knees quiver as she walks slowly toward her kitchen, moving like a fawn on new legs, or more accurately like a wench who's already been thoroughly pounded by my hard cock.

My need is rock hard and pressing against my leather trousers, and I lean against the door jam as she fetches two short glasses and pours us some wine.

I want this woman; I want her more than I remember

wanting any woman in my entire life. I should take her right now in the kitchen. Fuck her hard and fast, and then put her asleep to let her cunt recover as I drink from her vein.

It would be so easy to claim what I want—what I fucking *need* from her—and leave her none the wiser, ignorant of how I used her as a source of nourishment after the pleasure.

Vampire venom is what's kept our species a myth for millennia, what's allowed us to peacefully coexist with humans. Until recently, our two species' symbiotic relationship existed in the shadows, near-perfectly hidden, until our damned king revealed our existence to humanity, putting innocent vampire lives at risk.

Turns out, humans, although weak, are dangerous when armed with stakes, silver and ignorance.

Watching Ember from behind, my urges goad me to grab her, to lift that dress above her ass and plow straight into her, to drive until she can't take anymore and then to drink, to take what I crave even more than her cunt.

But for some strange reason, I want… Fuck. I want her to know who I am first, *what* I am.

*What is wrong with me?* I'm no rapist, but neither have I ever asked for permission to fuck or feed, never mind confessed what I am to a human. Never had to. The women I've wanted have been beyond keen to rut, and I always take what I want.

But something about Ember is making me hesitate. Clearly it's been too long since I've plundered.

Fear snakes through me, icing my veins.

Once she knows the truth—what I am—she may not

say yes, and then I'll be forced to *take* what I want, take it from her like the pirate I am.

Because I don't have the willpower to leave this apartment without having Ember—without totally possessing her vein and her cunt. But I'm also certain I'll regret claiming either without her consent.

It's the most foreign feeling I've had in my life. I know what I am—I am and have always been bad—but for the first time in my life I regret it.

We move into her living room, and she sits on the sofa, then nervously touches the cushion beside her, inviting me to sit close.

I sit at the opposite end of the furniture, bending up one leg and turning toward her, casual as all fuck, not a care in the world. I should get an Oscar.

She looks disappointed that I'm so far away.

"Sorry," I say softly, the word foreign on my tongue.

"What for?" She takes a sip of her wine, clearly trying to mask her emotions, her desire.

I slide my foot back to the carpet and grin. "Boots on the furniture."

"Oh!" She laughs, a spontaneous outburst that cuts the tension. "Don't worry about that. Your boots look clean. But—" She interrupts her own thought and frowns slightly. "Feel free to take them off, if you want. Make yourself comfortable. Please." She smiles softly, and then her teeth scrape the edge of her lip.

Her scent and her body language are making it clear that she wants me, perhaps as badly as I want her, but I'm enjoying making her wait.

Crossing my leg over my knee, I pull off one boot and

set it on the carpet, then cross the other leg, and pause with the sole of my boot facing toward her.

"Can I help?" she asks quietly.

Grinning that she caught my hint, I extend my leg toward her, my back braced against the arm of the sofa.

She pulls, and it's cute to watch her try to remove the boot that fits me like a second skin.

"I need more leverage." Still holding my foot, she slides off the sofa, and I pivot to lean against the back of the sofa.

Planting her feet, she tugs harder but then, slipping on the carpet, she tumbles back.

I catch her before she hits the floor.

Her eyes widen with surprise as she looks up at me, her weight supported in my arms, her lips parted and flush with her blood, as if *begging* me to devour her.

"How did you do that?" Her voice is breathless, and she pants from the effort of using it.

"Do what?" I smile, hoping to distract her.

"You moved so quickly. How?" She shakes her head. "Sorry. I should have just said thank you for catching me." Her hands slide from my neck toward my shoulders, and she bends one leg to brace her foot on the floor, readying herself to stand. "Can you help me up?"

I grin. "What if I like you in this position."

Unbalanced, supported in my arms with her head a couple feet above the carpet, she sucks in ragged breaths and her pupils dilate. She likes this position too—me dominant above her.

I could be inside her before she perceives any movement, plowing her hard on the carpet. My cock urges me to act. But her eyes change as fear overtakes her desire. One of her hands slides to the top of my chest and she pushes against me.

Shocked that I care, I snap out of my lustful stupor and lift her to her feet.

Startled by the sudden movement, she sucks in a quick breath, and then her chest heaves as she fights to return her breathing to normal.

Confused by the rapid movements, or maybe by what she's clearly feeling inside her cunt, she licks her lower lip and gazes into my eyes, seeking answers.

The air between us is on fire.

Stepping forward, she reaches up and pulls me into a kiss.

Hiding my surprise, I let her set the boundaries, keeping our kiss chaste, chaste by my standards, as she presses her lush lips against mine.

Using every ounce of my self control to hold back my fangs, I sense the blood pulsing inside her, her taste promising sweetness and mystery, and carrying some exotic flavor I've never tasted in the tens of thousands of veins I've sampled over my lifetime of travels.

Kissing her, I'm overwhelmed, fighting to concentrate as ecstasy muddles my thoughts.

Breaking the kiss, she looks into my eyes. "Is it…" She blinks. "Is it okay that I kissed you?"

Her uncertainty moves me. She misunderstood the hesitation in my kiss, and my inner pirate wakes from sedation.

Wrapping my hand around her waist, I pull her hard against me and kiss her again.

# CHAPTER THIRTEEN

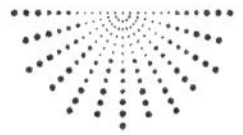

### *Ember*

RYKER PULLS ME CLOSER, and I gasp as my breath is stolen by his lips that crush mine and move as if starved—sucking and nibbling as if my mouth contains the source of all life.

I can barely sense my feet on the carpet. I'm floating, dizzy, my legs jelly, and I'm not sure how my body is staying upright. I'm being fully consumed, *devoured* by Ryker in a way that goes beyond anything I've ever imagined in my most sexy dreams. All of my focus is on my lips' response, moving to match his fervor and taking part in the frenzy as if they've always known how to perform this devilish dance.

And then, as if feeling neglected, my tongue flicks out to better taste him, and he groans, more like a growl, while his hard body grinds against mine. His thick, hard tongue plunges inside my mouth, stroking the side of my tongue, darting everywhere, tasting me, and it seems as if my tongue knows what to do too, our tongues easily playing together and waking even more parts of me, until my body's fully on fire.

Wantonly, I pulse against him as his hands reach under my sheer jacket to explore, their large size spanning every inch of my back, and then shifting lower to cup my ass and pull me even more firmly against his hard body.

Somehow my dress is now gathered up near my waist, and his hand slides over the backs of my bare thighs and then their fronts.

Shuddering, I can barely breathe through our kisses as his hand moves to rest over my belly and then circles downward toward my hot core.

I pull back. "Ryker."

"Fuck. Shit." He staggers back.

I almost fall, but his strong hand takes hold of my waist.

"Too fast." He shakes his head. "I got carried away."

"It's okay." Taking his hand, I stroke his palm with my thumb, marveling how even that part of him feels impossibly thick and strong. I never thought I'd find fingers so sexy. "It's just. I don't know…"

"Don't know what, luv?"

I look down. "I don't know what I'm doing…"

"Oh." He steps back from me. "You've changed your mind." The resignation and disappointment in his voice are obvious. "I understand."

I shake my head. "No, that's not what I mean. I mean, I *do* want…this. I do want…you."

His eyes darken, his pupils expanding as his eyes pierce me, like he can see directly inside me. But he doesn't move closer. He's waiting for a signal that I'm not sure how to send.

My mouth dries as nerves overtake me. Part of me wants him to know that it's my first time and part of me doesn't. According to things I've read, some men don't like the hassle of dealing with virgins, and I feel ridiculous that I've reached this age with so little experience.

"What is it, luv?"

I look down. I'm ruining this, and the only thing worse than passing up this chance to have sex, sex with Ryker, is that I might disappoint him.

His bent finger urges up my chin and I open my eyes to look into his.

"You're a virgin," he says softly.

"No, I—" I squeeze my eyes shut for a moment, and then nod.

"Oh, my innocent little dove." His fingers stroke my face and he peppers my forehead with kisses.

Disappointment washes through me. He's kissing me like a kid now, but then his hands drop to my shoulders and he pushes off my sheer jacket, sending opposite signals.

Looking up into his eyes, I wriggle out of the garment and let it drop to the floor, and then his lips shift to my throat.

He lingers there, close, breathing heavily as his teeth scrape over my skin, and then he shifts his lips' focus to my shoulder, to my collarbone.

The zipper of my dress slides down my back, his fingers grazing the bare skin at its side, lighting it on fire, and I suck in a shuddering breath.

"Do you want me to make love to you, little dove?" He looks into my eyes, with heat and concern.

I nod, not sure I like his new nickname for me. My mouth is so dry now, my mind so muddled, I don't even try to form words.

"Let me take care of you," he says softly. "Let me teach you about pleasure." His hands glide over my skin, almost gracefully, tracing from my neck to my collarbone and then back, over and over, as he presses soft kisses onto my cheeks, my forehead, my eyelids.

"Will you grant me that honor?" he asks, his mouth pressing against my ear. "The honor of giving you pleasure? Of teaching you the ways of physical love?"

"Yes." The word escapes my lips like a wheezing exhale, and then he captures my lips again, kissing me with renewed fervor, kissing me in a way I can feel through my entire body, but especially between my legs. The dampness and ache there is growing, and my insides pulse, tightening and releasing over and over like my sex is crying out for more—for him.

My breath shudders against his lips as my body pulses, and I've never felt anything so wonderful. And we've barely started—I hope.

I want this part to go on forever, his lips kissing, his hands exploring, the ecstasy of the feelings it all ignites inside me, but as much as I love this, my body craves more. The intense internal waves of contraction have slowed now, but the rest of me—it continues to move under his touch.

Out of my conscious control, I slide and press against

him, as hungry for his skin as his hands seem to be for mine.

A hand nudges the back of my thigh, and I lift my leg without thinking. Clearly my sex is making the decisions now, fighting to get closer to his hard body.

My action's rewarded, and he pulls me in tight against his leather trousers, his thigh even more rigid than I expect.

I moan against his lips as the new pressure sends even more pleasure coursing through me, tightening parts deep inside and sending sparks to the outer universe of my being.

My hips pulse against his leg, and his hand grabs my ass to press me in harder and I realize the ridge I'm feeling against my needy softness is…

"Ah!" I throw back my head and cry out, unable to contain the pleasure as I realize that it's his erection rubbing my sex, stroking me with only leather and the thin strip of my thong between us.

My body is completely flooded with desire now, and I tense for a moment, wondering if he can tell how wet I am, wondering if I'm soaking his trousers with my dampness.

He pulls his hips back and lowers my foot to the floor, but before I can process my disappointment, he encases my skull in one large, strong hand and kisses me again, while his other hand slides under my dress to caress my upper thighs.

I miss the strong pressure of his sex on mine, but this, this soft stroking so close to where I'm on fire, is divine—better than divine—and then my vocabulary utterly fails me as his fingers stray higher, teasing the junction that joins my legs to my torso, tickling my pubic hair and stroking softly over the thin silk covering my mound.

My breathing accelerates as my dress drops off my shoulders, and then, not breaking our kiss, he adjusts our bodies to let my gown drop to the carpet.

His thumbs hook into the elastic at the top of my thong, and he crouches as he pulls the flimsy garment down to my ankles. I lean onto his shoulders as he carefully helps me lift one foot then the other, to step out of the panties.

Rising again to tower above me, he guides me forward, hands grazing over my butt, the backs of my thighs, and I step past my discarded clothing. I'm fully naked before him now, but not cold; my skin blasted by an internal furnace and the heat of his hands.

I close my eyes as we kiss, and we start moving. It's not toward the bedroom, but I trust him to guide me; I'm not even sure I'd be able to see if my eyes were open. Then he turns me, and my back touches something hard and cold.

Opening my eyes, I find I'm naked against the window.

He breaks our kiss, and I'm about to object, but then his mouth distracts me, drifting lower and lingering against my throat. There, his teeth scrape my skin again and his lips latch onto my throat. He sucks gently as his tongue flicks against my pulse.

He groans, so deeply I can feel it travel through his lips and into my body, but then he breaks his seal with my throat, and moves lower, kissing my shoulders, my neck, my collarbones, my chest. And then his fingers and lips find my breasts.

Softly kneading my breasts, he tugs gently on my nipples, which tighten to impossibly hard points under his touch, and his increasingly sharp tweaks on my nipples tighten something deep in my belly, as if the nerves in my breasts and sex are connected. Perhaps they are.

Looking into my eyes, he flicks his finger over the tip of my nipple, and I've never felt or seen anything more intense.

His other hand slides between my legs.

My head snaps back against the window and he strokes over my curls, dampened with my sweat and desire. Embarrassment flickers, and I look back into his eyes. If he minds the dampness, he doesn't show it.

Instead, he bends over, latches onto one of my nipples and sucks while his fingers sweep along the seam of my folds. My body shudders, more like convulses, in a spasm completely outside my control.

His lips release my breast. "You okay?" His finger strokes my damp seam, and my hips won't stop moving. I've never felt so sensitive, like every nerve in my body is sparking at once.

"Yessss," I say. "Very okay."

He grins, and then his finger slides deeper, splitting my folds to drag through my most intimate place. His finger pad grazes my opening, and I gasp as new sparks of pleasure pulsate through me.

"You're so wet," he says, his voice deep. "So fucking ready." His finger continues to slide, forward and back, forward and back, dividing me over and over, and making me gasp each time he hits somewhere new down there.

He claims that I'm ready. But am I? The thought of that hard ridge I felt—so massive and thick—is terrifying.

But I want this, I want it so badly. I want to lose my virginity and I want to lose it tonight—to Ryker—yet at the same time I'm afraid, unable to imagine the reality of his huge hardness forcing its way inside me. Maybe it isn't as thick as it felt through his pants?

"Yessss." My word comes out on a shuddery exhale as his finger grazes my opening, and he moans in response.

He nudges my feet farther apart where we stand. And then kneels on the floor, taking my hips in his strong grip and moving his mouth to my mound.

"Oh!" I fall back against the window, but he catches me, softening my drop. Then he gently nudges one of my legs to rest over his shoulder, and I have no choice but to lean back on the glass, completely exposing my sex to his face.

His hand holds my thigh firmly over his shoulder, as the other strokes through my wet heat. He's looking between my legs with so much concentration and awe that I almost wonder if that part of me is strange, or made wrong.

My mind slowly registers what's about to happen —*oral sex*—but my comprehension is impeded by a thick fog. I tense up, unsure of what I'm expected to do, or what to expect from him, and I wish I'd washed down there after we got back from New York. But then his hand slides from my thigh to part my folds and all my regrets vanish as he breathes against my heat.

His breath tickles my pubic hair, alternately heating and cooling my damp skin, and he lingers there so long I start to wonder if this is it, if I've been misinformed and hot breath is the extent of oral sex.

Then his tongue flicks out, grazing my clit.

A shuddering breath escapes my chest, and my head strikes the window as his tongue circles and flicks over my sensitive nub, stealing my breath, my thoughts, my sanity. I've touched myself before but it wasn't remotely like this.

His tongue's strokes continue, varying hard and soft, moving around my clit's edges and then pressing hard over its top, switching course at just the right moment, almost as if his tongue and lips are under the command of my responses. But then I realize it's me who's under his control.

He's playing my body—now his, completely his—and I fully surrender to his mouth and his hands.

As his mouth's plunder continues, his hand strokes me, skimming over my opening and the pleasure is so intense that my hips jump forward with each pass, my entrance as sensitive as the clit he's flicking and rubbing with his tongue, and…and…oh, god, now he's sucking it.

My hips drive forward against the suction, and he nudges his finger inside me.

"Ah."

Breaking his latch on my sex, he looks up into my eyes. "Tell me to stop if I hurt you."

Unable to talk, I nod, definitely not wanting him to stop. I don't want any of this to stop, not ever.

His mouth moves back to my clit as his finger proceeds, sliding farther inside me, and the intrusion doesn't feel all that different from inserting a tampon, not yet, but then his finger moves, pulling almost out and then in again, pressing against my insides as it travels, and I can feel the hard edge of his ring. Each time he pushes, he lets more of his thick finger invade, and his mouth continues to torture my clit.

The sensation is overwhelming. My head rolls back and forth against the window and my hands slam against it. My body is completely overtaken by this mysterious pleasure. And still his mouth strokes and flicks and sucks, his finger plunges and circles and rubs, and then he slows his mouth's action, breathing heavily against me.

The pressure inside my body increases as a second finger slides alongside the first. For a split second the thicker intrusion hurts, but it's not really pain, or at least it quickly morphs into something I crave, something that makes me want even more thickness inside me. My body is shaking, and the tension building is so powerful that I'm not sure I can take it anymore—but neither do I want it to stop.

His other hand strokes my thigh, as his mouth renews its assault, alternately flicking and sucking, and I grab onto his long wavy hair, holding his head against me as my body detonates.

I cry out, barely recognizing my own voice, as pulses—no, massive waves—overtake my insides. My body is fully controlled now by the strings that he's pulling, the buttons he's pushing and sucking—strings and buttons I didn't even know I had—and I've never imagined anything so extraordinary, materializing from inside my own body.

I lose track of time and space, lose track of everything except my sex rubbing against his face, but then as I slowly regain my awareness, I realize both my legs are over his shoulders now, draped over him as I lean back against the glass.

His fingers continue to slide slowly inside me as his mouth gently kisses my inner thighs and my mound, but he stays away now from my clit that's on fire. His free hand guides one of my feet to the floor and then slides up my back to transfer my weight from the window. My other leg slips off him and onto the floor.

Keeping his fingers inside me, he stands and bends to kiss me, the sweet musky taste of my sex on his lips.

"You're so beautiful when you come," he says softly between kisses. "Miraculous."

"Thank you?" I say, my mouth dry, my voice cracking. "Thank you for saying that, for *doing* that… Ah!" I cry out as he draws his fingers out from inside me.

He raises those fingers to his lips, and I'm slightly mortified to see blood there, mixed in with the juices glistening on his thick digits.

Then, looking deep into my eyes, his gaze holds me captive, as he licks his fingers as if they were dipped in sugar, or the finest honey he's ever tasted. My mortification is amplified.

His eyes widen and his fingers plunge into his mouth as he sucks every trace of fluid from them, licking his rings, as if trying to clean off every last bit of me. He moans deep in his chest.

"Fuck," he says, after pulling them out. "Ho-ly fuck." His hand drops to his crotch.

My eyes follow the gesture, and I gasp at the sight of his hand sliding over the monstrous bulge there, its size even more intimidating than it felt while rubbing against me.

"Apologies, little dove," he says gruffly, "but I need to be inside you—now." In a flash, he undoes his pants—not a zipper but buttons—and then moans as he parts the leather and his stiff member springs forth.

I gasp, shocked at its size, at its color—so much deeper and redder than the rest of his skin—and at the sight of the thick veins that trace down its sides. His hand strokes its length, and a damp, even redder, tip appears from beneath the shroud of skin at the top.

His eyes are wild now, his face distorted as if he's fighting some invisible force. "Ember, you…Last chance to back out. I can't control…" His voice is strained.

He turns away. "I should leave. If I stay a second longer, I will fuck you. I can't bear this…"

Trembling, I inhale a ragged breath. "Don't go. Please don't go."

Wrapping his arm around my waist, he pulls me against him, and his erection presses against my body, hot and pulsing as if it has a life of its own.

"I don't want to hurt you," he says.

"You won't. I trust you."

He shrugs out of his jacket, so fast it seems magic, and the leather slaps against the wall on the other side of the room, pushing a painting ajar while he pulls his shirt off over his head. It's more like a blouse than a typical men's shirt, and I love how he has his own style, so unusual and high fashion, even though everything about him shouts male.

Taking my hand, he leads me to the sofa and then kisses me as he guides me onto my back. My legs fall open, one foot dropping to the carpet and he positions himself between my legs.

His face is bright red now, almost as dark as his penis, and his expression is distorted as if he's in pain. "I want to take you slow and gentle," he says, "but after tasting you… I'm not sure I can."

Reaching up, I stroke his face, my urge to comfort him overwhelming, even though it's me who's the virgin. My insides are aching with the memory of his fingers, and I'm pulsing and yearning to have that feeling again.

"You." His eyes close as his hand slides between us. "I've never tasted…" His voice trails off into a groan, and I feel the thick head of his erection parting my slick folds, and then pressing against my opening, now more sensitive than I imagined possible.

Eyes still closed, he pauses there, panting so rapidly that his chest convulses. If he weren't a virile young man, I'd fear he was having a heart attack.

I touch his cheek, and he opens his eyes, filled with anguish.

"Forgive me." His hips thrust forward, hard and fast, and I cry out as he tears me in half.

# CHAPTER FOURTEEN

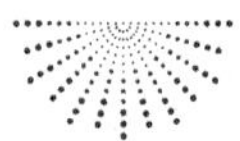

### *Ryker*

My brain explodes with gratification as I ram into her for the first time—harder and deeper than I intended—*far* harder and deeper.

She cries out in pain, and I freeze, holding myself still inside her, and it takes every ounce of power contained in my muscles to hold myself back as she adjusts to the massive intrusion. She's a fucking virgin and I just violated her with as much force as I've used on any wench. As much force as I'd use on a vampire, capable of quickly healing from tears or bruises.

Finding the will to open my eyes against the utter pleasure that's sealed them shut, I gaze into her violet ones. Her cheeks are bright red, her lush lips open, and she takes in shallow, ragged breaths as she looks back at me with wonder and surprise.

Relief floods through me as I see something in those magical eyes that goes beyond pain, but still, I don't dare move. Not yet. I don't trust myself. Not only is she human and fragile, it's her first time. I need to take her slowly, gently, but my body has other ideas.

*Fuck.* Her cunny is so tight, but also so slick with arousal, and it's pulsing around me as her body works to adjust to my cock's rude invasion.

"I'm sorry." I press a soft kiss on her forehead.

"Sorry?" Her forehead wrinkles and her eyes fill with confusion. "Why? Am I doing it wrong?"

"No." My heart snaps at her misunderstanding. "I meant—I should I have entered you slowly." My voice is tight. "I hurt you. That was not my intention."

Her tongue slides out to wet her lower lip, and my cock throbs in response.

"It only hurt for a second." Her eyes flutter shut and reopen as she tightens, hard, around my stiff cock.

*Holy fuck.* The breath vacates my chest.

"But it feels good now," she says touching my cheek as she massages me with her cunt. "I like how you're…*filling* me. And I'm glad that...that I finally know how sex feels."

Her hips shift under me, and I moan, the slight friction too much to bear.

"My little dove." My voice is so strained, I can barely talk. "You think *this* is sex? That a few hard pokes constitutes making love?"

Her eyes fill with worry, or possibly embarrassment. "There's more?" She tightens around me again.

Choking back a moan, I nod. "So much more. Are you ready?"

"Yes." The word comes out on a thread of air.

Bracing myself, I press a light kiss on her lips. "Tell me

if I hurt you. I will try to be gentle, but you…" I shake my head, unable to find the right words. "There is something about you…"

"What?" Her forehead wrinkles with worry again. "I *am* doing something wrong. Please. Tell me what to do."

"Ember." I kiss her softly. "You are the opposite of wrong. In fact, there is something about you. Something I can't seem to resist." My ass muscles release and tighten a few times, moving me ever so slightly inside her as I fight to hold my rod back. "I'm not sure I can be as gentle as I want to be."

Her lips part on a thready exhale that's clearly powered both by fear and pleasure. "That's okay," she says softly. "Make love to me. Please."

Unable to maintain my resistance, I pull back, sliding out through her tight channel as slowly as I can, and grimacing with the effort of keeping control.

"Does it hurt you?" she asks as she cups my cheek.

"Hurt?" I freeze with only my cock's head inside her.

"Your face…" She strokes my cheek. "I can tell that it hurts you."

"No." I swallow. "It's not pain you're seeing in my face, little dove. Quite the opposite." I thrust into her, hard.

She cries out, her breath shuddering as I hit home.

"Fuck!" I did it again, and my cock throbs inside her, even as I command it to be still again. It's like her body has some magic spice driving me wild. I've had more wenches than I could begin to count, but I've never felt anything like this.

"What's wrong?" she asks her voice full of concern.

"I'm trying to go slow…" I shake my head.

"It's okay." Her hips pulse, and she licks her lips, unaware of the seductive power of her tongue.

"If it's too much, tell me to stop." I withdraw slowly again as she nods. I can take away her pain if I feed. But I want her awake…

My body takes over my thoughts, ignoring my intentions and moving of its own volition. My back and ass muscles are no longer interested in intentions, they're only interested in giving me what my cock craves, giving me what her tight, soft cunt can offer, taking what my body demands.

Powered by more lust and passion than I've felt in my life, I drive into her, as hard and fast as I take female vampires, who have the ability to heal from the friction and force of the most punishing and rapid thrusts.

A high keening sound flows from her lips, and I open my eyes, unaware that I'd closed them and hoping to discover whether her sound is driven by pleasure or pain. But her eyes are closed, her cheeks bright red, her lips open, her head to the side, exposing her throat.

And my hips refuse to still, thrusting my cock inside her delicious tight cunt over and over and over. It's driving me mad. I should stop, at least slow down. I should check to see how she's doing, but my hips won't listen to reason and they drive with a force and pace I fear might break her.

Her breasts bounce with each thrust, bobbing so fast and hard they must hurt too, and so I take one tit in my palm to support it.

She moans.

Encouraged, my thumb strums her nipple as my cock

continues its plunder, ramming deep with each stroke and relishing the tight muscles responding inside of her, even as I try to convince myself to slow down.

I have no idea how much time has passed when I manage to ease up my unrelenting, inhuman pace.

She opens her eyes, and the sight makes me gasp, her beauty, her very soul on display in the violet depths of her eyes.

"Are you okay?" I ask hoarsely.

"I'm not sure, I—"

Ashamed, I stop pumping and drop my head down.

"I…I…" Her voice is shaking. "Are you finished?" she asks softly.

"I can be." I start to slide from inside her.

"No. Please don't stop. Not for me." Her hips swivel.

I groan with pleasure at her movement. I'm so fucking close to my climax. "Are you sure?"

Her head nods inside the crook of my arm.

Almost out now, I drive back into her hard and deep, and she's still so slick with arousal, so tight and warm, and as much as I've demanded from her body, mine still craves more. It's like her juices are addictive and my cock is a junkie.

Cupping her thighs, I bend her legs back toward her and rest her calves on my shoulders, opening her up to me even more fully, and then moving my hands to her shoulders I ram into her, each thrust hard and deep, my drives powered by as much of my vampiric strength as I'd use on an enemy, as I'd use to defend my life.

Her eyes close and her head turns as she explodes around me again, her pussy grabbing hard and fast with waves of violent contractions that I thrust against as if I'm fighting the strongest current, or sailing straight into the highest waves.

Her nails dig into my back as her body thrashes within its tight confines beneath me, increasing my pleasure even further, and then my own climax blinds me, stealing not only my sight but all of my senses. Not to mention any last pretense of control.

*Fuck, fuck, fuck.* I pound through my climax as my seed shoots inside her. And still, I go on, through an impossibly long release, and it feels like quarts of spunk erupt from inside me.

With one last hard thrust, I collapse and my fangs plunge into her throat.

I acted on instinct, but the moment her blood hits my mouth, regret slams my chest.

When I bit her, I released too much venom, its release mirroring the force of my ejaculation. Not only will my feeding put her to sleep, for hours, it will also rob her memory of our fucking, possibly our whole evening.

But that ship has sailed and I can't take the venom back, and....her blood is delicious, beyond delicious. The slight taste I had from bursting her cherry, was barely an appetizer to the main course. Ember tastes of summer, of sunshine, of flavors I'd long ago forgotten.

Her legs slip off my shoulders, and I cup her breasts as I feed from her vein, unable to stop myself, drawing long draughts of her blood and relishing not only her taste, but the pleasure it gives me as her blood absorbs into my body, nourishing every cell.

And to make it even better, Ember moans in ecstasy as

I feed. All humans feel pleasure during feedings, even after falling asleep, but her hands…Ember's hands are still moving over my body, almost as if she's awake.

Unconscious, she explores my back and ass, pulling me closer, and her other hand runs over my neck and through my hair.

"Ryker?" her voice is soft and throaty.

Licking my bite to close it, I pull back, shocked.

*How the fuck is she still awake?*

# CHAPTER FIFTEEN

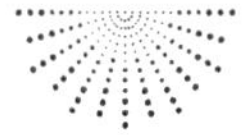

### *Ember*

A MILLION FIREWORKS explode inside my body, unconfined bombs detonating to release pleasure, euphoria, and…and something I can only identify as power. I've never felt so strong, so alive.

Moments ago, while Ryker had me literally pinned beneath him as he thrusted, I felt boneless—like I might never walk, might never move again, or at least like I might sleep for a million years before attempting any movement.

And then, after he ejaculated, I was so out of it I imagined he bit me. But now I'm alert—energized—my blood replaced by caffeine or something much stronger.

And speaking of blood. Ryker is wide-eyed above me, his lips wet with the dark red evidence that his biting my neck was *not* my imagination.

He did bite me—hard enough to break my skin! Is that a normal part of sex? I don't think so. It must be some kind of kink? If so, that's okay with me, as unexpected and strange as it was, I enjoyed it.

"Why?" It's all I can think to say. The word vampire flashes again but I know he's a man.

He leaps back off me. "Shit! What have I done?"

I reach up to my throat, and my hand comes away dry and I can't feel any wound. I rub the area, trying to find evidence of his teeth, but it's like I've already healed.

"You *bit* me." I wait for an explanation, because there must be one. I've never felt so stunned, so confused by what he did, and even more confused about my body's reaction. I liked it. The bite, the sex, both have left me wanting Ryker even more than before.

"Here." Ryker tosses me the fleece throw from the other end of the sofa and I wrap it around me as he buttons the fly of his pants.

The deep red blanket feels soft and warm, even though I'm not remotely cold, and I run my hands over its surface, as if I can sense every separate fiber in the fabric.

Wrapped up, I sit cross-legged at the end of the sofa as Ryker stands at its end, wearing only his leather pants and looking like he's just witnessed a murder, or a gory scene in a horror movie. Even though it was *he* who bit *me*, I'm overwhelmed by the urge to comfort him.

I pat the cushion beside me. "Talk to me," I say softly. "Please. Ryker. Tell me what's going on."

"You didn't fall asleep." He shakes his head as if in disbelief.

I tip my head to the side, fighting to comprehend this mysterious man I trusted enough to take my virginity, a man I still want to trust.

And even if I can't trust him I want him to take me again.

To *fuck* me again—right now. Because that was the best feeling of my life and I already want more.

"Do women usually fall asleep after sex?" I ask. "I mean, I've heard that men often do, and I did feel exhausted until…" I straighten my back. "Ryker, why did you bite me? Was that an accident? Did you get carried away?"

"You can say that again." He pushes back his hair, raking his thick fingers through his gorgeous long waves.

"Will you talk to me about it?" He's clearly upset, and I want to be understanding. I want to get past this before I invite him inside me again, something I want more than air at the moment.

"I'm not hurt." I reach up to touch my throat, verifying that there's no remaining wound, not even a trace. "In fact, I feel oddly fantastic." I draw a deep breath, tracing the air's passage through my body, noticing as it delivers its payload of oxygen to every part of me. I've never had such vivid awareness of my own body.

"There's something I need to tell you." Ryker looks down. "I meant to tell you before I, before we…"

"Tell me what?"

He clears his throat. "What Zuben told you. It's true."

"You're a pirate?" I laugh.

"And a vampire." He doesn't look like he's joking.

My back stiffens. "What?" I search his expression, scour his body language for proof that this is some kind of inappropriately timed prank.

He sits on the sofa beside me, and his weight shifts my

body toward him, so I brace my hand on the back cushions to keep at least some distance between us.

"I'm a vampire. So is Zuben," he adds quickly.

I shake my head. Up until now, tonight was perfect, beyond perfect, but now he's ruining it. The sex was better than I could have ever expected, especially for my first time, but his ridiculous claim has soured my euphoria.

My eyes narrow. "Is this your way to get rid of me?" Hurt and anger invade. "Is this how you get rid of all your one night stands?" My voice breaks. "*Was* this a one night stand?"

"No." He reaches to cup my face, but I pull back.

"No to *all* of that." He shakes his head. "And it wasn't the *sex* I thought would put you to sleep, it was my bite. Vampire venom does that."

"Does what?"

"Vampire venom relaxes humans—"

"So they can kill them." I frown.

"No." His head shakes vehemently. "Vampire venom relaxes humans, takes away their pain—and their memories—so they wake with no knowledge that they provided…food for a vampire."

"Bullshit."

His eyes open wider, and I feel blush bloom on my cheeks. I don't typically swear and even though we barely know each other, his reaction shows that he knows this about me already.

"It's not bullshit." He looks into my eyes. "It's very true. Most information circulated amongst humans about vampires is false. And the hate crimes committed against us—"

"Hate crimes?"

He frowns. "What else do you call it when innocent vampires are staked on sight?"

"Innocent? The police stake vampires in self defense, for public safety, to protect us from vampires…" My mind is reeling; I can't follow Ryker's logic. I'm not sure I want to.

"No." Turning toward me, Ryker rests his arm on the back of the sofa between us.

My body contracts in fear, but I take deep breaths and remind myself: this is the same man who took me to New York for dinner—in a helicopter—the same man I made love to not long ago. I should at least hear him out.

"Ryker, what you're saying makes no sense. Vampires are monsters. They kill." He is so not a vampire.

"Listen…" Ryker rakes back his hair again. "Do vampires ever kill humans? Sure. But humans kill each other too. Way more often than vampires do." His eyes narrow. "When humans commit murder at least there's a trial. Humans aren't just slaughtered on sight for being who they are." Closing his eyes, he draws a long breath, and his expression softens. "I didn't mean to raise my voice, or get into politics."

Looking into his eyes, I nod. His eyes haven't changed, and they still reveal so much emotion and goodness. Can my instincts be so wrong? Does he have some kind of delusionary mental illness like my mom?

"Humans and vampires," he continues, "our species coexisted in peace for millennia." His eyes narrow. "Most humans thought us a myth. We've always been hunted by slayers, but for the past twenty years it's been open season on my kind—wooden stakes through the heart left and right."

My teeth scrape my lower lip as I consider his words. I still can't believe what he's saying is true. He's making it sound like *humans* are the predators, not vampires.

And even if what he's saying is true, Ryker can't be a vampire. And certainly not Zuben. The idea is laughable.

"But you're alive," I reason with him. "Not dead, or undead. You're warm blooded. Very." I touch his leg and his eyelids flutter. He's as responsive to my touch as I am to his.

And I realize that my hips are swiveling, my rising arousal driving the motion beyond my conscious control.

My insides contract, and I suck in a ragged breath. Only minutes have passed since Ryker's hardness was pumping inside me, but my body already wants him again.

And as crazy as his claim is, my need for him is not only overwhelmingly powerful, it's more than just physical.

I want more sex, but I also want *Ryker*, I want to believe him and trust him, even if he needs psychological help or…

What if he *is* a vampire?

I close my eyes. I'm not thinking straight because I'm starting to believe him. And I'm more turned on now than before the sex. Did his venom, as he called it, also affect my libido?

"Have you put me….under your spell?" I ask softly.

"I hope so." Smiling, his expression darkens with desire, but then he blinks and shakes his head. "No. Not a spell. Not in the way you mean. Vampires have no such powers."

"But your venom… You said…"

"The venom makes feedings easier. It makes humans forget that it happened. But with you…" His shoulders rise as he inhales, and he slowly shakes his head.

"So…vampires *can't* control minds, or make women *want* you…" I'm too embarrassed, too unsure, to tell him how badly I crave him. "You can't control minds or cast spells?"

He shakes his head. "Afraid not, my little dove. Magic remains the sole domain of witches."

I suck in a sharp breath.

"What?" His hand falls to my shoulder, and I lean into its warmth. "What did I say?" His eyes are full of worry and curiosity.

I shake my head. "Nothing. It's just…this night…it's been so confusing." My hips circle, pressing my clit down against the sofa with each pass, my need rising so high now, I'm close to another orgasm. "Tonight's been confusing—and wonderful—but your mention of magic and witches…" I draw a long breath. "It brought back childhood memories."

His eyes widen. "What kind of memories?"

I smile. "Of reading the Harry Potter books."

Grinning, he nods, but I'm not sure he believes my explanation.

But no way am I offering more right now. I'm not sure that I trust my memories of childhood—of my mother's abilities, the way she disappeared—and even if I did trust my own mind, I'm not ready to share any of that with

Ryker, with anyone. Secrecy was something mother pounded into me as hard as my fear of the dark. I've already told both Ryker and Zuben too much.

"How can I convince you?" Ryker asks.

I draw a thready breath. "Convince me to do what?" Does he have some crazy sex act in mind? "I'll try anything."

He smiles and his tongue flicks out. "Convince you that I'm a vampire."

"Oh, right." I lick my lips. I'm finding it hard to focus on anything beyond having him inside me again. *What is wrong with me?*

"It doesn't matter," I say, hoping to get the topic back to sex. "And anyway, since you claim everything I know about vampires is fake news, how can you prove to me that you are one?"

His eyes brighten. "I have an idea."

I blink and he's gone. Or did I even blink?

"Where did…?" I glance around the room, trying to figure out where he went, and then he reappears beside me.

"How…?"

"Vampires can move very quickly." He grins. "Faster than the human eye can detect."

*He's holding a knife!*

I press away from him, scrambling back.

He leaps away, landing across the room.

"Ember!" He lifts both arms in surrender, dropping the knife to the floor. "I mean you no harm. I promise."

My heart is pounding so fast and hard I can barely hear, barely breathe. "Why?" I point toward the knife.

One hand still up in surrender, Ryker slowly crouches, maintaining eye contact with me as he picks up the knife. "I'm going to show you my vampiric ability to heal."

"What?" My eyes flit back and forth between the flash of the knife's blade as it picks up the light, and the rise and fall of his six pack of abs, maybe eight. How did I not notice them before? Clearly I had the wrong angle when he was driving inside me.

My insides pulse, ignoring my fear, or maybe because of it.

He steps back further, and I marvel at his abs' definition, how the muscles change shape as he moves. Then the blade moves.

He slashes his forearm.

A gash opens, so deep I see bone.

Blood flows from the wound, and shock traps a scream in my throat.

Dropping the knife, he holds his arm toward me, and his skin knits together, his wound closing like a film screened in reverse. He picks his discarded shirt off the floor and wipes his arm, then holds it toward me. There's no evidence of the knife's work.

"See?" he says. "See how quickly I heal? Can a human do that?"

I stare at his arm, at his whole gorgeously, powerful body, and my mouth is dry all the way down my throat. *Is it true?*

My mind's racing, but through fog I can't begin to form any words.

"Sorry about the blood." He disappears again, returning before I can blink, with towels from my linen closet, and he wipes the blood off the hardwood floor. "At least I missed the carpet." He smiles softly as he looks into my eyes.

The blanket slips from my shoulder, and I adjust it. The fabric grazes my nipple, and I gasp as a shudder of desire rakes through me. My hips pulse, mimicking the way they moved when Ryker was inside me.

My gaze drifts from his face to his massive chest, broad and dusted with just enough dark hair to be manly, and then down again to those abs. My tongue flicks out as I imagine tracing it through those hard ridges, wondering what his reaction would be if I did that, and then my gaze drops even lower.

His arousal is pushing against the flap of leather, not fully buttoned, the shape of him seeming impossibly large to fit inside a woman's body, even though I know that it somehow fit inside me.

I draw a ragged breath at the sense memory of how full I felt with him buried deep inside me, of how some of his early drives hurt, but then felt impossibly good, at how my body yielded, molded around him as if we were meant to fit together.

And how I want to feel that again.

But Ryker is a vampire.

I have to believe him—at least for the moment, at least until I talk him into taking me again, because I need him to do that so badly that nothing else matters. Any second I'm going to leap off the sofa and jump straight onto his… his cock.

I can think of no better way to say it and understand why people use the word.

Earlier in the evening, I was turned on, but this now…this is so much more.

My gaze rises to find him studying me intently, the slight curve of a smile kissing his lips.

"Your venom." I have to suck moisture from my cheeks to continue. "Does it make women…*want* you?" I let the blanket slip off my shoulders, and cupping my breast, I slide my thumb over my tight nipple, sucking in a sharp breath at the self-induced pleasure.

"Looks like it might." He steps forward slowly, his thick, heavy cock bouncing against the loose leather. "Venom typically puts humans to sleep, so I guess I've never had the opportunity to ask about other effects."

His cock slips fully out from between the fold of his pants. He grabs onto it and gasps, hissing as his fingers slide down to its base.

"Why do you ask?" His eyes are full of desire, and it throws fuel on my own.

"Because, even though we just…did it, I want you to…to *fuck* me again." I use the word, even though it's not normally in my vocabulary. "I need to feel you inside me."

His eyes widen, his expression heats and turns mischievious, as he continues to look into my eyes. "Where do you want this?" He strokes his cock. "Tell me."

"In my…my vagina."

"In your cunt."

I gasp at the word.

"I know it's sometimes used as a slur these days, but in all my years it's the best word for the female genitalia."

I nod, unsure I could ever say that.

"Say it," he says, deeply. "Tell me where you want my cock."

My hand slips between my legs and my finger grazes my overly-sensitive clit. I cry out. Panting as I rub myself, I try to gather enough air to speak.

"I want you, your *cock* in my…my *cunt*." My fingers slip through my throbbing wetness. "Now. Please!"

In a nanosecond, he's beside me, holding my face in his hands and kissing me with even more passion than before, stealing my breath and my sanity.

I reach down to find his erection, warm and hard, yet velvety soft as I run my palm down its surface. I didn't get the chance to touch him before, and my hand can't seem to get enough.

Moaning, he pulls back from the kiss and my hold, shaking his head. "I'll gladly make you feel good again." He winks. "Very good. But regretfully, I think we'd better put this bloke away for tonight." Grimacing, he tucks his erection under the leather and starts to button his fly.

"No." I reach my hand inside the flap to touch him. "Then why did you make me say it?" It doesn't seem fair.

He moans, his abs undulating as he catches his breath. I want to touch his stomach too, but sense that it might be too much while I'm still holding his cock. Too much for us both.

"Baby, you must be sore. I took you—hard—barely a half hour ago. Even if it *hadn't* been your first time… you're bruised inside, chafed. You'll be walking weird for a few days."

Squeezing him in my palm, I rise onto my knees and

kiss him again, loving how his groan vibrates my lips and quivers through my entire body.

"I don't *feel* sore." I look into his eyes, stroking him softly, wanting him to see that I'm telling the truth, wanting him to see the strength of my need.

"You sure?" He looks into my eyes as he slides his thick index finger between my legs, thrusting it inside me hard and twisting it, letting me feel his skull ring, as if he wants to prove me wrong.

I gasp in pleasure, sliding my hips forward to take in more of him, trying to recreate the earlier friction.

"See?" I say. "Not sore."

"My cock is bigger than my finger," he says in an almost growl, his expression conflicting with desire and concern as he grinds and twists his finger inside me.

I grip him more tightly. "I'm well aware of that." Tugging his cock, I pull him forward.

"Shit." He falls into me. "Fuck!" He hisses. He pushes my knees farther apart on the sofa and presses a second finger inside me.

I arch my pelvis, trying to pull him deeper.

"You're really not sore?" His eyes widen full of wonder and lust. "Most human women would be raw after that pounding."

I shake my head as my hips pump, sliding me over his fingers, pulling them deep inside me, loving how they're stroking my insides, even if they aren't satisfying me like his cock did.

My knee slips off the edge of the sofa and his fingers drive even deeper, joined by a third, and all his top knuckles strike my folds, almost like a punch. Awkwardly,

I thrust my hips against his hand and he keeps me from falling with his other arm. I am completely out of control. My body is fully driving the bus now.

"Okay, baby." His voice lowers. "Okay. Okay. Slow down." His tone is gentle, as if taming a wild animal, and that's how I feel. Wild, out of control, and so needy, so desperate. Not myself, but I don't care about that.

He pulls his fingers out and licks them, closing his eyes in pleasure.

"Fuck." He sucks hard on his digits. "Ember. I warn you. There is no way I'm going to be able to hold back this time."

# CHAPTER SIXTEEN

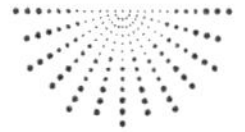

*Ember*

"I DON'T WANT you to hold back. Don't hold *anything* back. *Please.*" Lying on the sofa, I spread my legs wide as he removes his pants and tosses them away.

"I've never felt so alive," I tell him, "and so strong, so…so on fire."

Standing next to the sofa, he strokes my legs as he trains his gaze on my slick sex. His huge hands span my thighs, his fingertips meeting around my legs and then traveling down to my ankles and back, teasing my skin, making me writhe with desire. Slowly, his gaze travels up to meet mine.

Looking straight into my eyes, it's like he truly sees me, like I don't have any secrets from him, and I wish that I didn't. I don't think I can talk at the moment, but if I could, I'd tell him everything—about my mother, my recurring nightmares, my fear that I'm crazy.

Not only do I want him to know everything personal about me, I'd give him every one of my PINs and passwords, if it got him inside me more quickly.

Taking his cock in one hand, he kneels one leg on the sofa between my spread legs, and my insides pulse with anticipation, my wetness seeping out. Can he see it?

Trembling, I wait for him to move over me, to push that hard cock inside. But instead he reaches down and lifts me off the sofa.

In a flash, he lifts me into the air and brings me down hard, impaling me on his cock. The movement's so fast that my body reacts and I cry out, before my mind fully registers what he's done.

My hands land on his shoulders and then I cup one behind his head as we look into each other's eyes. I start to recover from the quick stab of pain and absorb his massive invasion.

"You okay?" he asks.

I nod, my body now adjusted to his girth and length, and the sharp pain of penetration morphs into pleasure, as he fills every last inch of me.

"You absolutely sure you're not too sore?" he asks.

Licking my lips, I shake my head.

"Because this time... Fuck, Ember, now I've had a taste of you...once I start..."

I tighten my inner muscles around him, a new trick I've learned, and he exhales through nearly closed lips.

"This time I can't be so gentle," he finishes his sentence.

*That was gentle?*

Excitement stirs inside me. I nod, but then fear joins my desire. Fear and dirty thoughts I've only had in my dreams. Dirty thoughts of being taken brutally for hours by multiple men taking turns. Thoughts of being completely dominated, unable to move as my body is used for a man's pleasure.

"My venom didn't put you to sleep," he says, stroking my back. "But maybe it had an effect on your cunt. Or maybe it was my spunk." His hips start moving, slowly rocking into me, and the subtle motion only makes me want more, so much more.

I tighten my legs' grip around his hips. "Your…cock definitely has a strong effect on me…" I gasp. "Down there."

"Where?" He winks and then gasps as I tighten around him.

"In my…cunt." I try to get used to the word.

"You have a strong effect on me too." He chuckles, low and deep, then he thrusts a few times, hard and fast.

I gasp, my breath stolen by the sudden intense movements, and then he stops again, his jaw clenched.

Shaking his head, he looks into my eyes with concern. "Fuck. It's like…like I'm driven to…to fucking *consume* you."

A shudder traces through me, and he pauses, breathing heavily, sucking in a few ragged breaths as if the effort to draw air is herculean.

"I feel this drive to fuck you," he says, "to fuck you harder than I've ever fucked anyone, but I'm afraid."

"Don't be afraid." I stroke his cheek. "I want you to do

whatever you need…to do anything—everything—to me. I want to feel it all, but especially your hard cock pounding deep inside my cunt." My words still sound strange on my lips, but I mean them, and I tighten around his girth.

His eyes fill with pleasure, but then his expression quickly shifts to something darker, something that scares me.

"I can take whatever you have to give me, Ryker." My voice is trembling with fear. "I promise."

I'm about to add some caveats to my bold statement—I barely just lost my virginity—but gripping my hips tightly, he starts pumping, thrusting his hardness deep inside of me, over and over.

He's thrusting so quickly I can't see him move. But I can sure feel it.

I grip onto his shoulders, my face pressed against his chest, as he uses the combined force of his torso and legs, against the opposing force of his arms to draw himself out and then slam back into me, so much harder and deeper and faster than before.

The force is so unexpected, so consuming, so wonderful, I can no longer distinguish pain from pleasure—I feel both with each stroke.

And still he accelerates further, moving so quickly my sex starts to burn, almost like I've been slapped down there—spanked—and that's how it sounds as our bodies slap together. Something rises to bump my ass in time with his strokes. Is that his balls?

That thought flies out of my head as an orgasm overtakes me.

My head snaps back and my body undulates as my sex explodes with hard pulses, but if he notices what's going on inside me he doesn't slow down. If anything, the force of his thrusts increases, their speed accelerating, and his grip on my ass cheeks tightens, as if he thinks that if he uses enough force to pull me down onto his cock, he can drive straight through me. Maybe he can.

But then he slows, letting me come down off the ceiling and back into my body, as the last aftershocks of my orgasm ripple through me.

Sliding inside me more slowly again, he lifts me almost off his cock and then carefully controls my speed of descent until he's fully seated inside me.

Over and over he lifts me slowly and pulls me back down, every inch of him abrading my burning inner muscles in the most delicious way.

I'm so sensitive now—finally understanding his expectation of soreness—and I can't think of words to describe this feeling—like pain and pleasure have married, joined forces to give me all the sensations I crave, sensations that radiate from our coupling to invade every other part of my body, my soul.

Moaning now, I lift my head to find him looking into my eyes, and the connection as we look into each other's souls seems even more real than the physical joining of our sex organs. And still, he continues to slowly lift me and slide me down, impaling me over his thick, hard shaft again and again.

"Still okay?" he asks, his voice hoarse.

"Very." I don't want this to end, not ever. Even though I'm sore, if anything, my climax amplified my desire. As magnificent and luxurious as his long, slow thrusts feel, my body craves more friction. Craves the feeling of his power dominating my body, controlling my senses, my mind, completely.

"Want to try something a little more adventurous?" he asks.

"Yes. Anything. Everything."

Again his eyes darken and fear shoots inside me. *What did I say?* My inner muscles tighten, as if questioning my boldness and making a futile attempt to hold him still. But my slight fear of this man, this man who claims he's a vampire, only seems to boost my desire, and instead of clamping down on him, my vagina—my cunt—involuntarily starts to massage him, as if it knows these tricks by instinct, and my juices build, my appetite for him growing.

His cock still buried deep inside me, Ryker walks us toward the window. Then, manipulating me like a rag doll, he lifts me off his cock and turns me to face out. As soon as my feet touch down, he pulls back my hips and drives into me hard from behind.

My hands slam against the glass to stop my head from going through the pane, but I realize there was no risk of that. He's got a tight grip on me, one hand on my shoulder, the other around my hips.

Our reflections shine back from the window, against the backdrop of lights of the city, and he slides in and out of me slowly, gently. Although this penetration from behind feels even deeper, almost too deep at first, I soon find myself pushing back to meet each long thrust, loving how I can affect the depth, make his strikes harder or softer depending on whether I rock with or against him.

I'm just getting used to this position, when his foot nudges one of mine farther to the side, spreading me open and putting me off balance.

His hands land on my breasts to catch me.

I can't even reach the glass anymore and any pretext of controlling the thrusts' depths has vanished. I'm completely dependent on him for support now, and he holds me where he wants me, kneading my breasts, rubbing my nipples with his thumbs as his cock slowly pumps.

Our reflection is clear in the window, and I love looking at him behind me, hoping I can make eye contact, but his eyes are closed tight, his face strained. Either he's about to climax, or he's once again holding back.

The answer to my unspoken question comes.

His drives surge to new heights—or I should say depths and speeds—and the force steals my ability to think or to see or to hear or to feel anything beyond his cock pounding inside me.

I can't think of words to describe how quickly he's slamming into my body now. And when I manage to open my eyes and glimpse our reflection in the window, I can't even see that he's moving.

*Vampires can move too quickly for the human eye*, he told me. He looks still, but my body tells an entirely different story than my eyes.

The friction inside me is overwhelming, and so is the heat on my nipples as his thumbs flick over them. I can't see his fingers moving either but I sure feel them. Boy how

I feel them. Over and over he drives inside me as he squeezes my breasts and abrades my tight nipples, and I gasp for air, unable to find the space to breathe.

My chest rises as he straightens my body. His drives lift my feet off the floor and he holds me aloft from behind, supporting my entire body weight with his hands on my breasts. And while I can't even see us moving in the reflection, I can certainly feel that we are, feel it in our other point of connection, my weight supported by his cock deep inside me as he continues to thrust with incomprehensible force and speed.

He slows to a point where I can see him moving—but still so quickly. Over and over he pulls his hips back as his hands on my breasts lift me, and then he slams me back down to meet his hard thrust. I'm like a rag doll, a toy he's controlling, but I don't mind, I don't mind one bit.

A deep moan rumbles from his chest, moving deliciously through me, and his thrusts slow again. But he's still moving faster than I thought a man could physically move, definitely penetrating me more than once per second, but I can fully see the act now, and the visuals heighten my desire.

I've never seen or imagined anything so sexy as Ryker holding me aloft as if I weigh nothing, manipulating me, using me, his powerfully strong body pumping me over his hard thick rod, holding my breasts, flicking my nipples as he drives his huge cock inside me.

Stepping forward, he presses my chest against the glass and one of his hands slides down my torso to land on my clit.

My hips buck back, and his mouth closes over my

shoulder, his teeth scraping, but not biting, his tongue licking as he sucks on my flesh.

Then his drives slow even more, luxuriously sliding inside me so that each one takes an eternity compared to before. One hand pinches my nipple lightly as the other mirrors that action on my clit.

I writhe against his squeezing of my clit and nipple, my hips' small involuntary actions the only illusion of movement I can control, as I remain trapped between the window and the force of his massive, strong body. I'm held off the floor by his hand and his cock, fully controlled by the pain and pleasure of his simultaneous pinches, both harder now and turning painful. Every nerve in my body is now focused on those two hard points under his unrelenting pressure.

He lifts his lips from my shoulder, leaving my skin feeling damp and hot. "You're going to come now," he growls against my ear, and the pressure of his pinching loosens slightly.

"Wha—?" The word doesn't even escape my lips before another colossal orgasm strikes, its explosions radiating from my sex to detonate in every part of my body. All the blood that rushed to meet his pinching is now flowing everywhere else.

I know the French call orgasms the little death, and I understand why. I feel certain I won't survive this intact. I can no longer see, no longer hear, I can't breathe. My toes, still off the ground, curl, and my back fights to curl too, fighting against his hold, my head slamming back against his chest as his fingers continue to expertly draw out my climax, rubbing and pinching both my nipple and my clit in some kind of torturous composition. This man is a maestro with my body, knowing exactly how to draw out the very best and biggest performance from deep inside of me.

And my orgasm continues, less intense now, but wave upon wave of contractions continue for so long I can barely remember how my sex organs feel when they aren't convulsing.

My body goes limp, turns to mush as Ryker continues to push himself slowly inside me, and I barely notice when he slides out, turning me and lifting me into his arms.

"You okay little dove?" he asks.

I nod against his shoulder. "Mmm hmm." I *am* okay, but my vagina seems scalded, bruised, but at the same time I feel so very contented. The sense memory of his girth filling me makes me want him inside there again.

"Can I—" he stops himself mid-question, and it takes all my remaining energy to lift my head to look into his eyes.

His expression shows worry, maybe shame, and he's holding his mouth rigidly shut.

I stroke his face to reassure him. "You haven't come yet, have you?"

"No, but—"

"Keep going until you finish," I tell him. It might hurt, given how I'm burning, but after all the pleasure he's given me, I want him to feel as fabulous.

I press a kiss against his closed lips, and they're tight, resisting, and I can't decide whether I'm relieved or disappointed that he's not already pounding inside me again.

I look into his eyes. "Was it something else you wanted to ask me?"

He opens his mouth to reveal—fangs. Long sharp teeth protrude from behind his incisors that definitely weren't there before.

"Don't be afraid." He looks into my eyes, but it's *his* eyes that show fear. "I need to do this." His voice is strained. "I can't…resist your blood. I can't resist anything about you."

I inhale sharply as I realize what he's going to do. He's going to bite me again. To drink my blood. It felt good before, even though I wasn't sure what was happening. In fact, it didn't just feel good, it felt great.

And every last ounce of my doubt is gone. Ryker is a vampire, and even though we only met last night, I know I can't resist him. I need him like nothing I've ever needed before.

Am I falling in love? I wonder as I look into his worried eyes.

That's ridiculous. It's too fast for that.

But even if this isn't love, whatever it is is strong and wonderful—the most I've ever felt for another person. I couldn't go on if he left me and I would do *anything* for him.

Tipping my head to the side, I bare my throat.

His breath is hot on my skin and my heart quickens. My blood gathers beneath his attention, rising to my throat as if it's eager to give itself to him too.

But instead of biting, he lifts me in his arms and carries me into my bedroom. He pulls back the duvet, lies me down on the bed, then slides in to lie beside me, gently cupping my head as he looks into my eyes.

Even though he did all the work, I'm exhausted from the sex and my body sinks into the mattress, my skin so sensitive that the sheets feel like velvet. The first time we fucked, I felt energized after, and wonder if the difference was like he said—either because he fed from me, or because he ejaculated inside me.

Lying on his side, he bends to kiss me, softly, tenderly, and it takes nearly all my remaining energy to react to his kiss, to even breathe as we lie in bed together, skin to skin, heart to heart.

I raise my hand to his chest, his soft hairs tickling my palm.

Pressing down, I feel his heartbeat. I made the gesture without thinking, but realize that my subconscious wanted proof of his beating heart. He was right. Most of what I knew about vampires was wrong.

My hand slides up from his chest to his ropey neck and caresses him there, but then remembering what he asked, I turn away from his kisses to once again offer my throat.

"Not yet," he says, so softly I almost don't hear him. "I want to devour every other part of you first."

*Devour?* A shiver of fear traces through me, but quickly evaporates. He doesn't mean that literally, I don't think, but even if he did I'd be happy to die for him right now, happy for him to consume me piece by piece as I lie here content.

"Are you cold?" he asks as his hand sweeps down my side.

I shake my head. "Just tired."

"I want to touch you, Ember. Touch you everywhere. I want to know every inch of your body, to worship you."

My eyes flutter shut as his hand traces down my throat then down the middle of my chest, so slowly, so softly, until it reaches low on my belly.

His fingers circle there and then trace back up. Soft moans escape my lips, beyond my control, as his hands carry out their explorations, touching every part of me so gently, almost reverently, and it's both relaxing and arousing.

I wish I had the energy to reciprocate, to explore his body in the same way, but I suppose, I hope, that there will be time to do that in the future. I'm not sure what I've done to deserve so much pleasure, but I decide it's okay to be selfish right now, to lie here absorbing his touch, his gaze, his gentle kisses that make me feel like a work of art, like a goddess or object of worship.

And each kiss, each lick, each touch, makes the wetness between my legs increase. I might not have the energy to move, but even with my soreness, I ache to have him inside me again, to have him use my near-lifeless body for his pleasure, and endlessly for the rest of my life.

But as much as my desire grows, as much as my need to have him inside me again increases, his caresses avoid where I most want him to touch, exploring every inch of me except that hot damp place.

Sliding down the bed, his tongue laps the inside of my upper thigh, and I cry out, caught up in the agony of desire, but still he doesn't offer me relief.

Instead, his mouth returns to my throat, his tongue

rigid, as the point of it traces over my skin, stroking, up and down, as if he can detect my veins and arteries, taste the capillaries beneath my skin, and then his tongue circles, spiraling everywhere, until I'm just as anxious for his bite as I am for his cock.

"Turn over," he whispers against my ear.

I mumble something unintelligible, meaning to tell him that I don't have the strength to roll, but he gently guides me onto my front, my face turned to the side on the pillow as he renews his inspection of my body, treating the back of me with as much interest and reverence as the front, kissing and touching me everywhere, the soles of my feet, the small of my back, the space between my ass cheeks, but still he avoids the places where I most want to feel his tongue, his fingers, his cock.

I am almost unconscious with pleasure when he turns me onto my back again. With sleepy eyes, I look into his, filled with so much need his gaze sears me, heating me as much as his hands have.

He strokes my throat. "I need to—" he stops short "—may I take your vein?"

"Yesss." The word hisses out of me, and it turns into a gasp as his fangs pierce my throat even before my word's fully out.

A surge of pleasure and joy races through me. My blood instantly catches on fire, like it's spiked with hot peppers, and my eager blood rushes through my body toward his lips.

But as he gulps down my blood, instead of draining me further, my energy returns, like a switch inside me was flipped. And the burning soreness between my legs changes too, transforming into an even more desperate ache. I can't even imagine how I'd feel if he drank while moving inside me.

With a gasp, he pulls his mouth from my neck, and his body goes limp as he falls asleep, one arm and one leg draped across me.

# CHAPTER SEVENTEEN

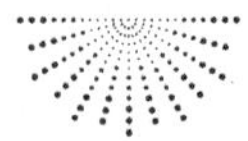

*Zuben*

"The CEO will see you now." A tall, slender vampire nods and gestures toward a large, ornately carved door. This floor of the DEFTA offices looks like something out of an Italian villa, not something you'd find on the top floor of most office towers, all audacious marble and showy antiques. The current CEO's taste.

Octavia took over DEFTA more than eighty years ago in what could only be referred to as a coup. Her interest in my personal research, which predated her rise to power, was flattering at first, but since that fiasco with the shifters, I've hidden what little progress I have made, and will most definitely hide my suspicions about Ember. I won't let Ember suffer a similar fate to those shifters.

I reach for the gold doorknob, but the door swings open before I can touch it, revealing her large office, decorated in rich reds of varying shades and textures, a strong emphasis on plush velvets and shimmering satins. It's not dark enough for my night vision to kick in, but the lighting is soft for an office and draws my focus toward the CEO herself, sitting behind a desk that seems to have been hewn from a single slab of white marble, intricately carved like Michelangelo or Bernini had done it.

Octavia stands and my heart skips a few beats. Objectively, beauty is a word that falls miles short of describing her physically, even though I have seen the ugliness in her heart. Her short, dark hair, almost black, wraps softly around her delicate features, in the flapper style so popular when she was human, and her olive-toned skin and flashing brown eyes seem to radiate light from within.

"Zuben." Her voice is soft, but somehow commanding. "So nice to see you again."

I nod and step forward tentatively. Involving her more than I have already is a risky move, but the stakes are too high. I must get Ryker away from Ember.

"I assume you have made progress on your research?" she says.

I step forward. "Nothing definitive." I choose the word carefully to disclose little without lying.

"Then why are you here?" Her voice has changed completely, her anger building. I must proceed carefully.

"I am here because I have discovered a thief, a pirate. One who has stolen from you—many times."

"You're bothering me with a thief?" She leans back in her chair and sighs. "I have a security department to handle such matters."

She flicks her wrist and five vampires emerge from the shadows, each of them massive and intimidating. Her personal security team members are also her mates, and rumor has it that at least one of them was Made by one of the Ancients, and possesses special powers beyond those of most vampires.

Something has to explain how such a young vampire as Octavia rose to such power in the syndicate, seducing the former CEO and then taking his place when he died, less than thirty years after she was turned in the 1920's. I met Octavia before she was CEO, and found her interest in my work charming and flattering.

Many of us question her rise to power, but few dare disobey her, and there is no doubt she has transformed DEFTA, made us all richer, and protected our members from the stakes of the overly zealous human police who now slay vampires on sight.

"I have previously brought this matter to the head of security," I tell her, "but he seemed unconcerned."

"Then why should *I* be concerned?" she asks.

"Because he has stolen from us—from you—and I cannot abide any vampire who insults you in this fashion."

She shifts, confirming I have taken the correct angle, making this personal.

"This vampire has stolen bonds, gold, countless millions of dollars, and now he dares show himself in your city—inside your syndicate's territory—flaunting the success of his crimes."

The door behind me opens, letting in a stream of cooler light, and I turn.

"You called for me?" Diederik strides into the room, bumping my shoulder on his way past, and then stands, legs spread, hands clasped behind his back, a few feet ahead of me—closer to the CEO.

"Zuben has discovered a thief," she says, sounding bored.

Diederik turns toward me and glares, a look so full of hatred I can feel it, but I look past him toward the CEO. If making an enemy of Diederik is the cost of freeing Ember from Ryker's clutches, so be it.

"I brought in his so-called pirate," Diederik says. "But Zuben lacked proof, and I think you'll agree that I was right to let this *particular* vampire go."

"Who is it?" she asks.

"Ryker Stone."

Octavia's eyes widen visibly.

"Ryker Stone is a pirate," I tell her. "And what Diederik does not yet know is that I have additional proof of this villain's crimes. He has—*had*—four gold bars in his possession, two with unique markings I can trace to our goldmine. And I am certain the others were also taken from—you." Even if she has a soft spot for Ryker, he is a thief and I need to make this personal, like he's insulted her.

The CEO steps around the side of her desk, her five mates continuing to flank her, as if they're attached and moving in tandem. There is no way Octavia could defend herself in her low cut shiny blouse, her tight black leather skirt and extremely high heels, but with her mates' presence she has no need. And her mates are beyond loyal and obedient, never leaving her side.

"Why come to me with this new evidence?" she asks. "Why not bring this proof to Diederik's attention?"

"I..." I raise my chin. "Diederik seemed unwilling to

arrest Ryker. I suspect they have made some *personal* arrangement."

Her eyes narrow, and she directs her gaze toward the vampire beside me. "Is this true, Diederik? Is the head of my security force a traitor? Have you taken a bribe?"

He widens his stance. "Of course not, but—"

"But what?" She glares at Diederik and his entire body is shaking.

"I knew of your personal relationship with this vampire, that he was your…friend—"

She steps even closer to us, so close that her alluring scent, sandalwood and frankincense, fills my head and scrambles my thoughts. "And you believe I let my friends steal from DEFTA?"

Diederik shakes his head stiffly, as if it's hard for him to move. "I didn't want to bother you with trivial matters. If the new evidence merits attention I'll make an arrest."

Frustration bubbles inside me. I can't take the risk that Diederik won't act on this. I need Ryker out of the picture—now—so that I can protect Ember.

"Madam CEO," I say.

"Zuben, are we not old friends?" She turns toward me with a seductive smile. "Are you not one of the few here at DEFTA who knew me before my promotion? Call me Octavia, please."

I nod as her attention fills me with warmth and unmistakable arousal. This is how she gets so many vampires onto to her side—her seductive power that makes others desperate to obey her. I am immune to such matters of the flesh.

"There is more," I tell her.

"Such as?"

I glance toward Diederik, then back to her. "It is a highly sensitive matter regarding a particular area of my research. I would prefer to discuss this in private."

Diederik grunts, but Octavia studies me, her gaze so penetrating and intense I can almost imagine that she is seeing inside my soul. "I thought you had not made any progress in that area?"

"Nothing definitive." I repeat my earlier words so I cannot be called a liar. "I didn't want to waste your time with my inadequately tested hypothesis, but if I had more time to study this vampire—"

"Diederik," she says sharply, her attention staying on me. "Leave us. Now. I wish to speak to Zuben alone."

He grunts again, but backs up a few steps, stiffly as if he's resisting the movements, and soon the light in the room changes as the door opens and he exits.

"Now." Octavia's hand slides lightly up my arm to my shoulder, and then her eyes meet mine. "Please confirm which area of your research we're talking about."

I swallow, hard, unsure of how much to share. I'd hoped to keep this about the gold, but Diederik has complicated that.

"My research into the Illuminator."

Her eyes widen. "Last we spoke of this, you claimed you had concluded that was a myth."

I shake my head slowly. "It is true that no Illuminator has been identified for over five hundred years, but I believe one is walking amongst us now, and in Philadelphia."

"And you think Ryker is the Illuminator?"

My breath catches in my chest. If I am strategic, I can use her incorrect assumption to my advantage.

"Ryker's arrest and detention will greatly aid my investigation." I smile inwardly. I have managed to keep to the truth, without fully revealing it.

"Well, Zuben." Her hand grazes my cheek. "This changes *everything*." The way she draws out the word *everything* makes it sound like a seduction, and for a moment I think she might kiss me, but she steps back and returns to her place behind the desk, her five mates moving seamlessly to take their places behind her.

"I will order Ryker's arrest," she says. "And instruct Diederik to detain any other vampires found in his company in case they are already using his blood to their advantage. Let's keep this quiet for now." She leans toward me. "Just between you and me."

I nod, not wanting to point out that her mates are standing behind her. Clearly she considers them part of her and trusts them completely. I cannot imagine feeling that way about another.

Taking a mate, never mind *multiple* mates, is not in my future. I have walked this earth long enough to know that love is a foolish emotion, an illusion even more fraudulent than those of a human magician—all smoke and mirrors and sleight of hand. I am too smart, far too logical to fall for such trickery.

Octavia returns to her chair, and the door behind me opens. My audience is over and was most successful. I back up a few steps, bowing before I turn to exit the room.

# CHAPTER EIGHTEEN

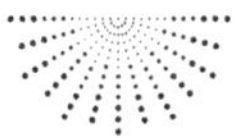

*Ember*

AFTER HOURS of gently stroking Ryker's hair, exploring his muscled back and arms and everywhere else I can reach as he lies sprawled across me, I finally fall asleep, but I'm the first to wake too, as a thin line of sunlight streams through the crack at the edge of my heavy bedroom curtains.

Speaking of heavy, Ryker's body is warm and thick, like the most comforting quilt but so much better as he breathes slowly and deeply against me. The hairs on his broad chest softly tease my skin, and my hands delight at the textures of his muscled back, the scars there seeming to me like purposeful decoration, even though I know whatever caused the many raised streaks must have been painful.

I can't have slept much, but I feel so awake, so energized. I'm still processing everything he told me last night, all that happened, and while I'm full of questions, I'm no longer afraid. Not of him. If he's a vampire, then mankind is definitely wrong about his species. Ryker is nothing like the monsters we've been taught to fear. Although I suppose he is a bit of a monster in bed.

His eyes flicker open and he bolts upright. "Fuck."

"Good morning to you too." I pull myself from under him and lean back against the headboard.

"Now *that's* a welcome sight." Taking me in his arms, he kisses me.

But I pull back and cross my arms over my naked chest. "You really know how to make a girl feel special."

"What did I do?"

"Swearing as you wake up next to me?"

He leans against the headboard beside me. "Believe me, that curse was *not* about you." Cupping my cheek, he turns me to face him. "It was about that." He tips his head toward the window.

"Oh!" I nod at the stream of light at the edge of my blackout curtains. "So the sunlight part is true?"

"Afraid so." He grins. "Looks like you're stuck with me till sunset."

I laugh.

"What's funny?"

"I've always been afraid of the dark, but you're afraid of the light."

"It's more than just fear, little dove. Sunlight is one of the few things that can kill me." Rising, he steps beside the window. His body braces, every muscle tightening, and then he swipes his index finger through the beam of light.

His head jerks to the side in shock. Then he flicks his finger through the sunlight again. "Strange."

I step up to his side. "What's strange?"

"The sunlight. It didn't burn me."

I stretch my hand toward the beam, and yelp, pulling it back in pain.

"Ah! What?" My hand is sizzling and the smell of burning hair and flesh fills the room. My knees crumple in pain, but Ryker catches me in his arms before I fall and carries me to the bathroom, cradling me in one arm as he turns on the tap with the other.

He passes my hand under the cold water, but the burn has already subsided, the sting almost gone, and I watch in awe as the wound fades to nothing.

We stare into each other's eyes. Clearly he's as shocked as I am.

"Am I…" My chest tightens around a ragged breath. "Am I a *vampire* now? Because you bit me?"

He shakes his head. "That's not how it works. Transitions are dangerous and take days, sometimes weeks. Nothing we did last night would come close to causing that."

"Then what's going on?"

He carries me back to the bed. "I have no idea." I slide my hand over a ragged scar on the front of his shoulder, wondering what caused it, but wanting to know so many other things first.

Turning toward the window, he slides off the bed. "Stay back." He holds up his hand toward me.

"Don't worry, I'm not going near that window again." Even though I miraculously healed, the burn's pain is seared into my mind—no way did I imagine that—and I never want to feel that kind of agony again.

Ryker tests the sunlight, first with a flick of his finger, then more boldly placing his entire palm in the path of the light.

"Holy shit." Taking hold of the curtain's edge, he turns back to me. "Get on the other side of the room. Stay away from the light."

I don't need to be told twice, and move to the side of my dresser. After seeing I'm safe, he pulls the curtain a few inches away from the window, and sunlight streams through, bathing his naked body in warm light and redoubling my admiration of his physique. But while his sunbathed body is impressive, it's the expression of pure joy and wonder on his face that truly captures my attention.

"The sunlight doesn't burn?" I ask, and he looks toward me, shaking his head.

"Why did it burn me?"

"I don't know." Closing his eyes for a moment, he draws a long breath as if he can inhale the sunlight, then he lets the curtain drop and carefully adjusts it so that no more light can peek through.

"What's going on?" I ask.

Shaking his head, he reaches out his hand as he walks toward me, and I fall against his hard body as his arms envelop me in their power and warmth.

"I wish I knew." He kisses the top of my head. "What's the curtain situation in the living room?"

"They're shear."

"Aw, then I guess we're stuck in bed today." His hand

traces down my spine, and my hips shift against him in reaction.

"I can think of worse ways to spend the day." My hand explores the solid mound of his ass, a few scars there too.

He growls, deep in his chest, and then he throws me onto the bed, landing on top of me on all fours.

I squeal in surprise. Even if he can take sunlight now, he hasn't lost his unbelievable strength and power.

We arrange some pillows behind us then he drapes his arm around me as we lean back against he headboard. He pulls the duvet to cover us both and then looks deep into my eyes, and my lips tingle, wanting so badly to kiss him again, but there's more than just lust in his eyes. He's looking at me…strangely.

"What *are* you?" he asks.

"What am *I*?" I frown, not sure whether or not to be offended. "You think this is about…*me*?" I pull back a bit. He is the one who's not human. "You're the one who bit me. Who drank my blood. Twice."

"Yeah, but, I've bitten…" He shakes his head. "Let's just say your vein was not my first and nothing like this has happened before."

My teeth scrape my lower lip. "But I didn't do anything…I don't know…Nothing about this makes sense."

"That's an understatement." His fingers tease my upper arm, and I snuggle in closer against him as we breathe together, absorbing each other in silence.

"You said your mother disappeared when you were a kid?" he asks, his voice low.

I nod against him. "What does that have to do with

anything?" Unease creeps inside me, as if part of me already wonders if my mother could be the key to what's going on. Her magic. Her claims that my blood was special. Something Zuben claims too.

"Your mother just vanished into thin air? His fingers trail across my collarbone. "What did the police say?"

I draw a long breath. "I never reported it to the police."

"Why?"

I close my eyes, trying to think clearly—to remember things I've tried to forget and have never told anyone.

"Don't you trust me?" he asks.

I open my eyes to find his scrutinizing mine.

"To be honest." I bite the inside of my lip. "I don't know."

He turns away from me, and I reach up to coax his gaze back to mine. "I *do* trust you, Ryker. It's just…I've never talked about my mom or about what happened—not to anyone."

He nods, his face full of anticipation as he waits for me to say more.

"I'm not even positive that I remember what happened. I have these strange nightmares…" Nightmares of another time someone was taken from me. "It's me I don't trust. I don't know which memories are real and which are dreams."

"And yet—" His expression is so serious. "In all those years, you heeded your mother's warning and never went out after dark. She is the one who warned you about that, right?"

"Yes."

He nods. "She knew." Stroking my arm, he shifts and turns toward me. "Your mother *knew* you'd be irresistible to vampires. That's why she wouldn't let you go out after dark."

Ryker pulls up the duvet, tucking it around me with one arm as he leaves the other draped behind me, and I realize that I'm trembling. But it's not the temperature that's causing my shaking.

"My mother…" I pause trying to gather the courage and words. "My mother could do things."

"What kind of things?" he asks softly.

"Magic things. At least magic is the only way I can describe it. She could move objects without touching them, lock the doors and windows so that no key or force could work, and…"

"And what?"

"I think she hid our house, the whole farm? It didn't occur to me at the time, but the house was on a main road, not that far from a small town, and yet we never had visitors. No one even came down our drive, not until…" The trembling intensifies.

"Until what?"

"Until the day they came."

"Who? Who came?" His voice is filled with urgency, his eyes too. "When? What happened to you?"

I shake my head. "Nothing happened to me. I was a coward. She told me to hide and I did. I acted on instinct, the way I'd been trained to. If I'd known it was real…" My voice cracks. "I could have saved her."

He strokes my back, my hair. "Hey, now. You were a kid. Hush." He holds me against his chest and the rhythmic thud of his heartbeat penetrates my body, filling me like a calming mantra, and I rub my cheek on his chest, loving the contrast between his solid muscles and the soft hairs there, loving the warmth and the smell of him, like musk and vanilla and rum.

I want to melt into Ryker, to be absorbed so I never have to live without his comforting arms and body again. Not since my mother disappeared have I felt this seen, this safe, this loved.

"So your mother." His fingers trace down my spine. "She was a witch."

I raise my head from his chest to be sure he isn't teasing, but his eyes show no such thing. "A witch?"

"You said she could do things, magic things."

"You're telling me *witches* are real too?" I'll believe anything he tells me right now.

"Most certainly." He shrugs. "But I haven't known many." A wistful thought drifts into his eyes and he glances away for a moment. "My best guess is that your mother cast some kind of spell on you. A spell that effects vampires and makes them want you."

"You mean I'm catnip for vampires?" Suddenly, my heart sinks. Does that explain Ryker's attraction? Zuben's too? Disappointment drags me down. They aren't attracted to me, just my blood.

"Zuben told me there's something special about my blood."

Ryker's eyes widen. "Did that asshole *drink* from you?"

"No." I shake my head. "Not like you did." Desire tugs inside me and I stroke his cheek as my eyes flutter shut for a moment. I wish I could go back in time, just a few minutes to when I thought Ryker wanted me just for me.

Ryker frowns. "But he did drink from you."

Crap. Telling him what Zuben did will only add fuel to his jealousy. "When I first met Zuben." I look into Ryker's eyes. "I cut my hand and he…he kissed my palm while it was bleeding. I thought that the cut was superficial. It healed so quickly, but…"

"Zuben healed your cut with his venom and he had a taste of your blood."

I nod.

Alarm invades Ryker's face, his entire expression and his body goes rigid, his arms tightening around me. "Does Zuben know where you live?"

I nod. "He was here."

His eyes widen. "In your apartment? When?"

"Last night. Before you came."

"Why?" His brows draw together.

"To warn me…"

"Warn you about what?" He shifts and looks down at me. "Listen Ember, you need to be straight with me. This is serious. You're in grave danger."

"Funny, that's what he said. He came to warn me about you." My body tenses. What have I done? Moments ago, I trusted Ryker with my body, my life, and now… I shift to get out of the bed.

His hand lands solidly on my leg, stopping me. "Ember, you aren't safe here. As soon as it gets dark we have to leave."

His normally teasing eyes are so serious, and he seems

genuinely concerned. I close my eyes as my mind swims through a swamp of murky contradictions.

Both Zuben and Ryker claim they want to protect me from the other. Each has made me uncomfortable and scared, but both have also shown kindness and I can't deny that I'm attracted to them both. If Zuben had won the auction, I would have happily gone out with him instead, and he might even have been the one to take my virginity, although it's hard to imagine it being as magical as it was with Ryker.

The two men are so different, one serious and steady, one joking and exciting; both have shown kindness and generosity and both are devastatingly handsome and shockingly interested in me. Although now I wonder if that's only about my blood.

I feel like I've been transported to a parallel universe I don't understand, but as I wade through all my thoughts and insecurities, one thing clarifies in my mind.

"Zuben would never hurt me," I tell Ryker. "If he wanted to hurt me, he would have already."

"It's not just him I'm worried about." Ryker shifts on the bed. "I might be a pirate, but Zuben works with some seriously shady vampires. DEFTA is one of the oldest and most powerful vampire syndicate in the new world and—"

"Syndicate? As in *mafia*?"

He shrugs. "Not all vampire syndicates are run like crime organizations. A lot of them are more like corporations or clubs to protect their members, but DEFTA is different."

"Different how?"

"DEFTA's enemies have a habit of vanishing. Especially over the last seventy or eighty years since the current CEO seized power." He looks away for a moment. "Now that humans know about vampires, DEFTA's made deals with the police, they've given up vampires who refuse to play by their rules."

"And then the police *stake* these vampires?"

He nods. "But even setting DEFTA's responsibility for those murders aside, their so-called business dealings are super shady. Zuben wasn't lying when he told you I've stolen from them, but not more than what's been taken from me." Ryker's brow furrows as if he's remembering some dark event from his past.

Then he takes my shoulders and looks into my eyes. "Ember, if Zuben knows what your blood can do… Or worse, if his *boss* knows, then you are *not* safe. DEFTA will take you. They'll use you."

He pulls me into a tight embrace. "As soon as the sun sets, I'm taking you away from here. Somewhere no one can find you. I'll keep you safe."

My entire body tenses in his arms. I spent my childhood hidden away and now Ryker wants to trap me again? And worse… "How do I know that *you're* not planning to use me too?"

He leans back from me, hurt flashing in his eyes. But then he shrugs. "You can't know that, Ember. Not for sure. But since I've already drunk your blood, seems I can face sunlight already, so what benefit would there be to my keeping you just for that?"

"I don't know…" I swallow hard, wanting to trust him, but I need reassurance. "You could loan me out to your friends, sell my blood."

*Did my own mother sell my blood? Is that why she took vials of it from me?* My gut contracts but I don't have time to tend to the wounds caused by my mother. I can see on Ryker's face that I've hurt him again.

But before I can say anything to fix it, his expression goes blank and he leans back and shrugs. "You're right. You have no reason to trust me. None at all. All I can offer is my word. Guess you're going to have to roll the dice."

Taking my hand, he puts it on his chest and presses it against him, and I swear I can feel the thump of his heart in my palm. "But I swear to you, Ember, I will do everything in my power to protect you—both from Zuben and DEFTA."

"But Zuben wants to protect me from you. Are you really a pirate?"

He grins. "My little dove, I am and have been a *lot* of things—few of them good. In truth, I am a bad, bad man, bad to the core, but I swear on my life I will keep you safe."

Looking into his eyes, every part of me down to my soul wants to trust him—so badly. I've already trusted him with my body and with secrets I've never shared with anyone.

"You're wrong," I say softly.

"About what?" His head tips to the side.

"About being bad."

His lips part like he's about to speak, but I raise my hand.

"When we met, I thought you were dangerous, but you're not. You're sweet and kind and gentle—"

"Not always."

He acts so quickly I don't feel the movement, but find myself on my back, under him on the bed with his hardness pressed between my parted legs.

I gasp as my hips rise against him. My body clearly trusts him, even as my mind is unclear.

"It's best you know the truth about me." His expression is dark as he holds himself over me, pinning me down. "Do *not* have any delusions about me, little dove. I am *not* a good man. And Zuben was one hundred percent right about one thing. I am dangerous."

I suck in a ragged breath, my body responding to the sensual pressure and his overpowering strength. My heart is racing. I'm shocked, but also more turned on than I thought possible. "Maybe I like it."

He grinds against me, his erection sliding hard against my mound and dangerously close to my clit.

"Maybe you like *what*?" he asks. "Tell me what you like, little dove."

"I like…you—" I gasp as his cock slides between my folds and grazes my clit. "Oh, Ryker."

"Tell me!" One of his hands encases my breast, and the other moves to my throat. "Tell me what you like." His expression's ferocious as he looks into my eyes.

"The danger." I gasp, through the grip he has on my throat. "I like your dark side, Ryker. I like the danger."

A devilish grin takes over his face, and his fingers scissor my nipple, pinching. I arch up into the pain, the sheer pleasure.

"Careful what you ask for, little dove," he growls as he plays with my nipple and strokes against my sex with his hardness. "Because I'm about to show you just how bad I can be."

His hips pull away, and then with one hard drive he's buried inside me. So deep I cry out at the pain, but it quickly turns to pleasure, by body eager to take whatever dangerous things his has on offer.

# CHAPTER NINETEEN

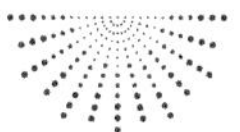

*Ryker*

STANDING between the parted curtains in Ember's living room, I marvel at the warmth of the sun on my chest and the colors of the sky as it sets. How long has it been? Three hundred years—more or less? I stopped tracking time.

And I'd certainly forgotten how direct sunlight feels—the heat of it, without an actual burn. Amazing. And even more amazing, it seems to be Ember who's given me this gift.

"Ryker?" her voice calls out from the bedroom, and I draw the curtains shut. "What time is it?"

"The sun's not down yet." I walk to the doorway of her bedroom and pause. "But it will be soon."

She nods. "Where will we go?"

"Another city," I answer. "I'm thinking Montréal to start." We can get there easily in a night and I've got a place in the Old City where we can stay.

She pulls up to sit against the headboard, and my dick

stiffens at the sight of her full body, a body I've enjoyed so many times and in so many ways in the past eighteen hours, I can't begin to count.

"I don't speak any French." Her bottom teeth worry her lip, and I leap forward, landing straddled over her legs on the bed, my hands on the headboard beside her.

I thrill at the reactions my quick movements provoke —her gasp, her dilated pupils, her flushed skin and tightened nipples. Reaching down, I press my hand against her sex and tease her.

"Doesn't have to be Montréal," I say as she wiggles under my touch. "We can go anywhere you like. Anywhere we can reach in one night, that is. No time to arrange long distance travel for tonight, but with some planning, we can go anywhere in the world."

"What about my job?" she asks softly.

"Call in," I suggest. "Do you have some vacation saved up?"

She nods. "Lots of it. But—"

I push two fingers inside of her, and she sighs, cutting off her sentence. "Oh, yes."

Her hips move, her wetness creating friction against my digits without my even having to move them, and I press my thumb against her swollen clit, loving the instant reaction I see on her face and on the skin of her chest, as her blood rushes to the surface of her most sensitive areas.

I am so drawn to this woman, pulled to her like a magnet for a million reasons, but the way our bodies click is definitely in my top five, if not number one.

Her hand takes my cock, and dances its fingers along its underside, turning the already rock hard shaft to a diamond, a diamond with electric nerve endings of pleasure.

"Fuck me," she says. "Fuck me as hard as you can."

I look into her eyes as she uses a word she would not have yesterday. Was she really a virgin last night? She's no vampire—it's easy to see she's all human—and yet her body responds with vampiric-like passion, with a vampire's libido and resilience. After sex, her body recovers so quickly, wanting more, always more.

She's taken more punishment from my cock than I've dared offer any human's cunny before—even during my hate-fucking stage—and the sense of power that rises inside me while we are joined…

It's exhilarating, terrifying. I've never fucked the same woman this often—but still wanting more. Not since… No, not even with Tavi did I feel like this.

"You sure you want it hard?" I stroke my fingers inside Ember. I love how her body undulates against my hand, how her eager nipples reach forward to rub on my chest hairs.

"Are you still feeling…energized from the last time I fed?" I plunge my fingers deep inside her.

Her lips squeeze together, and she inhales raggedly and nods. "Yes. Please. I'm on fire. And I want to feel your power. All of it. Please."

I don't understand it, but not only did my drinking her blood give me the ability to take sunlight and steal hers, it also seems to have given her a vampiric-like sex drive and healing ability.

Since neither of us have any idea how long these effects will last, or whether they will ever happen again, we should take every advantage of the time that we have.

Moving quickly, I pull her down the bed, shifting one of her legs over my shoulder. I fill her completely, driving in so fast and hard that my balls crash against her body, and I land so deep that my cock aches, bending at the impact at her tight tunnel's limit.

She cries out, but then latches her mouth on my shoulder, her teeth biting down. She hasn't broken my skin, but her suction is strong, as if she wants to draw blood from me too.

My hips plow forward, acting on their own and slamming endlessly, each pass better than the last, each one the best I've ever had, but still not enough. And the force of each drive presses her body down into the mattress, even as she struggles to arch into my thrusts.

She wants more. I *need* more. More than this position and the soft bed allow.

Pulling out, I flip her onto her belly, and kneel as I pull her ass high. Then I drive in from behind, tugging back on her hips for leverage, moving my body against hers so rapidly that I'm thrusting at several strokes per second.

My cock heats from the friction, assisted by what seems like an endless supply of her juices, forcing itself through her muscles that tighten and release, over and over, almost as fast as my thrusts.

She is fucking amazing.

Pausing deep inside her for a split second, I wrap my arms around her body and lift her torso, letting the weight of gravity hold her down onto my cock as I leap off the bed.

Bounding again, I brace her over the arm of an upholstered chair. One of the last sunshine free places I've yet to take her.

Leaning forward with bent legs, I trap her body between mine and the chair's arm and hold still deep inside her.

"Please," she murmurs. "More."

"Anything for you, little dove." Using the full force of my legs, I drive into her hard, and she shouts out her pleasure at the force and depth.

Like a wild animal, I pound mercilessly, pulling back on her shoulders, her hips, her hair, her tits as I struggle to find new ways to get leverage and heighten my pleasure.

A fierce climax is building inside me, but I don't want to come. Not yet. It's too soon.

We might not get the chance to fuck again until we reach Montréal, and even if I can carry her there in a few hours of running—that's a lifetime without being inside her.

Slipping out, I turn her and press her back against the wall, lifting her above me so her legs straddle my shoulders, her sex in my face. Latching onto her love bud, I suck.

Her head slams against the wall behind, and I inhale her, tugging with the power of a vacuum, intermittently breaking the suction to lick and swirl, feasting on her sweet juices.

"Oh, Ryker!" Her hips buck against my face, and I let up on the hard suction, flicking my tongue instead, and then dragging it through her wet folds, lapping up the taste of her, salty with her sweat and so sweet.

I drive my rigid tongue inside of her, wanting to drink her dry in more ways than one, but it seems like she'll never be dry, her body creating an endless supply of sweet lubrication to please us both. Her hips circle against my mouth, and then she thrusts, pulling my tongue deeper as she comes in another seemingly endless orgasm.

But I need to see her face, and my cock demands to feel her contractions.

Lifting her off my shoulders, I toss her into the air and impale her as she drops.

Gasping, eyes wide, she grabs at my back.

"Shit," she says. "I nearly hit the ceiling. I felt like I was flying."

Shaking my head, I look into her eyes. "Now we fly."

Pressing her against the wall, I drive up and into her, keeping her suspended off the ground, using the tag team of gravity and the support of the hard wall to deepen each pounding drive.

And still she is coming, her pussy pulsing in fast waves around me that are simultaneously fighting and inviting my cock's progress.

Taking her face in my hands, I kiss her, my tongue mimicking my cock, and her lips tighten around that part of me too, sucking on my mouth's thrusting appendage as her cunt sucks my cock.

My need heightens along with my intense sense of pleasure. I will never get enough of this woman. I'm losing my fucking mind.

And I need to come. With all the fucking, I haven't

climaxed since that first time inside her, and she knows it. But I hold it back. My orgasm will signal an end that I don't want to come.

I look into her eyes—so much need there, so much passion, so much trust. Do I deserve this? Deserve her? Of course I don't. How could I ever?

I slow my hips' motion, dragging my cock deliciously through her unbelievable tight hold, and she likes this slow action too. I can tell. Fuck.

Taking her this way, my cock can sense every wet inch of her, and every relative point of my penetration is different and equally wonderful: the tug of her tight entrance on my head; her shudder as I graze over her g-spot; the pressure and shape of her tunnel's end; and the hug of her contractions when I'm buried in deep. My cock couldn't possibly choose a favorite part of her cunny. I want—I need—every inch of her.

Her hand stretches down, finds my stones, and she fondles them lightly. "Do you like that?" She asks, her lips against my chest.

I nod, my throat too constrained to speak, to breathe.

"And how about this?" She squeezes my balls, just enough, stroking the sensitive skin with her soft fingers, and I can no longer stall my building climax. I'm way too close to the top.

My head tips back, and I roar as my hips thrust beyond my control.

Am I moving fast? Slow? Hard? Soft? I have no fucking idea what my hips are doing as a massive wave crashes into me, drowning me in pleasure as my seed erupts with more force and volume than I ever thought possible.

Regaining my sanity, I thrust more slowly, but still hard and deep, and she tightens around me, holding me inside her. It seems my strength to pull out expired with the final thrust of my orgasm, while her strength seems to have increased.

I'm her prisoner now, her arms trapping my shoulders, her legs my waist, and her cunny holding captive my cock. Slumping forward, I pant.

Finally finding the energy, I lift her away from the wall and run my hands over her back, hoping to soothe any bruises our violent love-making raised.

Fuck, I totally lost my head. What if she's hurt?

"You okay?" I ask, my voice emerging through gravel.

"Better than okay." Her fingers thread through my hair, and I lean back and look into her eyes.

"I think the sun's down," I say, reality sneaking back in. Our excuse to stay inside has ended, and now that it's dark, she's really not safe here. Zuben knows where she lives and that means others might too. The entire DEFTA security team might crash in at any moment.

"I wish this day could go on forever," Ember says. "And Montréal's fine. I don't care where we go, as long as it's somewhere we can be together, just like this. Somewhere we can make love night and day. Because I never want to do anything else ever again."

A contented smile drifts onto her lips, and it's clear in her expression that she both means what she said and heard its absurdity. And I'm with her on that. I'll find us a place where no other vampire can find us, where we can be alone together for as long as this feeling lasts.

Ember makes me want to be better, to change. Have I already?

Nah. I'm a bad man, bad to the core and always have been.

Ember makes me feel good, but my desire to hide her away from the world, totally fits with my pattern. It's not goodness or love that she's woken inside me, my feelings for her are just a symptom of my innate badness, my greed.

I want Ember because of what she can do for me, not to mention what she does for my cock.

"Come on." Already hardening inside her again, I pull out and set her onto her feet.

She emits a high tiny sigh. "I miss you already." She reaches down to take me in her hand, but I intercept her, entwining her fingers with mine instead.

"If we get started again, we won't stop until daylight. It's too dangerous."

Her other hand reaches down to stroke my cock. "I've recently discovered that I *like* a little danger."

# CHAPTER TWENTY

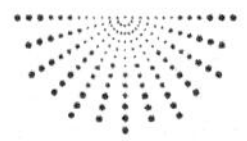

*Ember*

On the way down, I stand in the elevator as close to Ryker as humanly possible. I can't get enough of him and feel like I'd die if we parted.

Am I in love?

I smile to myself. I'm super naive about many things, but not *that* naive. People don't fall in love overnight. This feeling of ecstasy, of attachment—it can't be love. It's more likely sex hormones racing rampant in my bloodstream. Hormones that drive my body to do and feel and want things it had barely imagined before last night, and now that we aren't having sex, they've shifted tactics to trigger emotions, strong ones.

"How do we get to Montréal?" I ask.

"Once we get out of the city, I'll carry you and run. I don't want to draw attention now—not from humans or vampires." He glances around.

"We'll easily get to Montréal before dawn," he continues, "but first we need to swing by my hotel, pick up a few things, and as soon as we get out of DEFTA territory, I'll take you somewhere fabulous for dinner. We don't want to waste that pretty red dress you put on."

Even though I'd be happy with a cheese steak, I'm not surprised that he plans to take me somewhere nice.

I smile. I *am* starving for more than just sex, and it was Ryker who suggested I wear the dress from the night we first met.

And he convinced me not to pack much, claiming he could buy me whatever I need once we get to Montréal. He's carrying my small overnight bag, containing only a few of my essentials. We're all set. The message I left for Shana was short. I told her I had a family emergency and needed time off until further notice.

The elevator doors open, and Mrs. Hamilton from the fourth floor is standing in front of them. Seeing us, she startles, stepping back into the lobby from the elevator. I suppose she's never seen me all dressed up, especially not standing next to a massive man dressed in leather.

I smile at her, saying hello as we step off, and Ryker holds his hand to block the door's closing to let her enter. She slides into the cab, keeping as far from him as possible, alarm in her eyes as her gaze meets mine.

Apparently I'm not the only one whose first impression of Ryker was DANGER.

Keeping a smile on my face, I try to reassure her with my eyes. I don't want her calling 911—the police are a grave danger to my vampire lover. "Have a wonderful evening, Mrs. Hamilton."

She punches the button for her floor and then backs up against the wood-paneled elevator wall.

Ryker puts his arm around my shoulders as we walk toward the door. "Did you get the feeling she didn't like me much?" He chuckles.

Slinging my arm around his waist, I squeeze. "That's okay with me. I want to keep you to myself."

"That's a wish I can grant, little dove." He kisses the top of my head and then pushes open the front door of the building for me to walk through.

A light rain is falling, and so the street is quiet for this time in the evening. I tip my head to the sky. "Should have brought an umbrella."

"Rain doesn't bother me," he replies, "but we can go back up and get one of you'd like."

I shake my head, loving how the rain mists my face, cooling the heat that's been boiling inside me all day.

"Take my coat." He removes his leather jacket and it falls nearly to my knees when he slips it over my shoulders, surrounding me in his body heat and his scent. I inhale deeply, overwhelmed by intense and conflicting feelings of contentment, comfort and lust.

I look into his eyes. "If we've got time for dinner, maybe instead we should go back upstairs and make love one more time before going."

"You bad girl." He chuckles. "Seems I've awoken a monster."

I lean away from him. "You think I'm a monster?"

His gaze darkens. "Only in a good way."

I step forward to kiss him, but he takes my hand and starts to walk, and I have no choice but to follow.

He leans toward me as we walk. "Once we get somewhere safe, we'll have plenty of time to work on taming your monster."

Laughing, I shake my head, feeling giddy with happiness, but at the end of the block, Ryker stops and looks sharply over his shoulder.

"What?" I ask, pressing my hand against his chest.

He shakes his head. "Got a feeling we're being followed."

"Are we?" My heart thumps a little faster.

"Don't worry. You're safe with me."

It's not a direct answer, but it's all the answer I need, because I do feel safe with Ryker. So safe. I've seen how quickly he moves, seen demonstrations of his strength and power as he handled my body like I weighed less than a feather. I have no doubt he could protect me against whoever might be on the streets of Center City Philly tonight.

A few blocks later, he moves into a narrow side street, pulling me with him so quickly my feet leave the ground, and then he shifts me behind him as he peers around the corner.

"What's wrong?" I whisper, wrapping my arms around him from behind.

Turning, he leans against the brick wall at the mouth of the lane, and pulls me against his chest. "We are being followed," he says. "It's that fucker, Zuben."

"I didn't see anyone." I'm starting to think that Ryker might be a tad paranoid, but if we're going to be together, I'll need to discover and then accept all his flaws.

And even if it is Zuben, I don't think the tall Egyptian

man—not a man, a vampire—means me any harm. Maybe it would be good if he caught up with us, so the two men can air their differences.

I inwardly laugh at my fantasy. The idea that all would be well if they talked is too much to ask.

Ryker checks the street again, then takes my hand. "Let's get to Rittenhouse Square as fast as we can," he says. "Then we'll cut through the park to the hotel. The more humans around us, the better."

"Whatever you think."

He heads off, walking so quickly I have to scramble to keep up, and making me wish I hadn't worn my heels. I consider asking him to stop so I can dig my sneakers out of the overnight bag, but we quickly reach the southwest corner of the square. His hotel's not far now.

Ryker looks behind us, and I glance back too. A man ducks off the sidewalk into a building's alcove. It could be a coincidence? But no, Ryker is right. Someone is following us. And based on the man's height and shape it's possible that it was Zuben.

"Did you see that?" I whisper.

"Fucking Zuben."

"Maybe I should just talk to him?" I suggest.

"Believe me, it's not talking he wants from you."

I'm about to ask what he *does* want, but I already know the answer. Zuben wants me for my blood—he wants to use me for what it can do. But I can't deny that thinking of Zuben stirs something inside me, especially now I realize why he wanted to protect me.

Ryker tugs on my hand, and we walk across the street to enter the square. On this rainy night, there are barely a dozen people walking through the park, but also a large group of police congregated near the information booth at its center. Ryker heads straight toward them.

"Zuben will avoid the police," Ryker says. "They've got stakes."

"Then shouldn't *we* avoid them too?" The idea of a wooden stake through Ryker's heart causes mine to race.

"Cops don't scare me." He shakes his head. "Stupid fuckers think vampires skulk around in the shadows, hiding in bushes with their fangs hanging out. If those cops are here patrolling for vampires, they won't notice me."

A nervous laugh escapes my throat. Until yesterday, that's pretty much how I imagined vampires too. But yesterday feels like a lifetime ago. I'm a different person now, no longer afraid of the dark, and I'm starting an entirely new and exciting life. I feel safe with Ryker—safe and alive and brave.

The trees in the park are lit with tiny twinkling lights that sparkle on the wet paving stones, and the atmosphere is magical and romantic as we walk, hand in hand, toward one of the central fountains, not far from the group of police. It's gorgeous. I missed so much never going out after dark.

One of the cops turns toward me and nods in obvious appreciation. My red dress, slightly damp from the rain, clings to my body and I shrug off Ryker's jacket, draping it over my arm. With this dangerous looking man in his leather pants and loose white shirt, damp and clinging to his chest, I've never felt so sexy.

Under the shimmering lights of the warm evening, it's no wonder I've drawn the cop's admiration.

Keeping his eyes on me, the cop listens to someone on his radio and nods. The whole group of them shifts, moving as if called to action. Perhaps there's a robbery in progress nearby.

But who cares? These cops have no relevance to me and my sexy vampire lover.

Stopping near the fountain, I reach up to draw Ryker's lips down to mine. He hesitates, looking past me toward the police, and so I slide my hand between us to stroke his hard bulge.

Groaning deep in his throat, he kisses me, encasing my head with one strong hand, my butt cheek with the other, and I press my full body against him.

"Fuck, Ember," he says between kisses. "Never mind getting staked, you're going to get us arrested for public indecency."

With a smile, I look into his eyes. "I thought you weren't afraid of the police?"

He chuckles. "I'm not." He kisses me again, this time with more fervor, and he hardens against me, his sex pulsing through his leather pants and coming alive with the promise of pleasure.

I almost forget that we're outdoors—in a park, in public—and his hand parts my legs from behind. He drops my overnight bag and his leather coat slides off my arm onto the wet pavement. I tip my pelvis, my heat seeking his hardness.

"Get away from her!" a familiar voice yells, and I turn to see Zuben stalking across the wet paving stones.

He *was* following us.

I wave at Zuben, trying to reassure him, to help him see I'm okay, that everything between me and Ryker is consensual.

"Let's go," Ryker says against my ear.

I smile up into his eyes, but then searing pain envelops my body. The scent of burning flesh fills my nostrils and something metallic clangs against the paving stones around us.

Ryker cries out in pain as we both fall to the ground, and he wraps his body around mine as if he can shield me.

*What is happening?*

"Silver." Ryker's voice is strained against my ear. "Where's…my…leather…coat?"

I try to move my arm to where I think the coat fell, but the pain is too much. Every part of my body that's exposed to silver is burning. Why?

I've never had any reaction to silver before, but then I remember the sunlight this morning. Ryker claims that I'm not a vampire, but something has certainly changed.

"Not her!" Zuben's voice cries out. "Just him. You're only supposed to take him!"

"We've got our orders," another voice says. "Boss was clear. Any vampire found with him comes too."

"But she's not a vampire!" Zuben says.

"Sure as fuck burns like one," a voice says, and laughter rises.

Ryker shifts to put more of his body over mine. "Get under me." His voice is tight, full of pain.

Shifting, I see that Zuben is arguing with one of the police officers.

"You're drawing attention," the cop says to Zuben. "People are going to realize we aren't cops."

Not cops? Who *are* they? Fear and pain are so entwined in my mind I can't fully think.

"I don't care about anyone else in this park," Zuben says. "You can't take her. I forbid it. Leave her with me."

"*Forbid* it?" One of the cops grabs Zuben's arm, and then snaps a handcuff onto his wrist. Zuben cries out in pain, and smoke rises. Do they make handcuffs in silver too?

Shouting in pain, Zuben struggles to get away, and the cuff sears his flesh, so fully I wonder if it might burn through his wrist.

"Our orders are to grab any vampire found with the pirate," a cop says. "Seems to me, *you* fit that criteria."

A cop wraps a silver chain around Zuben's neck. His skin burning, Zuben drops to his knees, not far from where I'm trapped on the pavement. He lifts his free hand, reaching for his throat, but another cop grabs his arm and then locks his wrist into the cuffs.

Another cop injects something into Zuben's burned neck, and he collapses against the stone ground.

That cop carries the syringe toward us, and I tuck my head under the protection of Ryker's arm, but soon the weight of his body flattens me against the cold stones. Ryker's passed out too.

The silver netting lifts, and I scream in pain, feeling like it's taking my skin along with it. Someone shifts Ryker's body off me, and I struggle to get free. It might be futile, but I fight with all I've got.

But someone grabs my shoulder and head, stretching my neck to the side, and I feel a sharp prick, followed by searing heat that radiates through my body, burning like fire inside me.

The world goes black.

# CHAPTER TWENTY-ONE

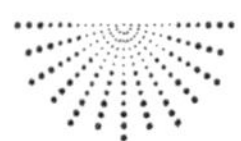

*Ember*

I WAKE IN DARKNESS, lying face down on something hard—stone, based on the damp, metallic scent. Am I still in Rittenhouse Square? Does the lighting go out late at night?

I want to lift my head to look around but the effort's too great, and my head spins, like I might pass out, so I remain still, waiting for the pain to abate and hoping to convince my brain to make sense of where I am and how I got here.

Through nearly closed eyes, I realize my surroundings aren't pitch black like I first thought. A faint glow of light flickers across the stone floor ahead of me.

"Look!" a male voice says with a scratchy voice, "one of the new ones is female."

Someone kicks my leg. "You awake?" asks a woman, presumably the leg kicker based on where the sound comes from.

But I have no intention of moving or talking. Not yet. I'm in too much pain to move much, and my mouth is so dry it's glued shut. But more importantly, I need to know where I am before these people realize I'm awake.

Sensing movement near my face, the air shifting, I open my eyes a crack to see feet and legs crouching beside me. They look female.

"Holy shit," she says. "She's human. She's got burns on her shoulder that haven't healed."

"Nah," the male voice says. "No humans in the dungeon. Only when they bring them down for food."

"Well, she sure as shit isn't a vampire, or anything else I've seen down here." The woman straightens, but doesn't move away.

Fear grips me, making me stiffen and causing more pain. I'm locked up in a *dungeon*—with *vampires*? Where is Ryker?

"Maybe she's a gift," says the scratchy voice.

"Don't be daft," says the female. "Why the fuck would they give us a human?"

"For blood," the male says. "And for *sex*." He kicks one of my legs to the side, then the other, spreading them apart. "Look. She's all dolled up for us too." He chuckles.

"Are you so hard up that you'd fuck a human, Corney?" the female says. "An unconscious one at that?" She whistles through her teeth. "Surely *someone* in this godforsaken place is willing to offer up a pussy or asshole for a pity fuck."

"Very funny," the male says. "And my name is Cornelius, Gracen! How many times do I have to ask you not to call me Corney?"

The female, presumably named Gracen, laughs. "You can ask all you want, *Corney*."

"What's this?" a deeper male voice says, as footsteps draw near. More than one set of footsteps, if I can trust my ears.

"Who is it?" the deep voice asks.

"New prisoner," Gracen says. "Looks human,"

"Human?" says another new voice. "No shit. The male they brought in last night is a vamp."

I gasp, learning that Ryker is in here with me—somewhere. As horrible as this is, that's a relief, and I send hope out into the universe that he'll find me, soon.

"She's gotta be here for fucking and feeding, why else?" says a new voice, one so gruff it sends tremors through my body.

"Nah," Corney says. "Don't make sense. She's gotta be a prisoner. Locked up too."

"Holy shit," Gracen says. "What the fuck does a human have to do to that bitch to end up down here?" She whistles again through her teeth.

"Maybe it's a mistake," Corney says.

"She doesn't make mistakes," Gracen says.

"Get her up," the gruff voice says. "I get first crack at her pussy."

"No way!" another voice yells. "You'll destroy her, Psycho. Let me go first."

"You guys are assholes," Gracen says, and I pray as another female she'll protect me. But instead, she nudges my shoulder with her boot, kicking me over onto my back.

My eyes open on instinct and I stare up into hers, which flash in the glow of golden light that must be coming from a flame of some sort.

Gracen smirks, slowly shaking her head as she looks down at me. "What the fuck did you *do*, human?"

"Get her ready," says the gruff voice.

"Psycho, put that thing away," Gracen says. "No one wants to see your fucking dick."

"Then leave," Psycho says. "Cause fucking is what *this* thing's gonna do."

*Enough! I will not just lie here and let myself be raped!*

Ignoring my pain, I turn over, scramble to my feet and run.

Still in heels, I move as fast as I can. But I know it's futile.

Assuming that gruff voiced male is a vampire, he can move faster than an Olympic sprinter, never mind faster than me—even without the heels and the pain. But I've got to try.

Carved out of stone, a long narrow passageway stretches forward, torches burning at intervals to provide faint sections of light.

Footsteps thud behind me, echoing along with laughter. I can't get away.

I know I'm in some kind of un-winnable game—a helpless rabbit surrounded by wolves, teasing me before they move in for the kill—but at least no one has grabbed me. Not yet.

Across from a wall-mounted torch, a large arch opens into a passageway on my right. Slowing, I glance that direction, and there's nothing but darkness. Maybe I can hide?

I take a few steps into the darkness, and something ahead of me moves and then snorts. A large shadow moves against the back of the cave-like space. Or is it just my imagination? I can't be certain.

But whoever is down there is massive.

Someone grabs me from behind, pulls me back and throws me against the wall opposite the cave's entrance.

It's Gracen.

"You don't want to go in *there*, honey." She shakes her head. "That bear is fucking *mean*. He'd more likely eat you than fuck you. Or..." she shrugs "...most likely he'd eat you *after* he fucks you."

*There's a bear in there?*

I stare into Gracen's eyes, unable to speak. She knocked the air out of my chest and my body shaking so hard it's hard to stand.

Deep cruel laughter comes from nearby. "Yeah, stay away from the bear," Psycho says. "They might call me a Psycho, but I've got no taste for human flesh—just blood and pussy." He laughs, like it's some hilarious joke, and then leers at me, his massive erection jutting out of his pants. The thing is far longer and at least twice as thick as Ryker's.

"Unlike the bear, I won't kill you." Psycho grabs his cock roughly. "Not on purpose."

"She's human." Gracen shakes her head. "If you fuck her with that thing you'll kill her."

Psycho lunges forward. "You gonna stop me?"

"Shit." Gracen shrugs, stepping away from me. "What

the fuck do I care? Have at it." Clearly saving me is not worth angering this monster vampire.

The monster strokes his cock, grunting, making his threat even more solid—and larger. Closing my eyes, I crouch into a ball.

*Think.*

I undo the straps of my heels. If I get the chance to run again, at least I'll be able to move more quickly. But I know enough about vampires to realize I can't outrun him. Or overpower him. There must be another way.

I'm in a dungeon that seems to be a prison for vampires—and bears? To survive, I need to stand up to the prisoners. Act tough, like Gracen does. But that idea seems a million miles out of reach.

"Hey, Psycho." The one called Corney draws my attention back to the group. There are at least a dozen of them now.

"Let me go first," Corney says.

"Why the fuck would I do that?" Psycho asks, and then he grunts, tugging on his cock with so much force I wonder if he'll pull the thing off. A girl can hope.

"If you tear her up," Corney answers, "no one else gets a turn."

"Again, who the fuck cares?" Turning toward Corney, Psycho points his stiff member toward him. "Maybe I'll take your ass first. Get me warmed up."

Raising his hands, Corney backs away. "Okay. Okay. Never mind. It was just an idea."

Psycho turns to face me, giving me a look that chills my already broken body and freezes my ability to move. Not that moving would do me any good. His eyes are full of a hunger that's so different from what I saw in Ryker's before we had sex.

It isn't desire, or even lust in Psycho's eyes. He's regarding me coldly, like meat.

And I suppose, to him, that's what I am.

*Is this how I die?*

My determination builds, heat and light rising inside me, like I'm lightning getting ready to strike.

Straightening my legs, I raise my hands toward Psycho, prepared to fight for my life.

He shifts back, as if pushed, and his eyes fill with shock.

It's almost like something pulled him away from me. Something unseen. I have no clue what it was but I'm grateful.

But even more than grateful, I'm drained, exhausted from fear, adrenaline, and dehydration. My tongue feels like sandpaper in my mouth, and I struggle to stay on my feet.

"Get away from her!" A voice yells. "Leave her alone."

Through my fog of confusion and fear, my defender's voice sounds familiar. But it isn't Ryker.

Zuben pushes through the crowd, moves behind me and places his hand on my stomach—possessively.

I retract from the too intimate touch, but that just pushes my spine against Zuben's body and his hand's pressure is constant and firm.

"Hey, handsome." Gracen smiles as she eyes Zuben, her gaze sliding up and down him as she walks around us. "You're fucking cute, newbie. What are you packing down there?" She traces her hand down to her crotch. "Wanna go somewhere and get better acquainted?"

Zuben ignores her, keeping his focus on Psycho. "This human is my *mate*," Zuben says firmly. "We were arrested together. She is *mine*." He says this last word with force and gives it even more weight by pressing his hand even more firmly against my belly. Heat radiates from his large palm and long fingers, easing just a tiny bit of my fear. But should I fear Zuben?

Psycho's eyes narrow as he considers Zuben's false claim. "You took a human as a mate?" His tone makes it clear that the idea is revolting.

"Yes."

"Is that why you're in here?" someone asks.

Stepping forward, Gracen touches Zuben's shoulder, tracing her hand over the shape of it under his wool suit jacket.

"What did you do, handsome," she coos, "to end up down here?" She touches herself through her tight jeans. "Come on, pretty boy. Have you been *bad*? *Really* bad? Tell Gracen what you've done."

"If you've been bad," she continues, "I can't promise I won't *punish* you, but I can promise it's gonna be fun. Your human can join in if you like." She licks the side of his face, but Zuben doesn't react, instead he keeps his hand firm on my belly and his eyes trained on Psycho.

"My mate is human," Zuben says calmly. "As such, she will not be a satisfying fornication partner for you." He nods toward Psycho's massive member, visibly pulsing now, unless my fear-induced imagination is creating an illusion.

But I don't think it is…

"I do not yet know the rules of this place," Zuben continues. "I do not know your customs, but surely, even down here the word *mate* means something?"

Psycho's eyes narrow, but he backs up a step. "Shit. What the fuck am I supposed to do with this then?" Grasping his member, he turns, pointing it toward the crowd like he's playing a demented game of spin the bottle.

Some in the crowd laugh, but others disappear in a flash.

"You looking to take another mate?" Gracen asks Zuben, running her hand over his chest and shoulder. "Or a little side action? Maybe a threesome?"

"No, thank you," he answers, without even looking at her. "Thank you for the offer, but not at the moment."

"Your loss." She pats his shoulder, then tips her head to the side, her eyes widening as she looks down to Psycho's threatening crotch.

"Can't lie, Psycho," she says. "I've always been curious… Ah, what the fuck." She whips off her jeans so quickly I barely detect the movement. "Do your worst. I'll heal."

Clearly sensing the opportunity, Zuben lifts me into his arms and carries me along the passageway.

Why is Zuben here? Where is Ryker?

I can't think… Confusion and fatigue have captured my ability to concentrate on anything beyond gratitude for how Zuben saved me.

A shout echoes through the hall, followed by, "Holy fuck, that thing is huge."

I look past Zuben's shoulder to see Psycho slamming into Gracen's body from behind, moving in and out of her quickly, but slowly enough I can see his massive cock glistening with what must be blood along with her juices.

Turning her head, she meets my gaze. *You owe me*, she mouths.

# CHAPTER TWENTY-TWO

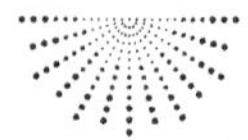

*Zuben*

My body vibrates with adrenaline and need. If I had arrived moments later, Ember would be brutally violated, most likely dead.

I was unconscious for hours, dosed with a concoction of colloidal silver, based on how I felt when I woke. My arrest was clearly a mistake. So was hers. That much is certain, but that does not answer where we are.

This is not the DEFTA prison. It's like no vampire prison I have ever known.

The security team was only supposed to take the pirate and any vampires found with him—no humans and certainly not me. I will sort out this mess, but have not yet located a guard to whom I can report this egregious error.

Ember is so weak, so cold in my arms, and the stunning red dress she wore to the gala leaves her almost naked. She clings to me, arms around my neck, her body soft, her scent enticing, and all of it makes me want things from her—things I haven't wanted for a hundred years, repulsive things I thought I'd never want again.

But I cannot give in. I will *not* use Ember for my gratification. If I take what I want from her—especially with her in this weakened condition—then I am no better than that animal who threatened to rape her.

"Where are you taking me?" Her voice is faint and scraped over sandpaper.

"To safety." If only I knew where safety might be. I have no knowledge of this dungeon and it's a far cry from the prison in the DEFTA headquarters with its simple but comfortable prisoner chambers. This is someplace much worse.

But I must be strong for her. Show her no fear. "We are underground. In a dungeon." We turn again and I mentally map all the twists and turns I have so far taken.

"I got that," she says close to my ear. "But why are we here?"

"It is a mistake," I tell her calmly. "I will fix it."

Sighing, she clings to me more tightly. "Where's Ryker?"

"I do not know." That is the truth.

Based on my conversation, Octavia thinks that Ryker himself is the Illuminator, and I'm not sure what she'll do to test that theory. But I cannot concern myself with him, even if I am responsible for his capture. All my concern lies with Ember.

Turning into a narrower corridor, I spot doors and kick one open. Inside, a group of vampires are copulating and feeding, writhing over a bed of Persian rugs, furs and silk sheets.

Ember stiffens in my arms, pulling in tighter against me.

Spotting us, one of the vampires beckons. We could hide safely here for a time, but there will be questions once they realize she is human, and although they are feeding from each other, some might also crave human blood, and I cannot allow any of them to taste her.

I turn away, pulling the door shut behind us.

"I wish you had not seen that," I say softly. "Not all vampires behave in such a hedonistic, animalistic manner." Over the years, I have learned to tame the baser instincts which are common among vampires, such as the raging need for copulation whenever we feed from each other.

"Were those *all* vampires?" she asks, her voice rough.

I must find her some water. "Yes. I believe so. I did not sense other species in that room."

"You can *sense* vampires?" she asks, pulling back to look into my eyes as I carry her.

I nod. "All vampires can."

"How? To me, you and Ryker look normal—I mean, like humans."

I kick open another door and this room is similarly furnished to the last, but unoccupied. A large, irregularly shaped mattress, more like a massive cushion, fills the center of the room, and it's covered in furs and silks woven into velvet and satin. Around its sides sit several pieces of furniture—benches, sofas and chairs—some plushly upholstered, some clearly meant for rougher and deviant sexual activities. My cock twitches, but I ignore it.

Mind over urges. I can control myself.

Carrying her inside, I kick the door closed behind us.

"It's so dark," she says, her voice revealing fear. "What…why did you bring me in here?" Her body shifts as if she's trying to escape my arms.

I set her down on a down-filled sofa covered in black velvet, and her hands frantically explore her surroundings, her gaze darting around in the dark, her expression confused.

"Vampires have night vision," I tell her. "There does not appear to be any electrical lighting in here, but I will ignite one of the torches so you can see your surroundings."

Calming slightly, she leans her back into the soft sofa and pulls her legs up into her chest, wrapping her arms over her shins as if she wants to hide herself from danger —from me.

Using the flint striker I find next to it, I light a torch, and the room fills with light.

Ember's shoulders relax, just slightly, and then a look of determination comes over her face. Letting go of her legs, she straightens her back, shifting forward on the soft cushions. But as strong as she is trying to appear, the effort of her movement visibly drains her.

"Where are we?" she asks, her voice scratchy. "What's going on? Where is Ryker? You were in Rittenhouse Square when we were attacked. What's going on? I need answers." Her voice breaks, so hoarse from dehydration.

"I must find you some water." I scan the room, hoping to find something liquid in here she can safely drink.

"Answer me!" she croaks.

My head snaps toward her, surprised by her fierce tone and pleased she has so much fight inside of her, especially given the circumstances. She will need that fight, until I can alert DEFTA management to the security team's error.

I approach her, and her body tightens and retracts, pulling away from me. But the movement is small. She's fighting to hide her reaction. She wants to appear strong and fearless, and I admire her for that.

"May I sit?" I gesture toward the cushions beside her.

She nods, stiffly, and I sink into the opposite corner of the sofa, turning toward her. She shifts to sit cross-legged, her back against the arm of the sofa, facing me, waiting for answers to her questions.

There is no way I can answer them all. I do not know the answer to some of her queries, and the ones to others will implicate me in her capture. I must withhold the truth, not for my self-interests, but to protect her. The less she knows about the circumstances of her detention, the more chance she will trust me, and she must trust me if I am to keep her safe.

But as I look into her eyes, flashing with a mix of fear and determination in the torchlight, I know that she deserves the truth.

I do not like to lie to anyone, but don't want to lie to Ember—ever.

# CHAPTER TWENTY-THREE

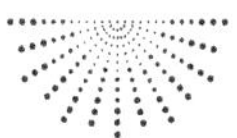

*Ember*

My back presses against the arm of the sofa, wishing it weren't so soft, wishing I could do something to help me seem stronger and hide how my body is trembling.

Zuben saved me from rape and probably bleeding to death, given the size of that monster's cock. I'm grateful for that, but need answers. Zuben knows what's going on here—knows way more than he's telling me at least.

I'm even weaker, more tired now than when I first awoke and it's a struggle to keep my eyes open, nearly impossible to focus with so many questions racing through my mind. I fight to set priorities.

The word priority puts my most important question back on top. "Where is Ryker?"

Zuben shakes his head, slowly. "I do not know."

"Bullshit!" My voice cracks and I struggle to find moisture to soothe my raw throat, the energy to sit straight.

Zuben's chiseled chin rises, his cheekbones catching the flickering light. Gracen was not wrong about his looks. As attracted as I am to Ryker, I'm not sure I've ever seen a more handsome man than Zuben. He's beautiful, really.

"Ember," he says calmly, "I do not know the location of the pirate, but I will tell you all that I *do* know. I promise."

"And what is your promise worth?" I ask, narrowing my eyes.

"My life," he says so earnestly it's hard to believe he doesn't mean it.

Even though I know he's likely manipulating me, there is something about his expression and the look in his eyes that urges me to believe he means what he said: to him, his word is worth his life.

"What happened last night?" I ask. "In the square. Were you following us?"

His chin dips. "Yes. I was."

I'm shocked at this blatant honesty. "Why?"

"To keep you safe."

"Safe?" I tip my head back. "You call this safe?" My voice scrapes out, each word drawing pain.

"No." His head bows slightly. "At that objective, I have failed miserably." He looks into my eyes again. "But if you can find a way to forgive that failing, I will do everything in my power to correct the egregious injustice which resulted from my error." He shakes his head quickly. "Correction. I will right this injustice whether or not you forgive me."

"Thank you." Why am I thanking him? He's just admitted that my being here is his fault.

"Why are you thanking me?" he asks.

My back stiffens. "Can vampires read minds?"

"No, most cannot."

"Can *you*?" I realize this man is not only cryptic, he's *very* literal, and his, 'Most cannot,' answer told me nothing. If he wants me to trust him, he's going to have to be more forthcoming.

"No. I cannot read minds." He shifts slightly. "In fact, at times I believe I am less skilled in this regard than most people on earth, no matter their species." His head twitches, just slightly, as if admitting this hurts him.

"And you did not answer my question," he continues. "Why did you thank me, given my actions caused you great harm?"

The raw honesty in his question, his need to understand my feelings, moves something inside me—shifts something profound in the utter core of me. "I was thanking you for stopping that Psycho guy from raping me."

"Ah. Yes." He nods as if I'm a magician who just revealed my best trick. "For that you are most welcome. I only wish that I could have spared you the threat."

"Back there…" I clear my throat. "Why did you call me your mate?"

He nods. "For that too, I must apologize. It was a presumptuous lie, but a falsehood designed to appeal to his values in order to stop him. I hoped that, even as a criminal, he might follow some basic rules of civility."

I cross my arms over my chest, feeling like an object that the two men made an ownership agreement over. "You mean… you appealed to his bro code."

He cocks his head to the side. "I do not understand. Oh!" His eyes light up. "Bro is short for brothers. Yes, that is correct, in a sense. I appealed to a code of brotherhood."

I want to ask more about what the word 'mate' means to vampires, but there are so many other things more pressing right now. And I need to conserve my hoarse voice and use it to find out all I can, before I pass out from fatigue.

I was alone when I woke, but the vampires who found me said I was brought in with a male vampire. I assumed it was Ryker, but now I wonder if I was brought in with Zuben? I remember when he was handcuffed in the square. "Why did you leave me alone down here?"

"I did not leave you. I would never do that." He leans toward me. "Not voluntarily. I too woke alone and had no reason to believe you were down here. My first priority was to search for a guard so that I could inform them that I was captured in error. But upon hearing a commotion, and the mention of a human female…" Closing his eyes, he shudders. "I rushed to investigate, on the remote chance that the human might be you."

My surroundings are clearer now as my eyes adjust to the light, but the better sight is not easing my fear. Some of the pieces of furniture look like they're meant for torture—or something—and the center of the room is a mattress, not unlike that room we passed with the orgy.

"You think there are *other* humans down here?" I ask.

"I do not know that with certainty, but no, I do not believe so."

Fatigue threatens to steal me. I can't sort through all

my questions. If this is a prison for vampires… "Why am I here?"

"I too am trying to ascertain the answer to that question." His dark eyebrows draw together and he pauses, as if thinking. "I have not yet fully recovered from the silver—" His eyes widen. "But I remember… You were trapped under that silver netting alongside the pirate. The silver burned you!"

Eyes wide, he shakes his head in wonder. "I do not comprehend why silver would harm you, but because of that, the security team must have mistaken you for a vampire. Still, that does not explain why the silver burned you, where we are, or why either of us are here. Nor does it offer any clues as to the pirate's location."

His candor takes me by surprise, increasing my faith in him. My gut instinct says to trust Zuben—I have no one else—but my skeptical side keeps urging me to test him.

Remembering that netting, I shift, and a sharp sting radiates from my shoulder.

He moves next to me in a flash. "What is causing you pain?"

I lean forward, revealing my shoulder and back to him, wishing I weren't still wearing this skimpy red dress that exposes so much of my skin.

"Your burns from the silver have not fully healed," he says. "That is most interesting."

Making a face, I look up at him. "My burns are *interesting*?"

He bows his head slightly, a soft smile on his lips. "Once again, I find I must apologize." He places his hands over his heart. "Your pain, Ember, causes me pain, and I wish I could take it away." Something flashes in his eyes, like he's had an idea, but it goes away as fast as it came.

"My interest," he continues, "is in *why* you burned. And why you seem to have partially healed, but not fully. Have you always had this reaction to silver?"

I shake my head, my throat so sore, my mouth seeming even drier now that he's so close.

He shifts off the sofa and kneels in front of me, putting his eye level with mine. "Ember, may I ask you a highly personal question?"

I nod. Just because he asks, doesn't mean I'll answer.

His head tips to the side, his brows drawing together. "If my suspicion is correct…" Closing his eyes, he shudders, as if his thoughts repulsed him. "I expect that you will not know the answer to this question, but nevertheless I must ask it."

Curious, I nod, encouraging him to just get on with whatever it is he wants to ask, but not wanting to waste the pain and effort of words.

"Did the pirate—did Ryker—did he drink from your vein?"

I clear my throat to answer, and cough. "Yes."

Anger flashes in Zuben's eyes, but then the obvious curiosity of another question takes them over. "How do you *know* that he fed from you? Did he *tell* you that he took your vein?"

"He didn't need to," I answer, remembering that Ryker was also surprised that I stayed conscious. I felt him bite me. I felt it while he drank. "I didn't fall asleep."

Zuben's eyes light up, sparking with interest. "Tell me more. Tell me *everything*."

I lift my hand to my throat remembering the pleasure his feeding gave me.

"Forgive me." He stands. "You are dehydrated, exhausted and clearly in dire need of liquid refreshment. There is none in this room, but I will find what you need. There must be water in this dungeon to satiate the non-vampiric prisoners."

My body tenses. Earlier he said I was the only human down here. "What—who else is down here?" It hurts to speak and I wish I could make myself stop talking, but I have so much to ask.

"I cannot answer your question with any accuracy," he says, "having just arrived myself. But based on my observations, in addition to mostly vampires, this prison contains all manner of what you humans would call supernatural creatures."

"Plus a bear." I swallow in a vain attempt to wet my parched throat.

"A bear? I doubt that." He takes a step back from me. "I will leave you now to locate some water." He's at the door in a flash.

"No!" The word scrapes out of me, and my body shakes, imagining what would happen if Psycho found me in here, or anyone else for that matter. Based on what I saw, the rooms in this hallway are used for sex, and drinking blood, and I have zero interest in being a participant, involuntary or voluntary, in any kind of a vampire orgy. "Zuben, please don't leave me alone. Please."

In a flash, he's kneeling on the sofa at my side. "But you must drink."

Again I see an idea flash in his eyes. His lips part and his fangs spring out.

I press back against the sofa cushions. "No..."

He shakes his head, offering reassurance with his eyes. "I am sorry for startling you. I have no intention of feeding from your vein. Instead, I mean you to feed from mine."

He bites his wrist and then presses the ripped flesh against my lips, moving so quickly I don't have time to react, or to seal my mouth closed before his wrist is there. The taste of Zuben's blood—coppery, salty, meaty—hits my tongue, and even before I swallow anything, a rush flows through my body unlike anything I've felt before.

The idea of drinking vampire blood, anyone's blood, is repulsive, but my lips part of their own volition, and I suck, gulping, drawing long draughts of the hot liquid that not only soothes my pain and my thirst, but my entire body, waking it, like an instant influx of energy.

But it's more than just energy. I've never felt so alive. It's not unlike when Ryker fed from me, or shot his seed inside my body—but it's different...even better. It's like there's a wind tunnel inside me, but the wind brings pure joy, pure energy, and unimaginable pleasure.

"Slow down. Careful." Zuben's voice is tender.

Gently squeezing my cheeks with his other hand, he forces open my mouth to release his wrist.

Too overwhelmed with pleasure to object, I close my eyes in ecstasy, licking my lips, running my tongue over my teeth and sucking at the insides of my cheeks—desperate to ingest every last drop of what he gave me.

Wanting more, I reach for his hand.

He pulls it behind his back. "You have consumed enough."

I nod as gratitude floods into the mix of emotions and physical delights racing through me. And other, stronger emotions pull me to Zuben. Shifting forward, I run my hand over his arm to his shoulder, wanting, *needing* to touch him, to be close to him, however I can. My thirst has been quenched, my burns seem to have healed, and I'm full of energy.

But beyond that, his blood has woken something else inside of me. Something I've felt only one time before in my life. And the feeling is perhaps even stronger now than it was with Ryker. It's impossible to deny that my body and mind are consumed with lust.

I try to fight against the raging need that's dominating my attention. It seems wrong. Not only do I have more important concerns at the moment, I developed feelings for Ryker last night—or whenever that was—strong feelings. So why do I now want Zuben so fiercely?

In little more than two days, I've gone from being a virgin, avoiding any situation that might turn sexual, into a nymphomaniac of some kind.

On the other hand, I've been attracted to Zuben from the moment I met him. Who wouldn't be attracted to his creamy brown skin, his thick black lashes, his chestnut eyes that look at me with so much intensity and interest—and his sharp, symmetrical bone structure that's at once beautiful and entirely masculine. And that's all ignoring his elegant frame, solid and muscular, belying his formal attire.

Objectively justifying my attraction is not helping to

quell my lust—my desperate need for this man, this vampire.

Zuben's hand shifts to cover mine, and I realize that I've been stroking his chest, my palm warm and tingling from the friction over the texture of his suit and the hard muscles beneath the fabric.

Turning my hand under his, I let our fingers entwine while I raise my other hand to his face. His eyelashes flutter when I make contact with his cheek.

"Ember." His voice is deep, rich like butter, and his skin is surprisingly soft, almost like velvet, and so warm to the touch as my thumb strokes his sharp cheekbone and my fingertips tease into his dark hair, which I now realize is longer than I originally thought, slicked back with some kind of grooming product.

Turning his head, he kisses my palm, like he did the day we first met, and desire vibrates through my body, tightening my sex and further heightening my need.

I can hardly believe how wet I am. I recognize *that* feeling at least, and my inner muscles pulse, calling out for his cock. I hope it can hear.

*What is wrong with me?*

Is this wrong? Maybe I deserve, maybe I *need* a little comfort, a distraction from the danger. And this doesn't have to have anything to do with my feelings for Ryker. We didn't make any promises, even if promises were implied—at least in my mind.

Zuben's tongue lightly licks my palm, and I sigh in pleasure, squirming with need on the sofa.

"I am sorry," he says, "about your body's unexpected reaction." In a flash, he takes both of my wrists and holds them firmly down by my sides, and the bold gesture amplifies my lust.

The heat and wetness between my legs builds. Whatever he wants from me, I'm up for it. Up for anything. I've had fantasies of being dominated by a man, but until last night I never thought that I'd want any of my sexual fantasies to merge into real life.

But it tracks that Zuben would like taking full control during sex. Does he plan to tie me up? It would suit his rigid personality, and I hope other parts of him are equally rigid.

Dropping my wrists, he leaps back from me, landing on the other side of the room.

I start to rise, but he holds up his hands, palms toward me. "I cannot allow anything sexual to happen between us."

He clasps his hands behind his back, and the action parts his jacket, revealing more of his torso and elegant slacks. And it draws my eyes down to his obvious erection, tenting against the wool fabric, foreshadowing its shape—long and stiff like the rest of him.

My hand snakes down the neckline of my dress, lightly caressing my skin and lingering at the edge of my breast. The involuntary movement feels lurid, like something Gracen would do, not me, but I'm unable to stop myself.

Standing, I walk slowly toward him, circling the edge of the massive mattress that fills the room's center, and my hips' exaggerated movements make me even more aware of the dampness between my legs—not to mention the deep, hot ache of need centered there.

Now that I've discovered sex will I want it *all the time*?

Want it in an all-consuming way that supersedes other needs, pushes aside common sense and discretion? I know I don't want *every* male.

I certainly had zero desire when surrounded in the hall by those vampires, or those fake police last night. But Zuben is a whole different ball game. A game I very much want to play.

Nearing him, I reach forward to touch what I most want, but he captures both wrists before I get the chance. My legs squeeze together, my hips making tiny circles I can't even try to make subtle, as my body fights for some kind of relief.

"Don't you want to have sex?" My tongue flicks out to wet my upper lip, and my wanton action shocks me. It's like I've been possessed by a different person, or an entirely different version of myself. "I can tell you're turned on." My eyes flick down to his erection again.

"Sex between us is not possible." Zuben looks over my head, now unwilling to meet my gaze, even though his cheeks have darkened and his breaths have quickened. He's fighting his desire as much as I am.

"Why?" I shift toward him, but his grip on my wrists tightens and he moves my arms between us, preventing my pelvis from reaching its desired destination.

"It is…against my moral code."

"Oh!" I blink in shock. "If you're worried about bro code, Ryker and I aren't exclusive."

He winces. "The pirate is most certainly not my brother. Please be assured that my reluctance has nothing to do with him." He looks into my eyes. "I do not wish to take advantage of you."

Relief floods through me, and anticipation heightens my desire. "But you wouldn't be taking advantage of me. Not at all. I consent." I smile. "I want this. I want *you*." I arch toward him, but his hands, holding my wrists, keep my belly from pressing into his hardness.

His gaze snaps down to meet mine, and I suck in a breath, seeing his obviously heated expression. He wants me as badly as I want him, even if he refuses to admit it.

Desire radiates, and my hips circle, driven by the pulsing need at my core, as if there's some kind of perpetual motion machine inside me I can't begin to slow down.

My cheeks heat, along with the rest of me, and I force down the last remaining thoughts at the back of my mind, urging caution and restraint. I will kill any thoughts that offer any reasons to stop this. My body doesn't care about reason, or propriety, or caution. It just wants satisfaction for my overwhelming need.

"Your sexual feelings," Zuben says firmly. "They are not real."

"Oh, they are *very* real." I step toward him, but he steps back, shaking his head.

"Who are you to tell me whether or not my feelings are real?" I don't want to get angry or offended, but he's not making it easy. His arrogance, his belief that he knows what's best for me is a turn off, but not nearly enough to turn off my physical desire.

"There are things you do not understand," he says.

"I'm not a virgin," I blurt, then bite my lip, wishing I could take back my outburst.

He blinks, his long lashes kissing his sharp cheekbones. “I did not suggest that you were.”

“Do you prefer men?” I ask. “Is that it?”

He shakes his head.

My gaze drops to the floor, along with my self-esteem. “You aren’t attracted to me.” How could I have read him so wrong? Has my lust been seeing things that aren’t there?

His hands release my wrists and land at the sides of my face, tipping my head up so our gazes meet. “Ember, my attraction to you is…it is *very* strong.” He exhales through his lips, his breaths coming more quickly now and reminding me of the other evidence of arousal I saw when his suit jacket parted.

“Then why?” I hate the desperation in my voice, but my need is miles beyond the point of transparency and edging toward pathetic.

Taking the lapels of his jacket, I grip tightly to keep my hands from stroking his chest or worse, grabbing his erection or letting my hands venture behind him to explore his ass. Touching him will make him move away from me—the last thing I want.

“Your physical need—” his tongue flicks out, barely grazing his lush lips “—your *desire* was caused by my blood.”

“It was?” I’ve already figured that out and don’t care, but he likes to explain things, so I’ll let him. “I can feel your blood’s effect on my body. It quenched my thirst, healed the rest of my burns.” I stroke my shoulder and upper back to confirm what I already suspected, and then drop my hands to my sides. “And your blood gave me a *ton* of energy. Does vampire blood have caffeine?”

Smiling, I reach for his hips, but he releases my face and steps back from me, slamming against the wall.

He disappears, and I turn, finding him on the other side of the room in front of an oddly shaped leather bench. I don't think I'll ever get used to how quickly vampires can move.

I cross the room, this time over the mattress, holding my arms out for balance and loving the textures of fur and silk against the soles of my feet, wanting to lie down and luxuriate in the fabrics. But even more, I want to reach Zuben, to pull him down into the heavenly softness with me.

As I cross, he moves away from the strange bench toward a nearby sofa, and when I step off the mattress, he sits, gesturing for me to sit too.

Resisting the urge to slide onto his lap, or even perch too close, I lower myself near the other end of the furniture and turn toward him.

"Let me explain more fully," he says, and I nod.

"Vampire blood has a…a *pleasurable* effect on humans."

"Like the venom?"

His head tips slightly as he nods. "Yes, I suppose that is correct. Ryker told you about vampire venom?"

I nod. "He said it usually puts humans to sleep."

"Normally it does, yes, but it also invokes pleasure, helping humans to relax so they do not resist the feeding in any way that might cause trauma or physical damage to their throats. The venom ensures that humans suffer no more than the small puncture wounds necessary to drink, and then it heals those wounds."

"I didn't fall asleep when Ryker fed." But I certainly felt pleasure. So, so much pleasure. Thinking back on my time with Ryker, it's hard to remember which was better, the feedings or the sex. It's all intertwined for me.

"I was very interested to learn that," he says, "and it makes me even more certain about the special nature of your blood. But at this juncture, I would like to focus, not on the pirate's taking your vein, but on *my* blood's effect on your…your *libido*."

His tone is pedantic, like he's a teacher and I'm his pupil. He's making it sound as if I have zero control over my own wants and needs, and… Okay, even if that's true, even if I'm starting to suspect the same thing, I feel like a fool being called out on it.

And I also hate knowing that my reaction must be something that happens to him all the time.

"Do you *often* give humans your blood?" I ask, hoping the slight jealousy I feel doesn't show in my voice.

"No." He shakes his head. "You are the first human who has ever tasted my blood."

I straighten. "Then how are you so sure that your blood is the reason that…the reason I want you?" And I want him so badly. Right now, my sexual need is in control of my body, my mind, in control of everything.

"I have seen this reaction before," he says. "I have seen other vampires give humans a taste of their blood."

I cringe, imagining vampires using their blood like a rape drug, and I'm starting to understand why he doesn't want to take advantage of me. "So, you're saying that vampires drug humans to have sex with them?"

"Not normally. No." He shakes his head vigorously,

then tips it slightly. "I cannot say I have never seen that happen, but that is not what I meant. I have witnessed vampires feeding humans small amounts of blood to save them from pain, or to heal them from life threatening injuries. But…" his head tips to the side "… while it was obvious that the humans felt sexual desire after those feedings, your reaction seems…unusually strong."

"You can say that again." My insides contract, a tiny orgasm that steals my voice for a moment. The effect of this man, without even touching me... "And *you've* never fed a human before? Not even to heal them?"

He shakes his head.

"Why?"

"Because I believe that it is unethical."

"Then why did you give me your blood?"

His cheeks darken. "I saw no other solution to your dehydration, and—"

"And what?" He clearly doesn't want to finish his thought.

He sighs. "When I bit my wrist, I released a great deal of my venom, knowing you would ingest it as you fed. As such, I thought you would sleep through any…these undesirable physical effects."

"Undesirable?" I feel punched. Rejected. "But I'd already told you that Ryker's bite didn't put me to sleep."

He nods. "I assumed the cad had held back his venom." He clears his throat. "Ember, please let me explain. I want to be as unambiguous as I can."

I nod. He keeps going around in circles, making excuses, stalling as if he hopes that if he talks long enough, frustrates me enough, I'll get past this overwhelming urge to have sex.

But in spite of my growing annoyance, my sex continues to pulse, so damp my thighs are slick.

"Since the day we met," he says, "I suspected that your blood's effect on vampires could be very special, but I did not anticipate that the effect of a vampire's blood on *you* would also be different."

He shifts, and his jacket falls open, once again exposing his tented pants. My breath shudders through me, and my hips pulse.

"Thank you for explaining." I shift toward him. "And now that everything's out in the open, you won't be taking advantage—"

"Yes. I would be. And I don't want you to ever have a reason to question my motivations with regard to you." Everything in his voice, his expression, his body language reads genuine. He cares what I think of him.

He doesn't want our first time to be tainted by artificially generated desire. The thought floods my heart and makes me want him even more. Now that I understand where he's coming from, we can get past the ethical dilemma fighting inside him. But how can I convince him that my desire is real?

"Zuben." I slide my hand along the sofa cushions, shifting ever so slightly toward him. "I appreciate your honesty and your…values. It means a lot that you don't want to take advantage of me."

His body visibly relaxes, his shoulders shifting. The tendons in his face release too, and his lips soften, making him even more handsome—something I didn't think possible. His eyes flutter shut and I marvel again at his thick black lashes. I want to kiss those lashes, or better yet feel them flick over my skin.

"I want to be fully honest with you," I say copying his serious tone. "No games between us."

His eyes snap open. "Games?"

"No…artifice."

He nods. "I appreciate that. Thank you."

"You're welcome, and I understand that some of the physical things that I'm feeling are…heightened because I drank your blood."

He opens his mouth to say something, but I hold up my hand, and he stops to let me continue.

"But you need to understand something too."

He nods.

"I was attracted to you *way* before I tasted your blood. I was attracted to you the first day we met. And everything you've done since then, the concern you've shown for me, has only made me *more* attracted to you. If you made love to me now, you wouldn't be taking advantage of me. I promise."

A muscle at the side of his jaw twitches, and he shifts on the sofa again. He's so staid, so controlled, and I want more than anything to see him unravel. To know how he looks when he comes.

My insides pulse at the thought.

"But there is another way I can use you," he says, "and I want everything out in the open before—" He looks down, draws a breath, and then looks back into my eyes. "If I am ever so lucky to… Before I even consider any kind of sexual activity, I want you to understand—"

From the hallway, comes a blood-curdling scream.

I shoot to my feet, heart racing. “What was that?”

Zuben shakes his head, stiffly.

The voice cries out again, clearly in pain, a scream followed by a loud curse, and this time I recognize its source.

I race toward the door, but Zuben gets there before me.

“You need to stay hidden,” he says.

I try to push past him. “No. We have to go. That scream, it was Ryker.”

# CHAPTER TWENTY-FOUR

*Zuben*

Ember's face reveals her terror, but also her bravery and determination, and her emotional pain smashes my heart into sharp shards.

But at least I am saved for the moment from the torture of resisting her infinite charms. My body is exhausted from the effort. My lips burn to kiss her, my hands itch to explore every inch of her lush body, and my stiff member is pounding, aching with need, especially as the wool of my trousers abrades its sensitive skin.

It has been more than a century since I have allowed such urges to intrude.

But until she knows the full truth—or at least everything I suspect—and until she is no longer under the lubricating effects of my blood, I will resist her, no matter how hard she tries to seduce me.

Ryker cries out in pain, and Ember throws herself against my body, trying to get past me to the door. In the attempt, she grazes my erection, and my breath expels raggedly.

"We need to help him!" she implores. "He's in pain!" Her eyes are so full of anguish that I feel it too. It hurts that she feels so much for this pirate, but her feelings for him make me feel even more strongly that I was right to resist her.

"I will find him." I hold her shoulders, keeping her firmly in place. "I will help him if I can, but it is not safe for you down here. No one else can—can know what you are."

She frowns, beautiful no matter what her expression, her skin so radiant and…

I tip my head to the side.

"What?" she asks impatiently. "You just thought of something. What is it?"

"You look like," I tell her, shaking my head, trying to talk myself out of telling her what I'm thinking. "I do not know how long it will last, but at this moment, you could be mistaken for a vampire."

She takes a step back. "Did drinking your blood…did it *change* me?"

"Yes."

Her eyes fill with fear. "Am I a vampire?"

"No." I shake my head. "No. But at the moment, you might be able to fool others into *thinking* that you are."

The horror fades from her expression.

"Holy fucking shitballs!" Ryker's voice shatters the air. "Do that again, Ricky, and I'll kill you!" He cries out in obvious pain, an agonizing wail too horrible to comprehend.

Ember winces. "We have to go find him," she says. "Now." The determination in her eyes is visceral, amplifying my admiration and desire for her, even though I would prefer if her concern was for me.

"Very well." I take her hand. "But stay behind me. Follow my lead, and I will do all I can to assist your pirate. But my first priority remains keeping you safe."

She nods, and we exit the room. Ryker cries out again, and her hand tenses inside mine.

"This way." I lead her down the hallway. Ryker saying the name Ricky proves Diederik is with him.

Sensing movement behind us, I turn to see that the orgy participants are filing out of the room we passed. At least they're heading the other direction. Likely Ryker's screams disturbed their activities.

Following the sounds, I lead her through a labyrinth of tunnels and then, as I peer around a corner, I spot two burly guards standing in front of a door to our right. Another scream fills the air. Very close now.

"Wait here," I tell her, but she shakes her head, telling me with her eyes that there's no chance that she will let me leave her behind.

"Please," I say. "Stay here. If you come, you will make it more dangerous for *him*, and for me." Arguments about her own safety clearly have little effect.

Sighing, she presses her back against the stone wall. But the look in her eyes does not reassure me that she will stay put. Alas, I cannot do anything to control her.

I squeeze her hand, before I leave her. Turning the corner, I button my suit jacket before I stride up to the guards, keeping my shoulders back, my face firm in a display of authority. This is a DEFTA facility—or I assume that it is. I am a senior executive and these men are prison guards.

"Let me through."

The guards widen their stances, fully blocking the door with their bodies. "No one gets in."

I scowl. "I am DEFTA's Senior Vice President of Research and Compliance."

The guards look at each other and shrug, clearly unsure what to do.

I raise my voice. "I demand entrance. Tell Diederik, or whomever is in charge, that Zuben is here."

The door opens behind the guards, revealing Diederik.

Not only is this confirmation that we are in some kind of DEFTA run secret prison, Diederik will know that Ember and I were incarcerated in error, and will release us.

I am about to beckon Ember to join me, but then Octavia steps up to join Diederik, and I pause. Better to err on the side of caution. Until I know what is going on, I do not want to expose Ember to Octavia, to anyone.

Alone in the hallway, the risk to Ember is high, but it would be many times higher if Octavia links her to my research. And I don't know how Ryker will act if he sees her. The pirate fed from her… Does he already know what her blood can do?

"Join us," Octavia says sharply. "Why did you take so long to respond to my summons?"

"Your summons?" The guards part, I step into the room, and the door is closed behind me.

Ryker is sitting in a chair about twenty feet away, bound with silver cuffs at his ankles, wrists and throat.

Naked, he is breathing heavily, clearly recovering from whatever induced his last round of pain.

"You!" He glares at me. "This is *your* fucking doing? I'll kill you!"

I do not want to point out that he has no chance of killing me while strapped to a chair in a dungeon. That truth is obvious and it seems cruel to state.

A guard, dressed fully in leather, including a face covering, steps up to Ryker and puts a gag in his mouth. The pirate struggles against it, but the guard pulls back on the silver around Ryker's throat and the pirate stops moving as smoke rises from the burns on his neck.

I turn to find Octavia glaring at me.

"I did not receive a summons," I tell her.

"Nonsense. I called for you as soon as we had Ryker in custody," she snaps. "What took you so long to arrive?"

"I have been in custody too. I have been down here in…wherever we are."

She blinks, and then turns toward Diederik. "Is this true?"

Diederik starts laughing, and although it has been a century since I have resorted to any form of violence, the urge to punch his smug face is overwhelming. Octavia glares at Diederik and he swallows his chuckles.

"I didn't know Zuben was taken." Diederik clasps his hands behind his back. "As you commanded, my team brought in any vampire found with Ryker." He gestures toward me. "Guess he was with him. My guys were just following orders."

Octavia shakes her head. "Well, you are here now,

Zuben. *Finally.* But it seems you were wrong about Ryker."

"No." I step toward her. "I am not wrong. He is a pirate. A thief. If you will allow me to show you the evidence—"

She shoots me a look so fierce I can feel it, and her lovers gather closer around her, with their menacing presence. "You know that is not what I'm talking about."

My jaw hardens. Has she told *Diederik* about my research into the Illuminant? Octavia swore me to secrecy, assuring me that she would do the same, and her obvious greed in wanting the Illuminant for herself, made me believe that she'd never tell anyone. Certainly not someone like Diederik.

But if Diederik knows, I have put Ember in far more danger than I realized, and getting her released along with me has become even more delicate and complicated.

What have I done?

My intentions when I arranged to have Ryker arrested were to get him away from Ember, to keep him from discovering the truth about her, but now…

"I ordered six different vampires to feed from Ryker." Octavia flicks her wrist toward him. "None of them… reacted as you claimed they would." She steps closer to me.

"Have you told—"

"I'm not an idiot," she interrupts me. "I only just summoned Diederik. He insisted he could soften Ryker up to tell me what he knows. But so far, nothing."

Clearly Diederik's interrogation techniques include torture. I am not certain that Ryker knows what I suspect

Ember's blood can do, but if he does know, he has not revealed it. If he had, Octavia would have her goons searching the dungeons for her.

"Now you're here," Octavia says. "You can ask the right questions."

My heart rate accelerates, but I reach inside myself to calm down. I am better than this, no longer driven by anger, cruelty and other base instincts. I will not let my emotions show. Revealing them will put Ember in more danger.

"Remove his gag," Octavia says, and the guard in protective clothing does as she asks.

"Fuck you, Octavia!" Ryker shouts as soon as his mouth is free and he starts to heal from the silver gag's burns. "Fuck you all."

Octavia flicks her wrist and Ryker is immediately flooded by sunlight that pours down through a hole in the ceiling, high above. He screams in agony, writhing in the chair, and the silver burns are now insignificant compared to his crisping skin.

She flicks her wrist again, and the aperture closes.

Ryker slumps forward, as much as he can slump within his constraints, and the acrid smell of burnt hair and flesh fills the room. If Ember's blood gave Ryker the ability to walk in the sunlight, even for a time, that time has passed.

Or am I wrong about Ember?

Octavia sashays toward Ryker. "You know I don't enjoy this, lover. Answer Zuben's questions so that we can put an end to all this…unpleasantness." She leans toward his burnt body, slowly starting to heal. "End this, so we can get on to matters *much* more pleasant."

She turns toward me. "Ask him your questions!"

I turn to Octavia. "I was wrong." I bow my head slightly. "Your experiments have proven that this vampire does not hold the key to my research. He is not the one." I already knew he wasn't the Illuminant, and I certainly do not want to ask him questions about Ember in front of Octavia and Diederik.

Her eyes narrow. "Are you certain?"

"One hundred percent." Nothing is ever one hundred percent certain, but I don't want to confuse Octavia with the finer points of statistics.

"Release Ryker's bindings," she says, her voice tight. "Then someone feed him. Quickly. He has suffered enough."

One of the guards removes his leather hood and leans over Ryker, exposing his throat, and the pirate's fangs spring out. He plunges them into the other vampire's vein.

Octavia moves to the side of the room as Ryker's feeding progresses, and her mates surround her. As they caress her, she kisses them, one by one, and I turn away from the intimate family moment. Octavia and her five mates have something I will never have, something I don't even want, but a strange longing opens inside me.

"What the fuck were you doing with Ryker when we picked him up?" Diederik asks me.

Ryker releases the vampire's vein, and he moans as his skin heals more rapidly.

"I was following him," I tell Diederik.

"Why the fuck would you do that?" he asks me. "You knew we had orders to pick him up."

"I needed to be sure that he did not flee the city."

Diederik crosses his arms over his chest and he shakes his head. "My team knows how to do their fucking jobs."

"If that is the case, then why was *I* arrested?" I say, but immediately want to take my words back. There is no use in antagonizing this man, and bringing up the arrest might remind him his team also captured a female—if he knows.

"I don't know why you were arrested." Diederik's eyes narrow. "Maybe because you can't keep your fucking nose out of my business!" His head tips. "You just reminded me. My team picked up *two* other vampires with Ryker."

*Fuck.*

He takes a step back from me. "One of them was you." He chuckles. "Clearly. But the other was female." He steps toward Octavia.

I grab his arm. "Do not bother her with this."

Diederik stares at my hand on his arm, and I release him. "It would be a waste of time," I tell him. "I have seen this female vampire, and she is of no consequence—one of Ryker's lovers in the wrong place at the wrong time."

Calling Ember a vampire is an outright falsehood, and I hope the lie does not show on my face. A negative side effect of learning to control my anger and lust—and my more wicked urges—is that I became less adept at masking deceit.

"Why remind the CEO of your blunder?" I whisper to Diederik, and I glance at Octavia to make sure she's still distracted by her lovers and not listening.

"Good point." Diederik nods. "Not like we could release the prisoner anyway, now she's been down here."

A tremor goes through me at that thought. For this place to stay secret—even from me who is head of Compliance—Octavia must not ever release someone once they're down here. But she must make some exceptions.

I glance over at Ryker. His skin is still red, blistered in places, but it is no longer blackened, and his features have become fully recognizable. Sunlight was used as a torture method for vampires in the past, but until today I believed that it had not been used for centuries, never mind by my own syndicate. Barbaric. So is this entire dungeon.

Octavia's mates part to allow her to pass, and they follow protectively behind her as she approaches Ryker.

"Can you stand?" she asks him.

Instead of answering, he rises, and although I can tell he's trying to hide it, his eyes reveal the pain caused by his motion.

"Get dressed," she says. "We will continue our discussion in my office."

"Are you letting Ryker go?" I ask, incredulous, but again wishing I had kept my mouth shut. My fear for Ember is making me reckless, shaking my usual calm and good judgment.

"That remains to be seen," Octavia answers. "Come. Both of you." She glares at me. "I would very much like to understand why you believed this vampire was the key to your research."

My heart rate accelerates. I should be glad to be leaving this dungeon but that will leave Ember unprotected.

Octavia and her mates walk out the door. Diederik and most of his team follow behind, two of them waiting for Ryker and me to exit.

*What am I going to do about Ember?*

As we leave the room, I turn and look down the hall. Ember's crouched, but rises as she sees us.

Ryker turns back to see what I am looking at, and then he grabs my lower arm, shooting me a look of dire warning. And as much as it repulses me to follow his lead, I know that he's right.

As much danger as Ember faces down here, Octavia cannot know about Ember. And clearly Ryker already knows or suspects more than I want him to.

I wish there was a way to offer Ember comfort right now, to let her know that my leaving is my best chance to help her, and that I will rescue her from this place, even if it means giving up my own life.

## CHAPTER TWENTY-FIVE

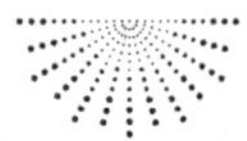

*Ember*

JOY OVERPOWERS my terror when I see Ryker exit the room along with Zuben.

Ryker spots me and I want to call out, but the look he gives me says not to. Zuben glances back too, and his look also screams that I shouldn't move, but it's all I can do to hold myself back.

Ryker's face is red, like it's been sunburned and his hair seems less full, but I start to question that observation as it returns to its normal lush state before my eyes. Has Ryker been burned? Is that why he was screaming? Why?

Ryker and Zuben are quickly surrounded by about ten other people, one a petite female, the rest male and huge—presumably vampires—and so I heed the warning looks the men sent me. Ryker puts one hand behind his back, and gestures down with his palm, like the way one might tell a dog to stay. Then he gives me a thumbs up and an okay sign.

The gestures flash by quickly, and then the group disappears in the dimly lit hall, but their meaning was clear. Both men saw me. And if it was safe to come with them, they had an obvious chance to tell me.

They disappear, swallowed by darkness and turns in the tunnels, and I press myself back against the stone wall, cold at my back. I fold my arms over my chest. I have no idea what happened to my shoes—I haven't seen them since I undid their straps while Psycho threatened me—and this skimpy evening gown does nothing to hold back the damp chill in the air. I should get one of the blankets or furs from the room that Zuben and I were in. Better yet, I should hide under the furs there until he returns for me.

Because he *will* return. Neither Zuben or Ryker would leave me down here.

I head back in the direction we came, but almost there, I hear voices coming from around the corner. I freeze.

A group of vampires, male and female and in various states of undress, are filing into the room Zuben and I were in.

Waiting until they're inside, I creep down the hall, moving past the closed doors, trying to listen from outside, hoping to find one that's empty. But it's too hard to be certain, and there is no chance I want to interrupt—or worse—get dragged into some kind of blood drinking sex orgy.

Thinking about sex, my insides tighten, reawakening my still unsatisfied urges, but as heightened as my sex drive remains, I won't settle for just anyone—only Zuben or Ryker will do.

Reaching the end of a passage, I hit a three way junction, and fight to remember the limited amount of the dungeon's layout I've seen. But Zuben was carrying me when we came this way before—assuming I *have* been this way before—and I have only my instincts to guide me.

Hearing faint voices from one direction, I follow my gut to choose between the other two, and then move quickly and quietly, stopping at each closed door, but too frightened to open any without knowing what's inside.

Around another bend, light streams from an open archway. Warmth comes from the opening, and a faint smell—almost like a campfire.

Drawn toward the warmth and the light, I creep forward, hoping whomever is in there is friendly. Until Ryker and Zuben get me out of here, I need a safe place and allies to protect me.

As I draw nearer, the scent intensifies. It's definitely wood smoke, mingling with the unmistakable smell of cooking meat. My stomach growls as my hunger wakens and I continue to creep forward. Vampires eat food, based on what Ryker told me, but they don't *have* to. Vampires eat only for pleasure and to blend in with humans. Are there other humans down here? I hope they'll protect me.

Zuben claimed I could pass for a vampire, but the effects of his blood might have worn off by now, and closer inspection would reveal my humanity.

Reaching the opening, I pause to gather my courage and then peer around the corner. Relief floods in to temper my fear. Humans. At least I'm pretty sure they're not vampires because a beam of sunlight shines into the cave-like space from high above, and no one seems bothered by it, calmly passing through the light.

If I spotted this group of mostly men on the streets of Philadelphia, I'd change direction, but here, even this rough looking crowd, tattooed, shaggy haired, and dressed like a motorcycle gang, seems safe. Or at least safer to me than vampires right now.

"What the fuck are you doing here?" One of the women glares at me, striding forward. "This is a vamp-free zone."

"I'm not—" The rest of my intended sentence is trapped inside of me. Three of the men transform into wolves.

Massive wolves, with bright shining eyes that seem to emit light from within and snarling lips revealing sharp teeth.

Turning, I run.

"That's right, baby vamp!" the female shouts after me. "You'd better run. And stay out of wolf territory you blood-sucking whore!"

Fear and adrenaline drive me to keep running, dashing recklessly through multiple turns until I have absolutely no idea how I would find my way back to where I started.

Rounding a corner, I hear a voice that freezes my bones and stops my heart, halting me dead in my tracks. It's Psycho.

"Fuck, I need blood," he says loudly. "Human blood. Hammering Gracen's cunt took a lot out of me."

"Won't be long," says a voice I don't recognize. "Only be a few days until we get humans."

"Can't wait that long." Psycho's voice echoes through the halls, making it harder for me to be certain which direction it's coming from. "Where'd that little human bitch go?"

"Why didn't you feed from Gracen when you fucked her?" the other voice asks, and I realize it's probably that guy named Corney.

"I *did.* Do you think I'm an idiot? It's *human* blood I crave now. And human pussy. Should never have let that little tramp in the red dress go."

Certain now of which direction his threatening voice is coming from, I head the other way, trying to think, to curb my panic. *Where can I hide?*

I turn into a darker passageway. Vampires can see in the dark, but maybe Psycho won't expect me to go into a place where I can't see. Keeping my fingers against the jagged stone wall, I question my plan.

I can barely make out the shape of my hand when I wave it in front of my face, but I keep moving forward, fingertips against the rough, cave-like shape of the space. As my eyes adjust, dim light from the passage behind me glints off facets of roughly hewn rock.

Sensing movement ahead, I stop.

Glancing around, I wish I could see, but instead I listen intently. Someone—or something—is moving. The footsteps are barely discernible, but I detect heavy breathing and, at erratic intervals, what sounds like a faint moan. It doesn't sound human. Is it my imagination?

I spin back toward the entrance, and the faint light from the hall seems too bright now, making me squint, but as much as I want to be somewhere I can see, I know with certainty that danger lurks in the halls I just left, grave danger, and whatever danger might be in here remains to be seen.

Better to go with the devil I *don't* know, than Psycho.

I turn away from the entrance, and something large crosses the space ahead of me. Moving from left to right, it's like a shadow within the darkness. I can now perceive a slight amount of light glinting off the far end of the cave.

Or is my fear tricking me into seeing things? I shake as my recurring nightmare of being trapped in the darkness haunts me. In that horrible dream, I'm in a hole in the ground, not the cellar under the farmhouse, another one, smaller, and above me others scream in terror.

It's not real, I tell myself. It's only ever been a dream. I need to get myself together if I'm going to survive.

"Hello?" I whisper, and then wait, but hear no response, see no further movement.

My options narrowing and my desperation growing, I continue forward into the cave, keeping one hand on the wall, the other extended in front of me.

My extended hand strikes another surface, more rock, and I realize I've reached the back of the cave, or perhaps a bend in it. So I follow along the back wall, moving slowly, carefully, until the opening into the main passageway is no longer visible.

Sensing movement, I freeze and listen. "Hello? Is someone there?" My voice seems so small in the space, and my entire body shakes, both from fear and the cold. With each step on the freezing, damp stone, my bare feet sting and pains shoot up my legs to penetrate my hips and tighten my back. My fingers, scraping along the wall, are nearly numb.

I'm going to die of hypothermia, if whatever is in here doesn't kill me first.

Something scrapes the stone floor, scratching, and I hear what sounds like a heavy exhale, almost a huff. It's an animal in here with me, but maybe a calm voice will soothe it.

"Who's there? Please. Don't hurt me." My voice sounds shaky now, my plea pathetic, but pathetic is all I have left, and each step forward is a bigger challenge, more painful than the last. I can only hope that whatever is in here takes pity on me—and that it isn't hungry.

My extended hand strikes another wall. This part of the cave is shorter than the first. At least I think that it is. I don't trust my perspective anymore and didn't think to count my steps.

I turn the corner, continuing to explore the space. If I don't find a blanket—or something—I'll die. One step. Two. Three.

"Hello?" I call out softly.

Something, or someone, groans, then huffs, and I stop.

Two small lights appear ahead of me. Almost like eyes, but they're too far apart and they can't be eyes because there's no light for the eyes to reflect. But my first guess is confirmed when the eyes blink, glowing when open like they are illuminated from within.

I scramble backwards, and my head strikes rock, the sharp impact followed by throbbing pain.

*The bear!*

Of course it's the bear. I thought I was in an entirely different part of this prison, but it seems I wandered into the bear cave. The one place that Gracen claimed would be worse than facing Psycho.

I cower, wanting to run, but the pain in my head has momentarily scrambled my sense of direction. I'm not even sure which way I came in. And isn't running the worst thing to do when confronting a bear? Or is that only wildcats? And do the rules of the wilderness apply down here?

The animal's shape is clear now, and I detect a faint glow coming from an arched opening behind the beast as the gigantic shape lumbers toward me. Even down on all fours, the bear is nearly as tall as I am, and I watch in terror as it plods ahead, one massive shoulder shifting forward, then the other more haltingly, followed by a muffled moan.

This is how I die? As a bear snack?

His eyes, like a sea of gold sparks, rise, lifting higher and higher, now several feet above my head.

Not sure what's real and what's my imagination, I survey the shape of the beast, a shadow within the darkness, a massive animal nearly twice my height now he's up on his hind legs.

His upper body lowers again, filling the space between us, and the bear howls when his front paws strike the stone.

His hot breath warms my body, but the sound sends chills into my heart. I don't know much about bears, but the cry sounded more like pain than a warning or battle cry.

His snout nears me, and I hear snuffling sounds as he takes in my scent, then his head turns, and one of his enormous shoulders presses against my body.

Firmly, but gently.

The bear's not trying to crush me, I hope, and the heat from his body and the softness of his fur makes me moan in relief.

My hands lift off the stone wall and fall onto his fur, and my upper arms soak in the warmth. If I'm going to die, at least I'll die warmer. The thought of fighting against this beast ridiculous. I could fight, but I'd lose.

The bear backs up a few steps and my hands slide out of his fur, then he rises onto his hind legs again, filling me with terror.

One of his paws lands on the stone wall above and next to me, the beast's chest now in front of my face, his scent musky, but not unpleasant—fur with a faint hint of campfire smoke.

His other paw lands on the stone near my waist and he tugs me, as if hoping to nudge me off the cold wall.

One of his claws presses hard against my flesh, and I jerk forward to avoid being punctured.

The bear scoops me off my feet, then rolls down and onto his side, enveloping me, completely trapping me in his powerful body and warmth.

# CHAPTER TWENTY-SIX

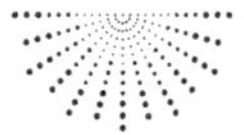

*Ryker*

SEEING EMBER IN THAT HALLWAY, I felt the worst terror of my life—and I've been through some shit.

Now, my fear has morphed into rage, but I mask my emotions. Every instinct inside me says that drawing Tavi's attention to Ember would mean she'd take my place in that torture chamber, or something even more horrible, so for now I must leave her behind.

Adding insult to injury, I have to walk alongside this Zuben asshole—the one who got us arrested.

I cannot *wait* to kill him. I'll tear him apart with my bare hands.

When I woke down here, I was stripped naked and strapped into that chair, my skin already burning from silver cuffs and my body aching from the aftereffects of whatever it was they injected into my bloodstream. I assume the same shit they used the first time Zuben had me picked up.

The masked guards had several vamps take my vein, and I was forced to watch them burn. Then my chair got dragged under that shaft of sunlight, Diederik showed up and my own torture started. The sunlight burns were horrific, so horrific I'm not even sure when Octavia entered the room, but I didn't give up a thing—especially once I realized they thought my blood would let vampires walk in the light, and who they were really after was Ember.

I thump my fist against my leg. I should have been more careful. It should have been obvious that those vamps in the square weren't cops. Distracted by Ember's kiss, I wasn't paying fucking attention.

Serves me right for thinking with my dick.

If I hadn't kissed her in the square, none of this would have happened.

But I need to focus on what's most important now. My urge to save Ember is strong, but I need to look out for number one. Always. Call me selfish, but I know who I am.

What's best for me always comes first.

We reach a huge metal door, and massive iron bars grind as they unlock, shifting to the side. One of the DEFTA security guards pulls a lever and the huge door itself slides, revealing an industrial-sized elevator cab. The group enters, Octavia encircled by her five burly lovers, who stick to her like erotic glue.

Once, several decades ago, Octavia wanted me as her mate, and I have to admit her offer was tempting—for about thirty seconds. As great as the sex was, once upon a time, no way would I ever give up my freedom to be with one woman forever. No fucking way.

*Ember*. Fuck. I wince as I think of her again. Right now, the idea of losing her seems even worse than being tied down to one woman. Is she the one who might make me commit?

Nah. Who am I kidding? I'm not wired for anything long-term, and even if I were, no way would I deserve someone like Ember.

That doesn't mean I don't want to get her released, and to do that, I need to talk to Octavia. I need to charm her, figure out a way to get Ember out without revealing what her blood can do.

Because the main thing today's torture exposed beyond pain, is that Ember's blood only let me take sunlight for a limited time. And if Octavia discovers a way to walk in the light, Ember will spend the rest of her life locked up, kept barely alive while being daily drained of her blood.

The elevator doors open, and we enter a long, dark tunnel, walking far more quickly than any human could fathom, traveling miles in less than a minute without running.

Where the fuck was that dungeon, and where are we now? Given Tavi and Diederik's presence, clearly it's all part of DEFTA, but for all I know, they've got buildings and underground facilities all over the state, all over the country.

We arrive at another large elevator door, this one more modern, like a hotel service elevator, and I step inside. I glare at Zuben, wishing I had the power to kill him with my eyes, but his are filled with so much fear and pain. I almost feel sorry for the dude. Not bloody likely.

After an ascent, the elevator doors open into a huge open space, concrete, with thick support pillars. Looks like an empty parking level under a high rise.

Looking back at me, Octavia licks her upper lip, upping my confidence that I'll be able to charm her into doing whatever I want. Shit. I'll even fuck her if that's what it takes. Not that fucking Octavia was ever a hardship…even if right now my body craves Ember.

We cross the open space toward yet another elevator, and this one is too small for the entire group.

"Diederik," Octavia says. "You and your team stay behind."

"But the prisoners—" the security head starts to object, but Octavia lifts her hand to stop him.

"I wish to speak to the prisoners alone," Octavia says. "If I have need for your services, I will summon you."

Scowling, Diederik bows his head and he and his team of guards stay back as Octavia, her mates, Zuben and I enter the elevator cab. Her tallest mate pushes one of two buttons and we start to rise.

Fuck. My mind scrambles through strategies. What am I going to say to get Ember released? How do I explain why they mistook a human for a vampire? Maybe I'll just make the security guys out to be idiots—so stupid they took a human by mistake.

No chance can I tell Octavia what *really* happened. Whatever that was. In truth, I have no fucking idea why Ember burned in the sunlight or under the silver netting.

And since I my ability to take sunlight expired, it holds that silver will no longer burn Ember.

The elevator opens directly into what must be Octavia's new office, but instead of going to her desk, she crosses to sit in a red-velvet, wing-backed chair, and her mates take positions around it, a wall of silent muscle.

I want to laugh at the suggestion I might have ever been her mate. No fucking way would I ever have let her tame me like this.

"Come." She gestures for me and Zuben.

I move toward one of the chairs opposite her.

"No," she says. "Come closer. Both of you. Stand before me."

Like a trained puppy, Zuben swiftly takes a position of attention in front of her, chin high, arms stiffly at his sides. Obedient. Subservient. What Octavia is used to.

"Whatever you want, Tavi." I saunter up and cross my arms over my chest, shifting my weight to one side and smiling. "Happy to fulfill your every *desire*." I hope my double entendre comes through.

It does. A smile teases her lips and she shifts on her chair, crossing her legs to highlight them through the high slit in her blood red skirt.

"We can talk about *desire*, later." She shoots me a knowing look. "First, I demand an explanation."

I'm about to make a quip about issuing some demands of my own, but she directs her attention to Zuben.

"You lied to me. You told me Ryker's blood held special powers, and because of that, I arrested an innocent vampire and had him tortured—all for nothing." The rage in her voice is clear, and I'm fucking glad I'm not the target. In Octavia's mind, I'm an innocent victim.

"With all due respect," Zuben bows slightly. "Ryker is not innocent. He's a thief, a pirate who has stolen much from DEFTA, from *you*. I have proof."

Leaning back into the chair, Octavia flicks her wrist. "You think I give a shit about a few bars of gold? You misled me! How dare you!"

Zuben raises his chin. "I did not mislead you. I had strong reasons to believe that Ryker had…had *access* to knowledge that is key to my research."

I turn toward the tall Egyptian vampire as he speaks. Zuben clearly knows about Ember's blood, *something* about it anyway, and I'm ready to throttle him if he even *begins* to bring up Ember.

I remind myself that he hasn't, not yet, and contain my anger.

Zuben makes Ember sound like a science experiment. Perhaps this has played out just as he planned. He tricked Octavia into capturing us, and now he has Ember trapped in a dungeon where he can do what he wants with her. Yes. He plans to keep Ember for himself and doesn't want his boss to know the truth.

"Zuben, you are either a fool or a liar." Octavia's eyes narrow. "And at this moment, I don't care which." She turns to one of her mates. "Fetch Diederik. Zuben needs more time to consider his actions, and I need time to consider his fate."

Diederik comes into the room, along with some of his guards.

"Take him back to the dungeon," Octavia says, pointing at Zuben.

Diederik motions for his team. They grab Zuben, who looks ambivalent about Octavia's orders, making me even more sure that Ember's capture was part of his plan.

Diederik grabs my arm, and I yank it away.

"Not him," Octavia says.

"But he's the one you told us to arrest," Diederik says, his voice tight. "My team only captured Zuben because he was with this clown."

"I'm not done with Ryker." Octavia eyes me like a tasty treat, her gaze telling me all I need to know about *why* she's not done with me. What she wants.

And now that I know I'm safe, I'll give Tavi whatever it takes to get Ember released without explaining how she ended up in that dungeon in the first place. Especially now that Zuben is going back down there to carry out his no-doubt horrific experiments.

The guards lead Zuben from the room, and he looks back at me with alarm in his eyes, as if he's trying to convey some kind of message, but I don't speak Egyptian Robot Code. *Asshole.*

"Leave us," Octavia says to Diederik.

"Yes, boss." The bulky Austrian nods. "I will remain outside should you need me again."

"Fine." Octavia flicks her wrist as she turns her attention back on me.

The door closes behind Diederik, and then she stands and sashays toward me. Her petite curvaceous form is objectively alluring and, as she moves, her dark hair swirls around her olive-skinned face, with its near perfect features.

I swear, even a gay man would find this woman sexy, and I am decidedly not a gay man. Sure, I have dabbled in that arena—what man who spent years on a pirate ship has not—but on a ten point scale from gay to straight, I'm at least an eleven.

"It's good to see you." Octavia eyes me up and down, her gaze lingering over my crotch. "It's been too long."

I shift my stance to make my semi-hard bulge more prominent, and the smile on her face tells me she thinks my arousal is for her.

In truth, I got hard while thinking of Ember.

"Looks like you're glad to see me too." Her hand lands on my package and squeezes.

Groaning, I lean forward, my lips close to her ear. "My cock's always glad to see you, luv."

Her hand strokes me again, and then she steps back, pushing forward her ample breasts. "While I am flattered by your stiff cock, *you* have been a *very bad* boy."

"Then *punish* me." I lick my lips.

As soon as I have her under my spell, I'll ask her to release Ember. She'll cave to anything once she's impaled on my cock. If it comes to that. My charm, a little flirting should suffice.

"Believe me, *pirate*," she says. "I do plan to *punish* you." Her hand cups one of her breasts, pushing it up.

She glances over her shoulder at one of her mates, and he moves in behind her.

Replacing her hand with his, he pulls her breast free of her blouse and squeezes her soft flesh, his thumb and forefinger tightening around her hard nipple as his other hand slides between her legs, parting and lifting the fabric of her skirt from behind to fondle her sex.

Ripe and ready as always, Tavi's scent fills my head. If forced to fuck her, I'll close my eyes and pretend it's Ember…

I step toward her, but one of her other mates shifts to block me.

"What the fuck do you think you're doing?" he asks, gruffly.

Leaning, I look past him toward Octavia. She wants me. I know it. Why doesn't she tell her mate to fuck off?

A new look arrives in Octavia's eyes. One of determination and power. "You know how I once loved your cock," she says to me.

The mate behind her hikes up her skirt further, and thrusts a couple of fingers inside. Rising onto her toes at the force, she moans and then strokes his face behind her, rocking her hips as she fucks his fingers.

"You had your chance, Ryker." Her tongue rests on her upper lip as her lover's hand pumps. It looks like he's added more fingers, maybe threatening his whole fist. But the skirt's hanging too far down in the front for me to be certain.

"But if you *ever* want to touch me again," she says, stroking her mate's face, "you must first tell me why Zuben had you arrested."

"The gold bars—"

"Bullshit." She breaks free from her lover and steps toward me as her mate licks her juices off his hand, damp far past his wrist. "I want the truth."

"How the fuck should I know why that robot does anything?"

"So, you know nothing of Zuben's research project?" Her breast still exposed and the scent of her arousal strong, Tavi circles me, her hand softly on my leather jacket as she makes her rounds.

"The robot and I aren't exactly friendly."

"I thought his pet project was a fools errand, based on a fairy tale," she says, "but it was in my best interest to let him pursue it."

I shrug as if it's nothing to do with me.

"Zuben assured me that *you* were the key he'd been searching for." Her hand slides up my back. "I've had your vein before, but not for many years, and I never thought to test…" She stops in front of me. So close I could lean down to steal her lips.

Should I? No.

"You're saying Zuben wants me for more than my gold bars?" I lower my gaze to her chest and rub my package. "Maybe he wants a taste of this too?"

It's best if I act like the Ryker she knows, distracted by her, all my thoughts and actions guided by my cock.

She takes a step back. "Look at me."

"Believe me, I'm looking." I lick my upper lip.

"Look into my eyes, you ass." There's a hint of amusement in her voice. A good sign.

As I look into Octavia's eyes, I think of Ember, hoping the woman I'm with will mistake my near-rabid lust as being for her.

"Clearly Zuben was wrong." She shrugs. "Or he

purposefully misled me. Who the fuck cares. Let him rot with the others in that dungeon."

"Who else you got down there?" I ask, seeing an opening but trying to sound indifferent. DEFTA has a legit prison for vampires who break our laws, one where prisoners have rights and proper sentences. That dungeon is something else all together.

She frowns. Asking questions, I'm walking a tightrope here. I need to bring up Ember without arousing suspicions—suspicions that would drive Tavi to keep Ember captive forever—or even worse, land me back down there myself. My chest tightens as panic threatens. I cannot be held captive again.

"My dungeon is not your concern." She returns to her chair and sits, leaving her skirt hiked up around her waist. Holding her tit in one hand, she fondles her sex with the other.

"Of course." She squeezes her nipple. "If you and I can come to an *agreement*, my business would be your business too." Bending up one leg, she rests her heel on the chair and lets her knee drop to the side, fully exposing her red, wet pussy.

My cock pounds as her scent reaches me even more strongly. As much as it's Ember I want, I *am* a fucking male vampire who recently fed, and "fucking" is starting to dominate my brain, dominate my whole body.

In spite of what she's done to me, it's all I can do to keep from whipping out my painfully hard rod and slamming it into Tavi right there on the chair in front of her mates. She loves a good hate fuck and used to piss me off just to earn one.

Memories of our time together race through my mind—the way she liked to be bound tight while I drove into her. How she liked sex to hurt.

"I have a dilemma." She traces her index finger through her damp folds, then plays with her clit, and I can't help but watch. "Now that you've been in my dungeon, I can't just *release* you, not without due process."

Absurd. There was no hint of "due process" involved in putting me into that dungeon. The place is clearly for vampires she wants locked up without the benefit of a trial or the relative comfort of DEFTA's prison.

*What is she up to?*

Pushing two fingers inside herself, she moans as she licks her upper lip. "I can't show you any *favoritism*, just because I crave your hard cock." Her fingers draw in and out, the wet sound heightening my building need. "But perhaps we can strike a deal for your freedom."

Anger and lust stir my brain, and I try to concentrate. To remember my objectives. To think about anything beyond wanting to punish Tavi with my cock. I want to take all the power away from the most powerful vampire in the city, the one who hurt me and trapped Ember. I want to control when she feels pleasure and pain, when she comes, when she breathes. *Fuck.*

More memories rage through me. When we first met, it was Tavi who was under my spell, but as she gained her mysterious power that allowed her to seize the top post at DEFTA, eventually I realized it was her who controlled me. That's when I got out.

"Is this what you want?" She lifts her other leg, spreading herself, and two of her mates take her ankles and lift them, stroking her legs and spreading them wide. Her long sharp nails scrape through her soft folds, drawing blood.

"If you want this," she says, her voice full of lust. "Take it!"

Releasing my cock from my pants, I move toward her. I'll fuck her if that's what it takes to free Ember.

But she holds up her hand to stop me. "Not yet." She shakes her head slowly and glances up to the males holding her legs.

They release her, and she shifts her position, crossing her legs and hiding my target. I squeeze my member, letting her see its girth, its exposed head and the seed already spilling from its tip.

She wants me. I know it. It's written all over her, I just have to figure out how to use that to my advantage.

"Ryker, my love," Octavia coos. "You're the only man who's ever said no to me. You're lucky I didn't have you killed for rejecting me."

"Like I told you back then." My voice is strained. "I can't be tied down."

"Oh, but I know that you *can*." Her eyes flash with mischief and lust.

I chuckle and then lower my voice. "You can tie me up —literally—but only after I bind *you* and fuck you senseless first."

Her cheeks redden and her legs rub together. "You're lucky I have so many fond memories of how you can use that cock." Licking her lips she stares at my pounding erection.

"Yeah?" I squeeze it. "How fond are we talking?"

"Fond enough to forgive all—if we can strike a deal."

"A deal sounds good." Stroking my cock, I grin. "But deals have two sides and I've got terms too. Something I need from you, before your cunt, ass or throat get any of this." I pump into my hand.

Her chest rises with a quick intake of breath, but she quickly regains her composure. "Do you want to hear *my* terms?" She leans back in the red chair and rubs her legs together.

"Shoot."

"I will grant your freedom, forgive your past transgressions and crimes, under one simple condition."

I stroke myself. "Is this condition stiff enough for you?"

Laughing, she licks her lips. "Refuse what I want, and you'll be locked in that dungeon forever."

My heart rate increases. She hasn't even said what she wants yet, but I assume it's my cock, and I'm ready to give her anything so I won't be trapped down there again.

"Ryker." Her voice rises in volume, and her body seems to expand in size. She's still physically tiny, but her power has grown in the years we've been apart, and she's terrifying now.

"I will *not* forgive another rejection," she says. "Be my mate, or spend the rest of eternity in my dungeon."

# CHAPTER TWENTY-SEVEN

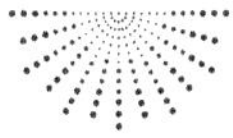

*Ember*

I WAKE FROM A DEEP SLEEP, wrapped in the heavy warmth of a bed that's firm but yielding enough to be comfortable.

My moment of comfort vanishes when I remember not only where I am but also the source of the warmth. I'm trapped in the arms of a gigantic bear.

His breaths come slowly. Very slowly. His massive ribcage rising and falling in what seems like intervals of fifteen to twenty seconds.

He must be asleep. Now is my chance to escape.

I shift, trying to use my shoulders to nudge away his huge arm, but just that one limb feels like it weighs a ton against my body.

Pressing down into his fur for leverage, I try again.

He snorts, and tightens his hold on me. Crap. I've woken the beast.

I lie still, hoping to fool him into thinking I was only moving in my sleep, but he turns over.

He's going to crush me.

I fight to get free, unwilling to suffocate without putting up a fight.

But the creature gently settles me onto the stone, my body retracting against the cold hardness after the bear's body warmth. He nudges me up to sit.

His breath is warm and moist, and as my eyes adjust to the darkness, his shape backs away from me, whimpering each time his left paw strikes the ground.

"Are you hurt?" I ask, even though it seems foolish to talk to a beast.

His head dips and rises, like he's nodding.

"Can I help?"

The beast exhales a sound, almost like an attempt at vocalization, but I have no idea how to interpret the sounds of a bear—even if I'm right and that's what he's trying to do.

"I can't see much." I fight to keep my voice calm, but it's equally scratchy and shaky.

He moves again, continuing to favor his left paw, and then gently nudges my body.

"You want me to stand?"

He huffs.

I rise onto my feet, and then feel the pressure of his snout at my hip.

"This way?"

He huffs again and, keeping one arm on the stone wall, I walk slowly, the creature moving alongside me, guiding my way.

He snorts and I stop. Then I feel the pressure of his snout pushing up one of my arms. I reach along the surface of the wall until I reach something different. My hands explore what it seems like he wanted me to find, and I recognize the shape from the ones I saw in the halls. A torch.

But how do I light it?

I fumble around, feeling everything, until I discover a thin, metal stick protruding from the base of the torch.

The bear snorts. I lift the stick. It releases from the base, and I feel its length, detecting a different texture at its tip. Is it a match? Or something like that?

Remembering a different texture on the wall to the side of the torch's base, I find that place again. Yes. There's a place on the wall that's rougher, unlike the smooth cold dampness of the cave walls.

The bear nudges me again and something brushes my other hand. The bear is trying to give me something. I take it, trying to guess what it is from the texture. Twigs? Straw?

Going on instinct and hope, I drag the stick's tip quickly across the rough spot. A spark! It's just a flash, but it confirms the position of the rough area to the side of the torch, and what it's for.

Excited, I raise the straw near as I strike the rough patch again. Then again. On the fifth try, the spark hits the straw and it lights, small flames flaring in the darkness.

I raise it and the torch springs to life, filling the space with light.

"I did it!"

The bear snorts and huffs, and my pride is flooded out

by fear as the mammoth creature comes into full view. Bigger than any bear I've seen on TV or the movies. He's several times the size of a human and his brown fur shines in the torchlight. But nothing outshines his eyes, amber that borders on gold with flecks of bright light that seems to come from within.

Should I run? No. He would outrun me. And if the bear plans to hurt me, wouldn't he have done so already?

I reach forward, slowly, and he moves until my hand is against the fur at the side of his head. Without thinking, I thread my fingers into the soft warmth, and he moans, a rumbling sound that transfers into my body and almost makes me pull back my hand.

But gathering my courage I continue stroking the bear's fur, and he rubs his head against my hip.

Then I remember why he wanted me to light the torch. Or at least why I wanted light. It's crazy how I've been attributing human traits to this animal. Anthropomorphizing. That's what it's called.

But my survival instincts, or something inside me, urge me to believe that this animal wants my help. That he might spare my life if I do.

"Your paw," I say gently. "May I see?"

He backs up to sit on his haunches and then raises his left paw toward me. It's massive. More than a foot in width, with pads across the top that mimic human toes from the underside. Above that, claws extend several inches, sharpened to points that could rip me in shreds without effort.

My body tenses, bracing for a flesh-ripping swat, but

the paw stops a foot ahead of my face and turns toward the light.

Something glints. Something metallic stuck between two of the meaty looking pads of his paw.

"That must hurt," I say softly. It looks like it would be like having a huge splinter between your toes, one that gets jammed further in with each step.

The bear huffs.

"May I?"

He nods. This is not my imagination. This bear understands what I'm saying. There is no other explanation for what's happening.

Less than a quarter inch of metal is protruding from the bear's paw and, without any kind of a tool, I'm going to have to touch what looks like thick, leathery skin.

I place my index finger and thumb of one hand around the spot to brace it, then pinch the same digits of my other hand around the metal. I tug gently.

The bear's bright amber eyes show so much pain it hurts my soul, and a low muffled howl struggles in his throat.

"I'm going to have to pull harder," I tell him. Maybe it will be like ripping off a bandage, the faster the better.

He dips his head again, then looks at me with what seems like gratitude or at least trust in his eyes.

I dig into the fur beneath the metal, moving my fingers as low on the shard as I can, then I inhale a deep breath and pull.

An inch-long piece of metal comes out of his paw. The bear howls in pain and backs away from me. Then he rises on his hind legs and makes a noise—half roar, half howl—

that penetrates every last part of me. He twists to the side, his back writhing as if he's in even more pain.

What have I done? Will he kill me now that I've done what he wanted? Or worse, did someone put that shard there on purpose to tame him into submission?

He backs away into a dark shadow at the back of the cave, and his body convulses, his spine seeming to crack and change shape before my eyes. His roars transform from howls into something more human, and his fur contracts into his skin. He seems to be changing shape.

But I can't trust my eyes. Once again he's only a shadow in the darkness, even harder to see in detail now that my vision's adjusted to the light.

My body is frozen, unable to act, and when I try to coax myself into movement, I'm not sure if my inaction is rooted in curiosity or fear.

Rubbing my eyes, I step forward as his body thrashes and turns, and the sound of breaking bones fills the air.

The beast collapses in a heap on the cave floor.

*Is he dead?*

"Are you okay?" I slowly step forward.

His back and shoulders rise and fall, rise and fall. He's breathing. He's alive.

"Do you need anything?" I know this beast has kindness inside him. He had an instinct to warm me when I was cold. I need to appeal to that side of his nature to keep him from eating me, and to protect me from the vampires out there.

Still shadowed, he rises, his back toward me.

Unsure what I'm seeing, unwilling to believe my eyes, I stop in shock.

Because my eyes claim to be seeing the back of…not a bear but a man. A very large man, his shoulders wider than any I've seen, and his butt cheeks like two perfectly round boulders of muscle.

In fact, now that my eyes are adjusting to the light, this man is entirely composed of muscle. Zero fat. It's like looking at a photo of a body builder in full pose, but less grotesque, more like an oversized sculpture of the ideal male anatomy carved out of marble.

My mouth is dry. Drier now than even before Zuben fed me. And I still don't trust my eyes.

The man, or whatever he is, turns toward me and walks forward—slowly. The front of his body is just as impressive as the back, including what's hanging between his legs, even as I fight to keep my eyes off it.

He takes a step from the shadows, and his body is bathed in torchlight that seems to want to lick every inch of him, to accentuate every dip and divot, every plane and mound of him.

Or maybe it's me who wants to do the licking.

His extremely broad chest is enhanced by a very manly dusting of dark hair, reminding me that moments ago he was a bear, and he runs his hand through a thick, matching mane on his head, pulling it back to reveal striking gold eyes and a ruggedly handsome face with a closely trimmed beard.

"Go!" he says, in a voice so hoarse and so deep that it consumes the space between us, rumbling through me with the force of an earthquake.

But I'm too shocked, too curious to run. "Who are you?" I ask. "More to the point—*what* are you?"

"Get out of here!" he yells. "Leave me alone or I'll have you for dinner!"

---

## WANT TO READ MORE?

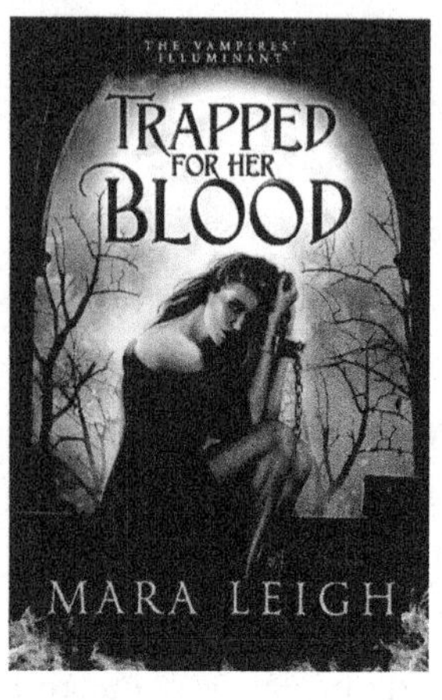


CONTINUE READING THE VAMPIRES' ILLUMINANT series with Book 2, TRAPPED FOR HER BLOOD.

**No one escapes from here.**

Trapped in a dungeon, three men with dark pasts vow their lives to protect me. Each of them is so different from the others--Ryker & Zuben, vampires who are night & day, and Axe, a bear shifter, who makes my heart stop.

I crave these men. Without them, I'd be dead. To find escape, we must work together.

Secrets slide around us like shadows in wait--some pull us together, while others threaten to tear us apart.

Something powerful is building inside me, something I know is bigger than I ever imagined.

My blood is only one reason I'm hunted, and the powerful vampire who runs this dungeon will stop at nothing to get me under her control.

Read now

---

## DID YOU KNOW???

THE VAMPIRES' ILLUMINANT series is set in the same world as my BOUND BY HER BLOOD series.

If you crave more vampires and haven't read that series yet, you should check it out too!

Read Now => Bound by Her Blood.

I've included a sneak peek of Bound by Her Blood at the back of this book. Just be warned that this series starts out a bit dark... The heroine in Bound by Her Blood goes through a lot at the start of the book. Trigger warnings for abuse.

Sneak Peek => Bound by Her Blood Chapter One

## ALSO BY MARA LEIGH

### PARANORMAL REVERSE HAREM ROMANCE

**The Vampires' Illuminant Series**

*Auctioned for Her Blood*

*Trapped for Her Blood*

*Desired for Her Blood*

*Devoted to Her Heart*

**Bound by her Blood Series**

*Bound by Her Blood*

*Bound by Her Passion*

*Bound by Her Destiny*

*Bound by Her Love*

*Bound by Her Power*

### CONTEMPORARY ROMANCE

*Bad Stepbrother*

**Downey Brothers Series**

*Bad Boy Next Door*

*Bad Habit*

*Bad Princess* (coming soon)

*Best Kind of Bad* (coming soon)

### SHORT EROTIC READS

**Fantasies Unleashed Series**

*Dirty Business*

*Surrender*

*Bedded by Strangers*

*Humbling the Boss*

# A NOTE TO READERS

Did you enjoy this book?
If so, you can make a huge difference.

Not only do reader reviews make my day, they help bring books to the attention of other readers. In fact, no marketing tool is more powerful or effective than honest reader reviews.

That said, I'd be very grateful if you could spend a one or two minutes leaving a review on this book's Amazon page. (The review can be as short as you like.)

**Believe me—your review matters.**

And thank you so much for reading!
xo, Mara

Be the first to hear about sales and new releases:
Sign up here
http://smarturl.it/MaraLeighVIPs

# ABOUT THE AUTHOR

Mara Leigh escaped from the corporate world and now hangs out in coffee shops, letting her imagination run wild. After living in various cities including Edinburgh, San Francisco and Philadelphia, Mara and her exorbitant shoe collection have settled in Toronto where she writes sexy, smart and satisfying contemporary and paranormal romance.

Follow her on:
Amazon: https://smarturl.it/MLAmznProfile
BookBub: https://smarturl.it/BookBubMaraLeigh
Newsletter: https://smarturl.it/MaraLeighVIPs
Reader Facebook Group: https://
smarturl.it/MarasReaderRoom

Or find her on social media @maraleighauthor

# SNEAK PEEK

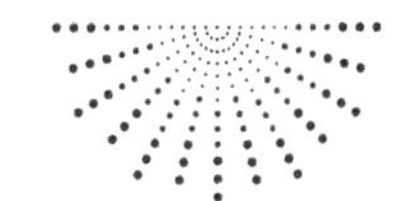

## BOUND BY HER BLOOD

# CHAPTER ONE

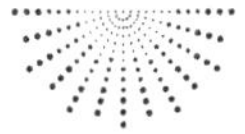

*Selina*

Today, I am going to die.

It's not the first time I've thought King Xavier would kill me. Not to mention the countless days and nights before my capture when I thought my end was near, but no matter how many times I've been close to death, it doesn't get easier—or more welcome.

And King Xavier's lost patience.

Each time I fail to complete the ceremony, the powerful vampire king grows more angry, his punishments more brutal—and on the last new moon he swore my next attempt would be my last.

No way will I survive another wedding.

"Come, Selina. Today's your big day." Jordina, one of Xavier's mates, gestures for me to step into the warm bath where she and Alexander are waist deep, their bodies' glistening like sculptures of a Greek god and goddess, and nothing short of magnificent.

Held captive at King Xavier's court for over a year, I'm still not used to the nudity and sexual openness here. My hand trembles as I unbelt my red silk robe.

"Don't look so frightened." Alexander smiles warmly, his deep brown eyes transmitting comfort. "You'll complete the ceremony this time. I'm sure of it, and then you'll be part of our family."

Although the king prefers females, Alexander is also one of Xavier's mates, and if I complete today's wedding ceremony, I'll be mate number nineteen. I'd rather die.

I drop my robe to the tiled floor, and the red silk spreads like fresh blood across the gleaming marble tiles, leaving my body exposed to everyone in the baths.

A loud exhale comes from a dark corner of the room.

I lift my gaze.

*Pike.*

My hands fly up to cover my body, and my belly tightens with fear. Pike's the most vicious of Xavier's King's Guard, and his immense size is a fraction of what makes this particular vampire so utterly menacing.

His huge body shifts, and his thick arms barely reach across his bare chest that's marred by a jagged scar that slashes red from one shoulder to slip under the waistband of the worn leather pants, hanging from his hips.

Pike's eyes, amber and piercing, penetrate the darkness. Shivers trace through me as if his gaze is visceral, scraping over my body, peering into my soul and adding salt to my many wounds.

Eager for cover, I accept Alexander's hand and descend into the warm, rose-scented water.

"Isn't she beautiful?" Alexander says to Jordina as if I'm

not there. "Such a perfect age when she turned." Lifting my hand over my head, Alexander twirls me around like we're on a dance floor, not in a small pool.

"Gorgeous," Jordina whispers near my ear.

Using soapy fleece mittens, she strokes up and down my arms, over my back and shoulders, and then slips the mitts under the water and over my butt.

*Relax*, I tell myself. *Allow yourself to enjoy the pleasant moments of this day*, but it's not easy, given I know what's coming.

Once Jordina finishes with my back, Alexander guides me onto the partially submerged lounging bed in the center of the bathing pool.

"Head back." Jordina holds up my lavender hair as I relax my neck into the cradle that seems designed exactly for me, even though I'm sure all of King Xavier's mates use this bath.

The female vampire pours warm water over my head, and I inhale the citrus scent of the shampoo as she washes my hair, giving my scalp an intoxicating massage. Weak from months of starvation and torture, my body yields to the warm water and the vampires' gentle touches.

As Jordina washes my hair, Alexander dons the soaped mitts and washes my throat, my belly, my breasts. His caress is firm but tender and sensual, and if I keep my eyes closed, I can imagine his are the hands of a lover, even though imaginary lovers are the only kind I've ever had. Not that I haven't been fucked.

Since I've been captive at court, I've been abused too many times to count, and although I've been blindfolded during most of those assaults, I feel sure the worst of them have come from Pike.

I shudder, knowing he's here in the room, his eyes on my naked body. My insides squeeze as if those muscles could protect me from his punishing member.

"What's wrong?" Alexander pauses, his hands on my breasts, and I open my eyes to find genuine concern in his.

"You know what's wrong," I say flatly.

"Selina." He strokes his hand down the middle of my torso to stop low on my belly, circling there. "Resisting will only bring you more pain. Give our king, give *us*, a chance. Is Xavier a demanding lover? Yes, he is. But I love him, and if you let yourself, you will love him, too." He smiles at Jordina and she nods, a blush rising on her cheeks.

"And you'll love being *our* mate," she whispers in my ear, then kisses the lobe.

Alexander backs through the water toward my legs, and his erection juts through the water, bouncing near his abs. Is his arousal for me, or because he's been talking about his mate?

It doesn't matter. And he's wrong. Even if I get through the ceremony—doubtful—I will never, ever, love King Xavier.

As Jordina massages my temples, Alexander lifts one of my legs and washes the length of it, spending extra time on my upper thigh. Then his mitten slides over my sex, stroking the plush fabric back and forth, way beyond what seems necessary to bathe me.

"Oh, Selina." His voice is throaty and deep. "I know

our king will have the privilege of taking you first, but I cannot wait to be inside you."

Alexander acts like he doesn't know what's been happening to me in the dungeons. Perhaps he doesn't. If he knew, how could he love King Xavier? How could any of his mates love the king if they knew what happens in his dungeon? Did any of them refuse the king like me?

As Alexander strokes the mitt over my sex, a wave of pleasure courses through me, in spite of the situation. In the less than two years since I transitioned into a vampire, my sex drive has multiplied exponentially.

When I was human, I totally avoided sex—any contact with men—but since I became a vampire I've found myself unable to control my body's reactions to stimulation—even when it's not welcome.

My supercharged libido is my least favorite thing about being a vampire and that includes drinking blood and missing sunshine.

But I can't lie to myself, being bathed like this by these two kind and beautiful vampires is arousing, even if my arousal makes me angry with myself. How can I be turned on after all that has happened, given what's *about* to happen?

I want my first *real* love-making experience, my first time that's *my choice*, to be with someone I love, but at this moment, I have to admit that the idea of sex with Alexander—or Jordina—is appealing, and being part of the king's harem would at least free me from being tortured by his Guard.

Can I go through with this? Marry the vampire king?

Luxuriating under Alexander and Jordina's skilled

hands, I can almost imagine my life as Xavier's mate, but then I remember the vampire king himself.

My entire body tightens.

"Poor Selina." Alexander kisses the multitude of round scars on my inner thighs, gifts from my stepfather.

Cigar burns were how my stepfather showed his displeasure when I showed mine at how he forced his penis inside me. He started when I was eight, less than a year after my mom married the monster.

I quickly learned how to check my mind out of my body whenever he'd visit me at night, but my compliance didn't please him either, and the monster found new ways to torture me besides penetration.

When I finally escaped the house at fourteen, I believed I was free, that I'd already suffered the worst things that could ever happen to me—to anyone.

Then I met King Xavier.

---

*Selina*

After my bath, Alexander and Jordina apply my makeup and style my hair while I hope for escape. I won't get through the ceremony, which leaves me two choices: escape or death.

"Do you like your hair this way, Selina?" Alexander asks, and I open my eyes for a moment. He's curled my hair into dozens of tiny ringlets that he's looping and pinning at varying lengths using tiny diamond-encrusted clasps that sparkle against my pale purple hair.

I nod, noting the heavy black eyeliner Jordina applied, the metallic silver eye shadow, and, of course, the blood red lipstick. Objectively I know I look good, but I hate it.

Beauty's a symbol of my captivity. My desirability's the trait that led to this misery.

If only I'd disfigured myself before I transitioned, but at twenty-two I'd been hopeful, no idea my physical self would be forever frozen in place.

And my lavender hair color, now permanent, came the very day I was turned. I was so happy when I splurged on that hair dye—a treat to myself for landing my dream job in graphic design.

After years of living on the streets and then in roach- and predator-infested rooming houses, I was on my way. Starting a job I knew I'd love and soon able to afford a real apartment. One where I didn't need to share the halls with roaches or registered sex offenders.

But the very night I dyed my hair, I was attacked by a vampire who nearly drained me and left me for dead in an alley. Somehow I'd turned all on my own—which is supposedly impossible.

Clearly it's not.

So many things I thought I knew about vampires aren't true. But one thing that's true—they thrive best in groups.

Surviving on the streets, a lone female vampire without a syndicate or kingdom for protection, wasn't easy. Still, I managed it for three months until the fateful night I met Santos and was tricked by his kindness.

Santos brought me here to Xavier's court, and

presented me to the king like a cat dumping a dead mouse on the kitchen floor for its human.

Seconds later, Xavier plunged his fangs into my neck. He fed from me until I was so weak I could barely stand, then the king declared I was his. Since that night, my life's been so full of torment and agony it makes my abusive childhood, my teenaged years on the street, seem idyllic.

One way or another, today is going to end all that. I only wish it didn't have to end in death.

Makeup and hair done, I stand still, and Jordina adjusts my wedding gown, this one even more elaborate than the previous twelve. In several hues of red, narrow panels of silk and crushed velvet intertwine as they drape my body, highlighting my shape and leaving my breasts mostly exposed, as well as my throat.

The embroidery thread is twenty-four-carat gold, as are the beads and tiny sequins hand-sewn along the neckline and slits, which reach from the floor all the way to my waist—front and back.

Jordina slips me into a thong. A triangle of red silk encrusted with tiny diamonds advertises my sex below the apex of the gown's slit. The string reaching back from there is fashioned from a series of large black pearls.

Jordina's fingers part my labia to position them, then she tugs up on the garment from behind, adjusting the length of the string until the orbs press hard into my sex, creating stimulation each time I move—or breathe.

I vow to minimize both at all costs.

Alexander takes a gold hoop from a tray and opens it. Without warning, he pierces my right nipple. I gasp, and my involuntary movement digs the pearls into my sex.

Alexander fastens the ring and slides it back and forth through the hole, then, using his finger, he wipes blood from my breast and pulls it between his lips, his eyes closing in ecstasy.

"Selina tastes delicious," he says to Jordina. "I can see why Xavier wants her so badly."

Alexander pinches my other nipple, making it hard, and then pierces that one, too, but this time I'm better prepared for the pain.

Jordina doesn't bother with her finger and takes my nipple, hoop and all, between her lips. She sucks, circling my nipple with her tongue several times.

"Oh, my," she says as she licks a few stray drops of blood from my breast. "You *are* going to be a very popular member of our family."

She crouches and her hand slides under the gown to circle my ass, then she tugs up on the beads from behind. I open my eyes to find her smiling, her expression swimming with desire.

Her hand lightly traces forward through my folds, then up the front of my gown as she straightens. "Selina. Please let love fill your heart today. Don't resist him this time. Please."

"Yes." Alexander puts his lips on my neck and licks the skin over my pulsing vein. "If you let him, Xavier will worship you."

"And so will the rest of us," Jordina adds. "Even if Xavier sometimes gets rough, we'll *always* make you feel good."

"So good." Alexander pushes his hand between my legs and fondles the pearls.

I squeeze my eyes shut, trying to fight my body's reaction. These two vampires are sexy AF, and the way they're touching me—tenderly, almost reverently, compared to the abuse in my past—drives my desire up to eleven.

Can I actually do this? Marry Xavier? Join this family?

Already powerful, with each new mate King Xavier grows more so. And as one of his mates I'll have protection for eternity. No one outside our family will dare touch me again.

Tired, hungry, tortured, I admit the idea is tempting.

"She ready?" A deep male voice invades the space.

Pike strides in, his heavy boots echoing around the dressing room.

My heart rate quadruples. Why him? Of all of Xavier's Guard, why do I have to be walked down the aisle by the most despicable, most cruel, most menacing vampire I've ever encountered?

"Just a couple of finishing touches." Alexander dips a brush in a pot of red powder, then carefully decorates my nipples, already fully healed from the piercing. If there's one advantage to being a vampire, it's quick healing, although that one thing doesn't make up for everything else vampiric. Not even close. I so miss being human.

I inhale the distinct coppery scent of the powder he's using, intoxicated by the unmistakable odor of dried human blood. Starved for so long, I wish I could bend to lick it off.

Jordina clips the end of a gold chain to my thong, tight against my clit. Where is the other end of it going?

"All ready," she says.

With horror, I realize the other end of the chain has a leather handle—and Jordina hands it to Pike.

Below bushy dark hair that falls to his shoulders, the massive vampire's eyes narrow as he ogles my body, shaking his head slowly and licking his lips. No doubt the beast is thinking of all of the filthy and painful things he wants to do to me. If I marry Xavier he won't get another chance.

His head turns, and I gasp. Caught at the right angle, Pike is handsome, in a brutish, ultra-masculine way. Even though his right cheek is scarred in an angry red mess, no doubt badly burned before he turned, I can imagine how he might once have looked. Standing before me, Pike's impossibly broad chest expands and contracts, each breath lifting pecs as solid and pocked as ancient shields.

Empathy rushes my heart. Are Pike's scars, the pain he suffered, what created the cruelty inside him?

No. I have scars and they didn't make me cruel. More likely Pike's wounds came from a woman trying to defend herself from him. I shake off my momentary softness.

Should I try harder with the ceremony this time?

I shudder at memories of my past wedding days. The very first time I walked down the aisle followed a period of relatively conventional courting—conventional for Xavier—and he made genuine efforts to win me over to his affections.

But that first time I refused to speak my lines during the ceremony.

My defiance led to a month of nightly assaults, like he thought he could use his body to force love into mine. But during wedding attempts number two, and three, and four, I again refused to recite the words.

After that, Xavier's distinction between punishment and coercion blurred, and his techniques turned more brutal. He moved me from the small room next to his into the dungeon where I'd be under the "care" of his Guard. His Guard made Xavier seem gentle.

The seventh marriage attempt followed a night after I was penetrated endlessly by Xavier's female Guard members equipped with huge dildos—the worst bachelorette party ever.

That time I gave in. I spoke all the ceremony's words. All I knew was I wanted the torture to end. That day I did resolve to marry him. I thought all it would take was saying the words, but it didn't work.

Since then, I've been defiant, and I've suffered for it.

If I try today, on lucky marriage number thirteen, if I try to *mean* the words as I say them, try to *feel* the words in my heart, then maybe this time will be different. Maybe today I'll end up one of Xavier's mates—married for all eternity to a vampire I'll never love.

As horrible as that sounds, it doesn't seem as bad as being dragged back to the dungeon by Pike—if Xavier even bothers with the dungeon this time. More likely he'll make me suffer some horrible humiliation and death in front of the entire court.

# CHAPTER TWO

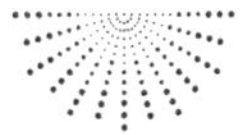

*Selina*

Four other members of Xavier's Guard stand outside the dressing room, all uniformed the same—bare chested with leather pants—and all carrying sharp wooden stakes. Two of them walk ahead of Pike, and two take places behind me, their stakes no doubt angled toward the left side of my back.

As we walk down the dimly lit corridor, my knees tremble and I grow short of breath. I haven't fed from a human vein since I failed my fourth marriage ceremony. Since I've been housed in the dungeon, I've had only thimble-sized sips of stale blood—barely enough to keep me alive.

I try to keep my eyes on the flagstone tiles, rather than Pike, but find myself mesmerized by the huge mounds of his ass cheeks, like steel pressing out against the worn leather, and by the undulating muscles of his back, fully engaged in keeping his huge mass upright.

Keeping the chain slack between us, Pike walks slowly enough for me to keep up, and twice the guards leading our procession have to stop to let us catch up.

But that small kindness ends when we enter the Great Hall.

The instant we're in sight of his king, Pike tugs hard on the handle, pulling it forward and up, pinching the tender flesh of my vulva and nearly pulling me off my feet as he jerks me into the room.

Dozens of crystal chandeliers hang over what looks like hundreds of vampires, all dressed in black and white.

Red, the preferred color at court, is reserved today for the bride and groom.

Flanking us, the guards continue up the aisle, our hideous wedding party walking more quickly now. Pike tugs on the chain when I don't keep up—or possibly just to be cruel—and by the time we near the altar, my vulva's burning and my clit's so sensitive I fear might come.

The guards in front part to stand at either side of the large marble platform. Pike tugs me forward until I'm mere feet away from the king, and then holds the chain taut, tugging aggressively against my sex.

Cruelly handsome, King Xavier's jet black hair is smoothed back from a strong-jawed face that frames lush lips, and his bright green eyes are accented by heavy but well-groomed brows. His red leather suit perfectly fits his strong, lean body and molds over the protruding bulge at his crotch.

All I see is ugly.

He smiles and pure evil emanates from every pore in his body.

*Try this time,* I coax myself. *If you don't marry him, he'll kill you.*

"I like the leash," he says to Pike. "Well done."

Pike tugs up on it—hard—and I gasp.

Xavier's eyes open wider. "That thing get her good and ready?"

"See for yourself, Your Majesty," Pike answers.

"No, you do the honors. Please." Xavier shoots me a look, full of malice.

"Your Majesty. I couldn't. She's yours." Pike's voice is hoarse and deep.

"That wasn't a suggestion," Xavier says. "Unless you'd like to exchange your living quarters for a stall in the dungeon."

Pike turns toward me, looking down, avoiding my eyes. Not that I want to see the cruelty I feel sure I'd see there.

"Spread your legs for my loyal guard," Xavier demands.

Before I can move, the guards behind me kick my legs apart so abruptly I nearly fall.

Pike presses his long, thick middle finger against his equally huge index one and shows them to Xavier, who nods.

Pike sucks in a long, ragged breath, then he slides his fingers between my legs, drawing back and forth a few times over the beads. I fight against my body's arousal as my breath expels in a thready burst.

"Do you like that?" Xavier asks, and I shake my head.

He chuckles. "Inside her," Xavier says. "I want to make sure she's prepared." He wants no such thing. He only wants to show his dominance—over me, over Pike, over everyone in the room.

Pike's chest heaves sharply in reaction to the king's command, and then he forces one finger inside of me.

I squeeze my eyes shut, trying to ignore my body's traitorous acceptance of the intrusion.

"Let me see," Xavier commands.

Pike withdraws, then holds up his index finger.

Xavier studies it for a moment and then licks my juices off its tip. "Not deep enough." He steps back. "All the way in. At least three fingers." He nods to the guards. "Secure her legs."

Pike's breath catches again as the guards take hold of my ankles and spread my legs even wider, holding them there.

Pike holds his pinky down with his thumb, making a rod with his three middle fingers and showing them to Xavier, who nods his approval. Then, with his other hand on my shoulder for leverage, Pike plunges his digits inside me—hard and fast.

I cry out. Even though I'm so wet, the sudden thick intrusion is painful.

Another effect of my rapid healing is that my channel has remained as tight and sensitive as it was when I ran away from home at fourteen.

Yes, my stepfather violated my body many times before that, but as I learned here at court, that monster was endowed with a pencil dick. Since my transition, each time I've been penetrated by anything thicker than a thumb, it's like my first time.

Pike pulls out his hand and shows his damp fingers to Xavier, who nods, smiling.

"Selina, my love," Xavier says. "Look at me."

I reluctantly raise my gaze to meet his, and he licks my juice off Pike's fingers, wet all the way to the bottom knuckle. Xavier sucks the large vampire's digits into his mouth as if tasting the most succulent dish. Pike looks angry, probably wishing he could have used his whole fist.

"Very nice." Xavier steps toward me.

I almost fall back. The guards are still holding my ankles.

"Let her go," he tells them and then he cups my face in his hands.

"My beautiful Selina." He kisses my forehead and looks into my eyes. "I cannot wait for you to be my mate, to share myself with you daily in wedded bliss."

I shudder.

"Darling." The look in his eyes turns almost compassionate. "You don't yet understand how magnificent it is to fuck and feed from your true mate, the power we'll *both* derive from our pairing." He presses a light kiss against my mouth, then slides his lips close to my ear and whispers, "Yield to me, Selina. Love me and I'll protect you forever."

He straightens, leaving no evidence of his tender plea on his face as he gestures for the priest.

The priest leads me onto the marble platform and wraps a sheer white silk scarf around my neck, letting the ends drape down my back. Then he does the same to his king.

At each of the past ceremonies, my white scarf ended up soaked in my blood, or torn from my body, or both.

Xavier's neck has yet to be pierced. If I pass today, will I be capable of plunging my fangs into his neck as he fucks me to complete the final step of the ceremony?

My intense hunger for blood rises at the thought.

I can sense the power of the king's blood as it pumps through his veins, and I fight a battle inside myself. In spite of my revulsion, my body hungers for Xavier—in more ways than one—and my survival instinct wants me to comply, to do all I can to make this work.

Listening to his blood gush inside him, I force down my hatred as desire floods through me. I want him to feed me, to fuck me. Fuck me here and now in front of everyone.

I shake my head quickly. What is happening to my mind?

I do want to live. Do I want it badly enough to go through with this marriage?

"My children," says the priest. "Do you come here today of your own volition, without coercion or threat?"

I glance at the wooden-spike-wielding guards, still aiming their weapons at my heart. "Yes, we have," Xavier and I respond together.

Hearing our voices in unison, my unwelcome feelings for Xavier grow. I certainly feel lust—both blood and sexual—but love?

"And is your love true?" the priest asks.

"It is," we both answer.

The vampires at court exhale a collective sigh, and the crystal chandeliers seem to brighten, filling the cavernous space with warmth and light.

"Do you promise to love and protect each other for all of eternity?"

"We do."

"We do, too," Xavier's other mates say in unison as they gather closer, and I can sense their blood pumping, too, feel their desire for the king, for me, for each other. I concentrate on those positive feelings. They all love him, can I?

"Do you promise to worship each other, your bodies, your eternal souls?"

"We do," I respond to the priest. I've said all these words before, but today's the first time I've said them earnestly, desperately wanting them to be true. It's the only way to survive.

"Then it is time." The priest gestures.

Two small vampire boys approach. They look around ten years old, but I learned from Jordina that one of them is over two hundred, frozen in time, just like I'll forever look twenty-two.

Each of the boys holds a small golden cup and the priest places a large golden bowl, ornately carved with scenes of mating couples, on the floor between us.

Xavier steps toward me, and the hunger in his eyes is so powerful I can taste it, *feel* it in my bloodstream and between my legs. At this moment I believe that Xavier loves me, in spite of his cruelty. And in this moment I want him, too. I want him to feed from me, to fuck me, to call me his mate. In spite of my weakness, my fangs tingle, wanting to come out.

Xavier sweeps me against him, pushes my head to the

side and plunges his sharp fangs through the silk scarf and into my vein.

I moan. It feels like the force of a thousand horses are pulling blood from my veins, pulling every cell in my body up and off the ground, and the rush is almost as good as the first time I fed myself.

But the feeding is over almost as quickly as it started and leaves me even weaker.

Xavier releases me, and I stumble back.

"Kneel, my child," the priest says.

I kneel on the cold marble.

Lifting the scarf, the priest holds my head to the side as one of the boys collects the blood that drips from my open vein, catching every drop in his cup, until the puncture wounds close.

King Xavier kneels opposite me.

One of his mates, Sylvia I believe, approaches and kneels beside him. They look deeply into each other's eyes and it's impossible not to see their mutual desire, plus what looks like genuine love between them. Will I feel that, too? Can I?

Xavier holds out his wrist to her, and she slashes it open with her fangs, drinking a few long gulps before holding his wrist out for the other altar boy to collect the royal blood in his cup. She kisses Xavier with her blood-drenched lips.

"Thank you," the priest says to Sylvia.

Xavier breaks their kiss, licking the last of his blood from her chin, and then she stands, backing into the shadows as the altar boys each hand their cups of blood to the priest.

It's the moment of truth.

If our love is real, if the words we spoke were true, then our blood when combined in the ceremonial bowl will combust.

My heart thuds in my chest, unsure of which outcome I want as the priest speaks incantations and raises the bowls high above his head. Slowly, he tips them.

The blood seems to flow in slow motion, one drop at a time descending toward the larger vessel below. The thick liquid strikes the bowl's surface on both sides and drains toward the bottom, the streams sliding slowly toward each other to determine my fate.

The first drops touch. Xavier gasps. Then our bloodlines completely intertwine and turn into… a small pool of blood.

"Liar!" he shouts. "You don't love me at all, you conniving little whore!"

One of the guards lifts me roughly to my feet and immediately all four of the wooden stakes are pointed directly at my heart—two points in front, two in the back, one so firmly against me that blood trails down my exposed skin at the front of the gown.

"Shall I grant you an easy death, Selina?" Xavier glares at me, hatred completely replacing the flash of love I saw earlier. "Should I command my men to penetrate your heart with those stakes right now?"

Eyes narrowing, he shakes his head. "What a waste that would be. It only takes one stake to kill you. Perhaps the other three should penetrate you first—in all of the places I've fucked you."

"One down your throat." He pushes his finger forcefully between my lips, then walks behind me. "One in your cunt." He bends me forward and forces his fingers inside me. "But first, I think, one in your asshole."

I hear gasps and cheers from the crowd, then something sharp scratches my anus. No. He won't. Even Xavier wouldn't do that.

Even this starved of blood I'd heal, but it wouldn't make the injury less painful or humiliating.

"Let me!" Pike's heavy boots shake the platform, and I close my eyes bracing for the pain. "Let me take care of her, Your Majesty. I will be sure that she suffers."

Xavier laughs. "Very well! Take her out of my sight, Pike. Use her as you wish and then kill her."

---

Keep reading => Bound by Her Blood

Made in the USA
Las Vegas, NV
27 February 2023

68250292R00177